Chapter 1

She came to herself—whoever she was—running in panic, gasping for breath, tripping over tombstones and stumbling into holes through a dark cemetery.

Where was she?

Smoke drifted past her from the darkness between flashes of light that outlined a stand of trees ahead of her. A red haze rose through those trees.

Why was she running? Was she being chased? She ran faster, harder, glancing over her shoulder to see if someone was behind her, but there was nothing. No one.

Another flash and explosion made her cry out. She stumbled to a stop, hugged herself, held her breath. Stars of red and green shimmered in the sky and filtered to the ground.

She closed her eyes, weak with relief. Not a war zone. Fireworks.

Calm down. Take a deep breath. Another.

Heart still practically in A-fib, she heard disembodied shouts and laughter. Whistles and applause filtered through the forest. What day was this?

Independence Day celebration? No. Too cold. This wasn't July.

Confusion cascaded over her fear, mingled, settled in the pit of her stomach. What year was it? How could she not know?

An explosion and whistle brought her eyes wide open again, and more lights formed a brilliant white star that spread across the sky, accompanied by a flute playing *O Holy Night*.

She recognized the star. But she felt no sense of familiarity when she looked down at her own hands. Amnesia from a fugue state could do that to a person. How did she know that?

Another explosion and screech unnerved her, but for a moment she was able to stand still, force herself to think instead of simply react. Fugue state. Yes.

Why was she here in this cemetery at Christmastime? The harder she tried to remember the more she trembled. Something black and deadly hovered in her mind, dammed by a thick barrier she could not force herself to penetrate.

She turned and looked behind her again, and this time she saw a line of cars parked along the cemetery drive. A red Mustang lurked amongst the others. She shuddered, as if a menace waited for her from inside the windows of that car.

Why did that thought terrify her? What if someone was chasing her? Had she been drugged? Injured?

She reached up and palpated her skull and neck, her shoulders and face. No injury there.

Another explosion made her cringe. She tried to breathe more slowly, evenly.

Something about this section of the cemetery held her here. But why? She stepped sideways and stumbled against a black marble tombstone. A tingle raced up her arm. She snatched her hand away, and for a flicker of a second the lights in the sky illumined the name etched in shadow. Dustin Grooms.

She caught her breath and held it, scrambled away from the stone, eyes wide, afraid to turn from it. That name...why did it affect her?

She continued to back away, then swung around and glanced at other stones. Something about this setting felt familiar all of a sudden. The aroma of spent explosives hovered in the air with the resultant smoke and fog. Trapped. She felt trapped. Where could she go? She certainly couldn't force herself to take a step toward the forest and the explosions beyond.

Monuments around her seemed to inch closer. She shut her eyes, whimpering, hugging herself. Had to keep her sanity—or what she had left of it. The smoke thickened. A headache intensified its steady rhythm behind her eyes as it mingled with the frustration, the confusion.

This won't last. I'm not losing my mind.

The words did nothing to comfort her. Why was that knowledge so instinctive, as if she'd used the same reassurance in times past?

More cheers and louder laughter drifted up the hill—and yet,

Dandelion Moon

Hannah Alexander

Dandelion Moon

Published by Hannah Alexander Books
PO Box 378
Monett MO 65708

Cover created by Angela Hunt
Edited by Lissa Halls Johnson and Nancy Toback
Interior Created by RikHall.com

how could she know the forest was on a hillside? She didn't move to see more; for a moment she felt as if her body was telling her not to try. Her body? Or something in her mind?

The finale filled the night with loud bursts of sound and eye-stabbing colors. A streak of pain etched itself down the back of her head. Tension curled in her stomach like heat from one of those firecrackers. She covered her ears and closed her eyes against the cacophony of the show. Her legs weakened. She dropped beside a tombstone on the cold ground and sobbed.

***

Joy Gilbert climbed the steep road from the park, trying to keep up with her mother, who had obviously been working out. "You did it."

"Did what?"

Joy paused to breathe. "First of all you came to the fireworks display, an actual community social. Then you stayed for the whole thing. I think I even heard you greet Wilma Rush as we left."

"Notice she ignored me." Mom's voice had regained some of the musical lilt that she'd lost last year.

"She ignores everyone. Good ol' Wilma, always there with a nasty attitude and a knife for someone's back, yet you greeted her anyway."

"It's biblical," Mom said. "You know, kindness to your enemies, hot coals on their heads."

Joy chuckled as she was expected to. "How long has it been since you participated in a town gathering? Town hall meetings? Social meetings? Parties? You're doing better. Admit it."

"Not doing better, just doing it now."

Joy could almost feel her mother shuddering beside her, and she smiled. "I know it's got to be hard to get back out into the world and face old friends and—"

"And enemies?" Mom shrugged. "It's hard enough to search for a decent church and face the gossips at the grocery store every week."

"Every town has its gossips. For that matter so does every church."

"Don't remind me."

"What you need is selective hearing loss. You did great work when you were on the town council. Nobody could distract you from your goals and you made Juliet a better place to live."

With a gentle smile at Joy, Mom shook her head. "In case you don't recall, most of the town council consisted of men, and back in the day…well…"

"Are you implying the men only listened to you because you were easy on the eyes? Come on. They could see your wisdom past the pleasing exterior."

"I never intentionally 'worked it' to get what I wanted, believe me."

"I know. Who can help being beautiful?" Joy chuckled. "But you've grown in wisdom—"

"And girth, and age."

"You've lost fifty pounds."

"Doesn't matter. I'm no longer part of the town meetings and don't want to be. That part of my life is over."

Joy knew her mother had never enjoyed the limelight. "Maybe it's just begun and you don't know it yet," she teased.

"Joy Marie, don't start."

"How about the hunt for the perfect church? Have you found one yet?"

"I'm narrowing it down, and you know as well as I do that nothing's perfect. You?"

Joy grimaced. "Working Sundays."

"Don't even try that with me. I heard you asking Zack to give you those Sunday shifts, and I know why. You're convinced every congregation will be the same as our old one. I refuse to believe all churches are filled with gossips and judgmental jerks. You just have to find the right one."

"The right gossip? Or the right judgmental jerk?" Joy scowled. Church busybodies had become thorns in the path for her last year. When Zack broke their engagement she'd blamed her church and left the congregation. Now she knew the real reason for that break, but the behavior of the people she'd thought of as her church family continued to make her distrust churches in general.

She and Zack had reconciled. Still, she occasionally wondered if he trusted her. And how could she trust another church after the way they'd treated her mother?

Mom also left their church last year. She'd asked to teach a Sunday school class and was turned down because Joy was illegitimate. It didn't matter that Joy was also a grown woman with a doctorate now; the trustees didn't believe it would be a good example to have an unwed mother in a position to teach children about Jesus. Small towns had their drawbacks. Quite a few of them.

"There are weeds in every wheat field, sweetheart," Mom said.

Joy knew what she meant. "I know all about the parable of the tares and the wheat, but my concern is with the actual wheat. Just as scientists have altered the original grain until it's unrecognizable and causes celiac disease, the same goes for toxic Christians."

"Toxic Christians are now causing celiac disease?" Mom asked dryly.

Joy paused again to catch her breath. She needed to find out her mother's exercise plan. "They wander from the truth. You proved your love for God from the time I was old enough to understand."

"Not all of them wander. Besides, when we avoid the fray we're allowing the weeds to take over, and then the wheat is drawn even further from the original truth."

"I'm not weed killer."

"And so you work in the ER on Sundays, where you have to judge between drug seekers and legitimate patients in pain. You hate it."

"They're all patients in pain, but too many of them try to self-medicate with the wrong thing."

"When do you plan to join Zack in his practice?"

Relieved by the subject change, Joy picked up her pace again. ""He's barely making enough to handle overhead, and I can't see it growing until he hires staff. He can't afford that."

"Then help him finance it with your half of the investment."

"A basic practice, including staff and start-up time, would be more than half a mil. You think I could possibly have saved that much since May?"

"You could talk to your grandpa."

Joy knew her grandfather would gladly give her the money to get a practice started. He would also take out ads in the paper and spread the word and tell all his friends, and then he would proceed to tell her and Zack exactly how they needed to run things.

"We'll do it on our own or not at all. Besides, we've got a wedding to plan first, and I already regret the decision to have a fancy affair instead of getting married the week after Zack proposed. It would've been so much easier."

"You needed the time."

"For what? We've known each other since anatomy lab."

"Even so, you still have some questions about this engagement."

"Since when did you become omniscient?"

"You're saying I'm right, then."

"No." She wasn't saying that at all. She might be thinking it, but not as often as before. Zack had his own family issues to work out last year. Seeing his parents divorce left him doubting everything in his life.

"Good, because if you two don't know each other well enough by now you might as well give it up. You don't want to rob your grandfather of the opportunity to give his granddaughter away."

"That isn't why I'm getting married."

"He never got to do that with me, and he still grumbles about it."

Joy sighed. Molly Gilbert had always been a force of nature, beautiful, vivacious and kind, but she took after her father a little too much. Last year was the only time Joy had seen her falter. Losing her only child to the city, losing her job, being forced to accept Joy's financial aid for the first time in her life had knocked the exuberance from her. Now that she was bouncing back she was getting a little too personal.

"Thanks for coming with me tonight," Joy said.

"I like fireworks," Mom said.

"You wore your earplugs."

"I like to watch them, not hear them. Besides, you just said I needed selective hearing loss. The plugs also block out the whispers and rumors that seem to follow me wherever I go."

"You set yourself up. Bricking that old shed is enough to stir up anyone's imagination."

"Only because they make it their business to snoop on my

private property."

"You know what they're calling it, don't you? A brick cat house."

"Cat shelter, not cat house. It's no one's business what I do on my own place. It isn't visible from the road, and no one has the right to trespass."

"You know this town." Joy shrugged as she veered to her left onto the paved drive of the cemetery, relieved that her mother was no longer leading the way in both distance and conversation.

For an instant she thought she heard a cry over the chatter of the small group of partiers behind them. She slowed her steps, out of breath. It really was time to start an exercise program.

A quick glance behind them showed her that the people following were laughing and acting silly, filled with eggnog and Christmas cookies. No tears there.

She frowned. "Did you hear that?"

Mom slowed beside her. "What?"

Joy scanned the shadows, unable to see a thing besides the shapes of tombstones and cars. "I thought I heard someone crying."

"Coyotes out in the field?"

"No. Listen."

They stood in the cold night air. The crowd caught up and filed around them. When conversation lulled for a few seconds Joy was sure she heard a woman sobbing.

Mom switched on her tiny keychain flashlight, which seemed to glow in the cemetery darkness almost as brightly as the show they'd just seen. "Over in the protestant section. Let's check it out."

Joy followed. When the light bounced off a familiar red bumper in the line of cars, she reached for her mother's shoulder. "Hold it. Aim that thing back to the red car. See it?"

"Hmmm. Nice. So?"

"Have you seen any red Mustangs in town lately?"

"I'm seldom actually in town if I can avoid it." Mom strode off through the cemetery.

"Myra Maxwell got that red sports car last month," Joy called after her.

"She lives half a state away."

Joy sighed. "Just look for Dustin's monument. This is the second Christmas since his death and she might have felt a need to visit." But Joy had just spoken to Myra on the phone yesterday. She certainly hadn't been crying, she'd been celebrating the continued recovery of Sarah Miller, one of their favorite mutual patients. The poor young woman had battled post traumatic stress disorder for years. Last night she'd made reservations to eat out at a nice restaurant and attend a company party.

Mom stepped across the crackly winter grass. "Hello?" she shouted. "Anyone out there?"

The chatter behind them stopped, then some young girl tittered.

"There's plenty of someones out there," a guy muttered. "Is Molly going to start holding séances now?"

Another idiot laughed.

Joy turned and glared as the crowd spread out to their separate cars. She caught up with her mother halfway along a row of monuments.

"Myra's parents are buried out here, too. Last night was the anniversary of her mother's death." Mom stopped suddenly, light raised, and Joy nearly collided with her.

The beam landed on the slender shoulders of a woman huddling beside the Maxwell tombstone. The woman had black hair, a long denim duster that looked familiar—and far too thin to protect her from the cold.

Mom stepped closer and shone the light near the woman's face.

"Myra?" Joy called softly. "Why didn't you tell me you were coming down? And where's your coat?"

Her friend didn't respond.

Mom dropped to her knees and aimed the beam of light against the headstone to reflect and widen the glow. She placed a hand on Myra's shoulder. "Sweetheart, are you okay?"

Myra looked around, her cheeks streaked by tears and mascara.

Joy pulled off her own jacket. "You're shivering." When she tried to cover her friend, Myra scrambled aside, eyes wide with terror.

"Stay away from me! I don't know you." She hunched her

shoulders, burying her head against her knees.

Joy stood holding the coat, fear stiffening her fingers and cutting off her air. She looked at her mother, who stared at Myra, still holding the light on her.

"You might not know us," Mom said softly, her voice shaking slightly, "but we know you. We're friends, and have been for a long time."

Myra shook her head. "Please go away. I don't want to know...I can't do this."

Joy swallowed hard, shock transforming into something more like horror. "At least take this jacket, please. We're not going to hurt you. Myra, I'm afraid something's happened to you."

"I don't know who Myra is."

"That's your name. I'm Joy Gilbert, and this is my mother, Molly."

"Please don't—"

"We can't just leave you like this," Joy said, feeling the quiver in her voice. "Something's obviously happened; you're in a state of amnesia and we're here to help you. Please Myra, just trust us."

"And first of all," Mom said, taking the jacket from Joy, "you need to get warm. Put this on before you freeze." She held the jacket toward Myra without getting close enough to frighten her further.

"You can't spend the night out here in the cemetery," Joy said. "You can stay with us at Mom's house. There's room." Joy glanced at her mother, tried again to swallow away some of the fear that paralyzed her, and went weak with relief when Myra finally took the jacket.

Joy stared at her best friend and forced herself to remain strong, but inside she wanted to scream out to the heavens. What was wrong with Myra?

Chapter 2

Weston Cline stood on his back patio in freezing temperatures listening to the ring tone of the Bluetooth in his ear as he waited for the fourth time tonight for Myra to answer. Again it went to voice mail. He could be warming his hands before a blazing fire inside—or by the outdoor fireplace, for that matter—but for some reason freezing half to death outside took his mind off the worry that gnawed at him.

Extravagant lights from the neighbor's Christmas display reflected warm jewel tones across Weston's plate glass window and indoor pool as the air pulsed in rhythm to Christmas music. Should he call Tressa to come spend the night with him so she could swim and enjoy the show? She used to love Christmas.

His daughter had become more precious to him as the months passed and they got to know one another again. But she was spending the holidays with her mother's family and Sylvia's new fiancé; Sylvia might lose her festive spirit if he called and tried to share their daughter. He wasn't about to fight for custody. Never again. If only he could convince his ex-wife of that.

He gritted his teeth as the sharp north wind shot needles of icy air down the back of his neck. Where was Myra? She never turned off her cell phone, never ignored calls, because as she'd once explained there was always the possibility that the call could be from a patient in trouble.

"It's me again," he said into voice mail. "I don't want to crowd you, but I'm worried, especially after I heard you left work in a hurry today." That wasn't like her at all. What if she was sick? What if she'd been in a wreck? All he could get from the secretary was that she'd received a call. But from whom?

"Would you let me know you're all right? If you don't want to talk at least text me to let me know you're safe." There. He'd sunk to begging for crumbs. He disconnected, staring at the glitter of lights on the pool, at his dark reflection in the glass.

His mirror image, surrounded by the brilliant Christmas lights, certainly didn't resemble the billboard ads all over Kansas City. Now of all times, the grandiose front-page newspaper articles, the pictures of the great billionaire Weston Cline on periodicals touting the benefits of fame and fortune, they dug at his gut. The world worshiped a fictitious man—someone he'd never wanted to be. Kansas City honored him for opening a clinic last year, as if they believed it to be a free clinic to treat all comers.

Why did the world try so hard to make him a savior just because his family had always used charity for promotional campaigns? How quickly he'd trade all his wealth to wash away the guilt of past actions.

He stepped from the patio and paced the length of his backyard, catching a glimpse of the line of cars driving by his neighbor's house to see the light display. Since Keegan's death, the outward show of Christmas celebrations depressed him. Keegan used to love Christmas.

But thinking about his son's death only made everything seem hopeless. He needed to focus on finding Myra right now.

He glowered at his reflection. He couldn't blame her for refusing to take his calls. He didn't deserve her time or attention. The fact that she'd allowed him to take her out to dinner weekly, and lately twice a week, showed her heroic heart, not his companionable presence.

Their latest dinner had involved a heated debate about her inability to detach herself from the struggles of her patients, to the point that their dinnertime conversation was almost always interrupted by a call on her cell phone from a patient in need. She felt their pain too deeply. It wasn't healthy.

He sank down onto the picnic table, shivering in the winter chill. Did he dare let her know how much she meant to him? What if he couldn't maintain a lifelong relationship? Wasn't one destructive divorce enough for any person?

He'd once been accused of having a heart of stone, but that wasn't true. If he could do anything to see Myra happy again he would do it, even if it meant she would choose not to continue seeing him.

But after today everything was different. Myra had left her

practice in the middle of the day, leaving her assistant scrambling to cancel appointments. Had it been any other day besides Christmas Eve there would have been a lot more calls to make, but the clinic was scheduled to close early. Abandoning patients meant something awful had happened.

He thought about calling Zachary Travis. How pathetic that the only person he considered to be a possible male friend was Zack, one of the people his actions had wounded so deeply last year. And yet Zack had been one of those who'd seemed most likely to forgive, and Zack might know if Myra was in trouble.

Chilled to the bone at last, Weston gave up fighting the cold and strolled into the pool house. The relief was exquisite as he inhaled the humid, chlorine-scented warmth that greeted him.

Before he could talk himself out of it he tapped his Bluetooth. "Zachary Travis."

Zack, of all people, should hate him. The price of deception was a high one and Weston continually lost sleep over his behavior. The only hope he had that the man would answer this call was that Zack had forgiven him long enough to save his life this summer.

He stepped around the edge of the indoor pool and entered the main house as he listened to the trill of the Bluetooth.

He strolled past the great-room mantel that held photographs—memories of happy times. Even after four-and-a-half years he felt a fresh throb of grief when he looked at the image of Keegan's smiling face. How desperately he wished he'd known Zack Travis and Joy Gilbert when his son was alive. Even as fresh med-school grads, they were sharp, educated and caring enough they could have diagnosed the line of family deaths and saved Keegan.

Zack answered the phone on the fourth ring. "Weston."

Rushed and tense. Obviously at work. "Did I catch you at a bad time?"

Zack gave a short, humorless laugh. "When isn't it a bad time during ER rush hour?"

"I'm sorry," Weston said. "I thought I might find you at home for once. You know, I don't think the administrator intends for you to be a slave to that ER 24/7. I still have influence with the board. If you want, I could—"

"That's okay." Zack's chuckle this time was genuine. "We'll make do."

"Why should you have to when I can help?"

"Because we're a physician short, and as the director I have to make up the difference. The board can't help with this."

Weston felt foolish. One moment he was brooding about his past behavior and the next he was attempting once again to use his influence and money to buy a friend.

The clatter of a keyboard, the ringing of phones and the chatter of staff on Zack's end of the line told Weston how busy the ER was. "Hold on a second," Zack said.

Weston listened as the doctor apparently covered the phone receiver to speak to someone. If not for Myra, Weston would have apologized and disconnected so Zack could get back to work.

"Sorry about that," Zack said seconds later. "I'm waiting for some test results so I have a few minutes to talk. What's up?" There was a slim thread of tension in his voice.

"Is everything normal in your town tonight?" Weston asked.

"As good as it gets on Christmas Eve."

"You and Joy are keeping in touch with Myra, aren't you?" Weston asked.

"They're on the phone together at least a couple of times a week. Why?"

"I'm worried about her. She got a call at work that obviously upset her. She left and didn't return. That isn't like her, and she isn't answering my calls. I can't convince her assistant to give me the number from caller ID."

There was a long hesitation. "Myra left and missed your appointment today? That's not like her."

"I didn't have an appointment, I called thinking I'd catch her between appointments." Weston paused for the right words. "I'm not actually seeing her as my psychiatrist. Not in the traditional sense."

"But Joy specifically asked her to take your case and she agreed."

Weston remembered the work he'd been doing with Myra on the importance of honesty. "We've been meeting for dinner one or two times a week, and she—"

"Dinner?" There was no missing the concern in Zack's voice.

"We share a meal and talk, then we go our separate ways." He should have known Zack would be protective of Myra, his fiancé's best friend.

"Last I heard Joy had to do some convincing for Myra to even agree to office visits." The tone had cooled considerably.

"I pay for dinner and she doesn't have to worry about the specter of my suing her for malpractice." He meant it as a joke, but Zack didn't laugh.

"How did you manage that?"

"I didn't. She invited me nearly five months ago stipulating that I was going to pay for both our meals."

"She invited you?"

"Maybe invited is too weak a word. She told me if I wanted counseling we would do it after hours at her convenience and if at any time I made her uncomfortable she would stop the meetings."

Zack gave a low whistle. "Myra can be straightforward, can't she?"

"During our first meal she wanted me to understand exactly how much damage I'd done to you and Joy, and to remind me that if I had been a physician I could have lost my license after firing Joy in May. If Joy had sued me for sexual harassment in the workplace, she'd have won. Myra told me if she'd been you, she'd have beaten me half to death, and there were times she wanted to, herself, except the man she was so angry with wasn't the real Weston Cline."

Zack laughed, and it didn't sound entirely friendly. "So a little hostility there?"

"I gave her half my lobster, all of my steak to take home with her, and believe me I was glad we'd met in a public place—albeit we were in a private room."

The laughter died. "Not the real Weston Cline? What did she mean by that?"

He shouldn't have been surprised by the hard tone in the man's voice. He accepted it with as much grace as possible. "She's still seeing me, and it's by mutual agreement, so you might consider that she took the time to look for something decent in a vilified man."

"Okay." There was a question in Zack's voice.

"My daughter told her I'd been trying to make some changes

in my life and she wanted to see if it was authentic. I think she took pity on me for Tressa's sake."

"Joy never mentioned any of this."

Weston winced at the edge in Zack's voice. Still that mistrust. "You know my reputation. You probably wonder if I'm—"

"Not my business."

"No. It isn't your business but I'm sure Joy will make it hers. I'm calling you to ensure Myra's safety, I'm not attempting to seduce her. It really is just dinner and conversation during which I turn off my constantly buzzing cell phone and we talk. Sometimes we even laugh. She never turns off her phone, which has me worried now. She hasn't answered any of my calls."

"Look, I'm sorry," Zack said. "I guess you can tell I'm still having a little trouble with the forgiveness thing."

"I don't blame you, but right now—"

"Have the two of you had a recent disagreement? Women have this thing called the silent treatment and man, it's a bear to break past that barrier if they dig in feet first."

Weston sighed. For a brilliant doc, sometimes Zack didn't pick up on the obvious when it came to real life. Time to spell it out once more. "She left work without a word. No little disagreement with me is going to make her do that. She had more appointments today and her assistant had to reschedule because Myra never returned. That isn't like her. Something else is wrong."

There was a long silence and then Zack released a hiss of air. "No, that isn't like her."

"Have you spoken to Joy? Maybe Myra called her."

"She hadn't heard anything as of four o-clock today or she'd have said something. I called her when things slowed down here."

The buzz of another telephone sounded at Zack's end of the line. "Where have you searched?" he asked.

"Everywhere I know to look. Even her house, her hair stylist, massage therapist, her favorite restaurants, her jogging trails. But no matter where she goes she would always have her phone."

"Unless she lost it or it ran out of juice."

"I thought of that, but if something happened that upset her badly enough to abandon patients she'd have called Joy or me, maybe Laine."

"Do you know her brother's number?" Zack asked. "What if

15

something happened to him?"

"I called him. He's fine. Now he's worried about her too."

At the other end of the line a female voice softly called out, "Dr. Travis."

Zack excused himself for a moment. Weston shamelessly eavesdropped as the faceless female relayed the quietest of messages. "Joy's bringing a friend in."

It was enough for Weston to make plans for Christmas.

When Zack returned to the line, he said, "I might have a lead."

"You think Myra's there?"

"You know I can't divulge patient information even if it is her."

"But you can tell me if it isn't."

"Yes, I'll do that."

"Thank you." Weston sank to the sofa in front of the cold, dark fireplace. Federal privacy rules struck again, because there was no way he would be able to get any news about the friend Joy was taking to the ER. "If it's Myra would you let her know I'm on my way?" Myra still thought of Juliet, Missouri, as home, and he'd come to know her well enough to believe that was where she'd go if she needed help.

"What?" Zack said. "Wait, you're coming here?"

"I'm not the only one who benefits from our dinners. We're friends. Good friends. I want to be there for her, and I need to...I've been wanting to...are you on duty tomorrow?"

"No, but—"

"May I take you out for a late lunch?" Weston asked.

There was a long pause. "Um, you do know it's Christmas."

"I'm sorry, you probably have plans with Joy tomorrow."

"She's on duty then we're having dinner at Molly's."

Weston shook his head. The man was scrambling hard to avoid a meeting. "I'm going to check a couple more places here in the city, then I'm out of options. If you don't call me back I'm driving to Juliet tonight," Weston said. "I'm not doing anyone any good here in the city."

"Your daughter—"

"Is with her mother and grandparents where she should be. And even if I'm wrong about Myra, I still need to have a nonhostile talk with a man of integrity because there's more to this situation than either of us has time to discuss right now."

Zack was silent for a moment. "When and where?"

"Thank you. I'll make it easy for you. There aren't any places in Juliet that will hold good memories for us, obviously. We can have German Christmas lunch downriver in Hermann if you wish. That's not a long drive. Or we could do breakfast, anything you want."

"The forests and roads are infested with deer at night, even at this time of year. You need to wait until—"

"I'll take my chances."

Zack's heavy sigh reached Weston over the line. "Perhaps new memories can wipe out the old ones. If you care for a walk after I get up tomorrow I'll give you a call. It isn't necessary for you to drive in the dark."

"Call me on my cell when you're ready in case you don't get any sleep tonight. If you don't call me about the patient Joy's bringing in, I'll be in town."

"Okay."

"I'll see you tomorrow." Weston tapped his Bluetooth as he climbed the stairs to the master suite. He had no idea how long he'd be gone, so he pulled out the suitcase Sylvia had given him on their final Christmas together—it was huge, as if she'd been hinting even then that she would help him pack and leave.

He'd furnished his suite at the Cline Research Wing in Juliet last year when he was spending a lot of time at the medical school, so it would be waiting. He hadn't returned to that wing since last year's tragedy, and he probably wouldn't feel welcome there for long, but he didn't care. Not everything was about him.

He would spend Christmas looking for Myra. He couldn't help believing she was in trouble even if she wasn't the one on her way to the ER with Joy. But he hoped she was, because if not, where on earth could Myra be?

Chapter 3

Her name was Myra Maxwell. She tested it silently, forming the words with her lips and tongue. It felt strange, totally unrecognizable, but this time when Joy Gilbert sank down beside her on the cold ground, Myra resisted the urge to withdraw.

"You can trust us to do whatever you need," Joy said.

"I don't know what I need." She gestured to the tombstone. "I suppose these are relatives of mine?"

Joy hesitated. "Maybe I spoke too soon. You might not be able to trust me. I want to do and say the right thing, but I don't want you freaking out on me if I mention something that upsets you."

Myra looked up at her in the glow from the flashlight. "You can tell me. Obviously they were my parents or other family members."

Joy nodded. "Parents. You loved them very much."

Joy's mother, Molly, patted Myra's shoulder gently then circled around the tombstone. "We won't leave you alone. I think it might be a good idea to get you to the ER, but I think our doctor here needs to check you out first."

Myra looked at Joy. "You're a doctor?"

"I'm presently an employee at the local emergency department, and I think it would be a good idea to have you checked out there. Nothing like this has ever happened to you before."

"You're sure about that?"

"I would have known."

"I noticed I didn't bring any identification with me." Myra spread her hands. "So perhaps I'm afraid to know more about myself? The car? The red Mustang? Something about it terrifies me now that I'm out of it."

Joy shivered and Myra reached up to pull the coat from her

shoulders. "You need this."

Joy pressed her hands against Myra's. "You need it more."

Molly took her own coat off and handed it to her daughter. From what Myra could see in the flashlight glow Joy looked very much like her mother, with thick dark hair and dark eyes. They were both beautiful women. To Myra, though, they looked like strangers. She suddenly wanted a mirror. It wasn't right that she knew what these two women looked like but she wouldn't even recognize her own reflection.

"I have an extra jacket in the car," Molly said. "I'll bring back another flashlight."

"Mom, bring my stethoscope?" Joy asked.

They both watched as Molly plowed a bright furrow through the night toward the only two remaining vehicles in the cemetery.

"That's my mom," Joy said with affection. "Molly Gilbert, rescuer of all lost and hurting beings whether beast or human—and on some occasions a combination of both."

"You know some beastly people?"

Joy laughed softly. "Yes, but Mom gets along better with her rescued animals than with beastly people. Some of her cats are practically human."

"Some?"

"At last count, there were fifteen left."

"Fifteen cats!"

"She had more but my cousin Dawn ran some ads in the paper about adopting well-trained pets, and now my poor mother's having to say good-bye to some of her loved ones."

"She must really love cats."

"And dogs, a goat and various kinds of domesticated and wild animals over the years. She presently has raccoons but they'll be old enough to go out into the wild soon."

Myra shook her head. No wonder Joy held her mother in such awe. "I'm sorry for the trouble. You do seem to know me but I still can't place you."

"Another reason to get you to the ER."

"I have no discernable injury. I've checked."

"So you remember to do that?" Joy asked. "To check for injury? And you realized you were in a fugue state so your training seems at least somewhat intact."

"Lovely. I know my training but I don't know what it is. I also apparently knew where to come and I recognized the fireworks but not my own clothing. Am I a doctor too?"

"You're a psychiatrist."

With those words the darkness threatened to close in again. Myra gasped and covered her face. Something about her profession frightened her?

"Hey, I know you don't know this." Joy laid a hand on Myra's shoulder. "In the real world, outside this fugue state, you and I tell each other everything. In fact you're usually the one who keeps my life right side up. Let me help you through this. It's only fair I help you out for once."

Myra instinctively trusted this woman, but she didn't trust what her own response might be when she came out of this state of denial. "Something about being a psychiatrist feels like a threat."

"Tell me how."

"I feel as if I'm being hunted by something huge and terrifying, and if I don't know what it is it can't hurt me."

"Isn't that what a fugue state is? Avoidance of some horrible knowledge?"

"Yes, but I don't even want to think about what it could be."

"Then don't. But running a CT scan on you won't force back your memory before you're ready, it'll just let us know if you've had an injury or something going on inside your brain to cause this."

"Give me a minute, please. Tell me a little more."

***

Joy sat shivering in the dark. Part of her foundation had crumbled and she was afraid of every word that might come out of her mouth. How much damage could she do here if she said the wrong thing? Even after Zack broke their engagement Myra was supportive despite her own tragic loss. After Weston fired her Myra was the first person she called.

"Joy? Talk to me."

"I'm not sure what to tell you. Anything I say could trigger a memory and I have no idea how you'll react."

"We're good friends. Tell me about that."

That shouldn't cause any wrong switches to flip. "We've been best friends for…let's see…since high school. You have an older brother who was grown before you moved here with your parents, but you keep in touch with him by email and telephone." She paused and was reassured by the quiet sound of Myra's even breathing. "You entered Juliet High in tenth grade, and your parents moved you here specifically because you wanted to attend Juliet School of Medicine." She waited to see if there was any reaction.

"So we're sitting on the ground in a cemetery in a town called Juliet? Or were both schools named after a person?"

"The town's named after the wife of one of the first German settlers in this area who discovered the native grapes we call Norton, which once saved the French wine industry."

"A history lesson." Myra sighed. "Safe topic. Come on, I'm not that fragile."

"We have no idea how fragile you are. We live on the Missouri River, which you would have had to cross to get here." That thought terrified Joy. Was Myra on autopilot the entire the time she drove here?

"What else? Talk to me. If I can get my bearings at least a little, maybe it won't be such a shock to me when I recover."

Joy sent up a silent prayer that Myra would regain her memories. Some people never did, or the memories were patchy. "You used to live near the park just downhill from here. We hold the fireworks just past the trees. You and I used to watch the show from your upstairs window. If the trees weren't in the way we'd be able to see your old house from here in daylight."

"How did we meet?"

"Math class. You were a year ahead of me in school, but we became friends almost instantly when we discovered we were both bound for med school. You loved spending the weekend at my house because you love animals."

"And your mother obviously attracts animals."

"You helped us bottle feed an injured baby coyote."

"I wish I could remember that."

Joy slumped. Nothing. "Something you didn't love was discovering that you had to understand geometry in order to take trigonometry, and you didn't sign up for the right class. So you spent the summer before your senior year learning geometry from me."

Myra released a quiet sigh. "Thank you for telling me that. You were obviously a very good friend."

"That's what we are," Joy said softly. "Good friends. Do you know you're part Cherokee?"

"I might get a clue if I knew what I looked like."

"You have black hair, beautiful olive skin with high cheekbones and green eyes. Your father was half Cherokee."

"My father." There was a quiet sigh. "From reading this tombstone I see that my parents died months apart."

"You sure you want to talk about that? It was a hard time for you."

"But long ago according to the dates on this stone."

"You dropped out of college before your final year because of your father's death and your mother's illness," Joy said. "That's how we ended up graduating together. Until you and your brother sold the house I stayed with you or you stayed with me because you didn't want to be alone."

"Why did we sell the house?"

Joy couldn't afford to hesitate. "You needed the money to complete med school. You didn't want to have to pay off school loans forever." It was part of the truth. Myra wasn't ready for the whole story.

Myra breathed deeply. Maybe she was beginning to relax. "Tell me about that tall monument behind you."

Joy sighed. How tangled could this story get? "That death was much more recent."

"I'll let you off the hook," Myra said. "I already know it means something to me, I just don't know what."

"Well then Dr. Myra Maxwell, you would know better than I whether it's safe to tell you how important he was in your life. He died over a year ago."

"When I touched the stone after I first arrived here I felt a tingle run down my arm."

"Pretty frightening."

"But I'm not having that reaction now. Dustin Grooms? The last name's different from mine, so he wasn't my husband or my brother. Tell me."

"Your fiancé."

A long pause, then, "I was engaged?"

Joy paused. "Any problems with that name?"

"Nothing."

"He was a fellow classmate in med school, and we worked together on a research project for a MRSA serum after we finished our residencies. He accidentally got infected from a particularly virulent strain of the MRSA, and—"

Myra's sudden intake of breath attempted to suck all the oxygen from the cemetery. "Oh boy, maybe we should hold up there. Deep water."

Joy shifted uncomfortably. It was no surprise that Myra couldn't go there yet. Their experiences last year were nightmarish enough to send all of them into a fugue state. "It was a difficult time. We can talk about it when you're ready."

"Was I ever married?"

Joy smiled into the darkness. "No. We saw too many friends divorce during med school and residency so we made a pact to keep each other from any romantic relationships until we were free from the hardest part." Joy settled more comfortably next to Myra.

"Are you married?" Myra asked.

"I would be if my fiancé hadn't broken our engagement last year."

"I'm sorry."

"It's fine. We're planning the wedding now." It made sense that Myra could talk about Dustin but not his death or the research project that killed him. She'd practically hyperventilated when she learned her medical specialty. "Any idea why it frightens you to know you're a psychiatrist?" Joy asked the question with hesitance, hoping she didn't stir things up too much.

"Denial of something but I don't know what, and right now I don't want to."

"Honey, I sure wish I knew what happened to you," Joy said. "But you obviously came here for a reason. Maybe it was to escape something in Kansas City?"

Silence.

"Tiffany Springs," Joy said. "Suburb of Kansas City. Your practice—"

"No! Please. Don't say anymore."

Startled, Joy placed an arm across Myra's shoulders. "It's

23

okay," she said gently, listening to her friend's quick breaths. "I won't push you." What horrible thing had Myra come here to escape? She must have instinctively known she'd be welcome here. Or maybe she'd come here to the cemetery like a child running home to her parents, terrified of something beyond her power to fight.

Myra was silent until her breathing slowed to a more normal rate. "Troublesome."

"You've always had a gift for understatement," Joy said. "We spoke just yesterday and all was well. Sarah Miller has finally begun recovery."

"Sarah Miller." She said the name as if testing it.

"Anything?"

"Is she a friend of ours?"

"A patient I referred to you," Joy said.

Myra didn't reply, didn't ask about their discussion yesterday. In fact, she seemed to switch off for a moment, though it was hard to tell in the darkness.

Two bright beams from flashlights pierced the night and outlined Myra's face, her eyes fixed far beyond them.

"Ready to come with us to the hospital?" Mom called.

Joy stood up and watched Myra as she blinked, frowned, and finally turned her attention to the beams.

"Myra?" Joy said softly. "Everything okay?"

"Sorry." She shook her head as if puzzled. "I guess I zoned out there for a minute."

"All the more reason to get you to the hospital."

Myra glanced toward the Mustang and took a shuddering breath. "I don't want to get back into that car."

"Good, because you have no business driving, anyway." Joy accepted her stethoscope from her mother, and under the glow of both lights she had Myra breathe, listened to her heart rate, even checked her neck arteries for a possible blockage. All was clear and normal except for a slightly elevated heart rate.

Joy wrapped the stethoscope around her neck. "I'll drive your car and you can ride with Mom in my Explorer. Wait here a minute, Myra." She handed her friend the flashlight and nudged her mother out of earshot. "Take her to the SUV," she whispered. "Get her to the ER, but if she hesitates don't force her to go in. It might help her to ride around and talk for a few minutes. Don't wait on me."

"Why?"

"She's afraid to get into her own car, and when I mentioned Kansas City she panicked. What if something happened while she was driving in KC?"

"For instance?"

"What kind of thing happens in a car?"

"You're saying she might've hit someone? No way she'd have pulled a hit-and-run."

"Of course not, unless that brought on this fugue state. Just take her the long way to the hospital, would you? I'll drive her car and call Zack."

"I already called."

"Good. I'll meet you there. You know this problem could be as simple as a nasty electrolyte imbalance."

"If so Zack will find it. You'll need these." Mom handed her Myra's keychain. "She left it in the ignition and her purse is in the passenger seat. Her fear of the car could be as simple as knowing her purse might contain information she doesn't want to know. Maybe a cell phone."

"Or a bad memory. I'll see you at the hospital." Joy turned toward the Mustang.

Mom distracted Myra as she walked her to Joy's SUV. True to form, she'd given Joy the brighter flashlight. While Myra was focused on getting into the SUV and listening to Molly's chatter, Joy walked around the front of the Mustang and aimed the light along the grill. No dents, no stains.

She cast a glance at the other car, noted they weren't watching her, and dropped to her knees to aim the beam through the grill. It was clean. She stood up and walked around to the driver's side, then stared after the vehicle that carried her mother and her friend from the cemetery.

The churning in her gut did not diminish, but she couldn't take time to be sick. Her best friend had lost her mind and Joy had no idea how to help her find it.

Chapter 4

Joy arrived at the Juliet Hospital Emergency Department three minutes after leaving the cemetery, and she didn't see her SUV in the parking lot. Good. Mom was taking a long route to the hospital, giving Myra time to settle a little, and avoiding the home where Myra once lived—and where her parents both died.

No one could calm a person's fears better than Molly Gilbert. She was also likely talking about her animals, telling funny stories about them, because Myra loved animals, too.

Joy had used a slightly heavy foot with Myra's dream car to arrive first. Maybe she should've chosen one of these little muscle cars for herself instead of that small bus she could practically live in.

She parked next to Zack's Outback. Three vehicles pulled out of the emergency patient parking area as she got out of the car. Yes! Maybe she'd have some time to talk to Zack if patients were actually checking out instead of in. She'd barely had time to lay eyes on the man she loved in the past few days, and unless she received special Christmas dispensation tomorrow, she'd likely be too swamped to even share a meal with him until they met at Mom's after work tomorrow night.

The glass door swished open and she entered in time to see him stepping from the emergency department entrance into the waiting room. His golden brown eyes lit with welcome when he saw her.

"Busy night?" She walked sedately toward him, badly as she would prefer to fly into his arms and feel them around her, strong and reassuring. After her shock over Myra tonight she needed his strength more than the air she breathed.

She also wanted to nuzzle his neck and kiss him right there in front of staff, patients, everyone. They'd understand, right? Hadn't everyone been in love at some time?

He invaded her personal space just slightly and looked down at her with an expression of such longing that she smiled up at him, indulging in the warmth she felt emanate from him. Whose idea was it to have a long engagement?

Oh yeah, that had been hers.

He glanced outside. "Where are the others?"

"Mom's bringing Myra."

"So it *is* Myra?"

"She didn't tell you?"

"I got the news second hand."

She frowned. "Second hand? Who else could have told you?"

He took a slow, deep breath, took her arm and walked her down the hallway.

This wasn't good if he was getting her away from prying eyes. "Zack?"

"Weston Cline called me in a panic about her."

She stopped walking. "What? Why him?"

"He told me Myra received a call at work today and left obviously upset. She didn't tell anyone why. That's all he knows."

Joy couldn't speak for a moment. "Again, why him?"

Zack met her gaze steadily. "It appears her counseling sessions with him have been taking place after hours over dinner. He tried to call her at work today, probably to apologize for an argument they had last night, and learned of her abrupt departure. He's pretty worried."

"But she never told me for sure if she was seeing him as a patient."

"You asked her to, didn't you?"

Joy sighed. "Yes and she reluctantly agreed. Now I'm sorry I asked. But over dinner? What's with that?"

"It's already happened and we have to move forward." Zack smoothed her hair back and rested his hand at the nape of her neck.

Joy took comfort from his touch as she gave herself a moment to breathe. "Why did he call you of all people?"

He gave her a sideways frown. "The most likely person to know her whereabouts is you. Would you rather he'd called you?"

She swallowed at the sharp look he shot her. Could he still be harboring unresolved questions about her time with Weston? "I don't want anything to do with him."

"Then maybe that's why he called me."

Joy tried again to focus on her breathing, on Zack's gentle touch, on anything but thoughts of Weston Cline. Had to calm down. "Please tell me he isn't here."

"Not yet."

"Yet!" Oh Lord, please no. "You mean he's coming?" Couldn't Weston just disappear from their lives?

"I was on the phone with him when Molly called the front desk." Zack hesitated, grimaced. "He apparently picked up enough overhearing the message from Molly that he guessed Myra might be the friend you were bringing in, and at the time I didn't even know it was her. He's been looking for her all afternoon."

"He must have been frantic to grasp at that straw."

"Caring for someone in trouble can make a person desperate."

"I don't like the thought of Weston caring about Myra, or behaving out of desperation. He's likely to do anything."

Zack sighed as he combed his fingers through her hair, obviously hoping to calm her. It worked for a few glorious seconds. She closed her eyes and relished his touch.

"Step back from the situation a moment," he said gently.

Her eyes shot back open. "We trusted him and look what happened. I don't want to make that mistake again. The man's liable to do anything, pull strings, offer bribes, threaten careers, and how can we know he wasn't the reason she left the city in the first—"

Zack pressed a finger to Joy's lips. "Slow down freight train," he said with affection. "What matters right now is that he apparently knows more than we do, and that might help us to help her."

"But I don't understand why he'd know anything about her, even if she has been counseling him after hours." Joy frowned at Zack. She knew that look. He was holding something back. "What am I missing?"

Zack paused, then sighed. "They've become friends, and from what he said it sounds as if the friendship is deepening."

"No." Joy held her hands over her ears. "Don't tell me that."

"Wouldn't you go to any lengths to look for a good friend who's obviously in crisis?"

"Of course."

"He's been seeing her for dinner, several dinners, obviously, which he told me serve as counseling sessions, but I gather he's investing more than words and money into these dinners."

"Emotions, as well, then." Not good at all. "But she's too smart to fall for a man like him."

"Sweetheart." Zack took her hands and drew them down to her sides. "Would you remember that it's Christmas? Time for some peace on earth, wouldn't you say?"

She felt the streak of warmth shoot up her arms and filter throughout her whole body. Closing her eyes, she focused on his touch for a long moment. But too soon another thought occurred to her.

She opened her eyes. "You said she received the call at work? On her work phone?"

"That's correct."

"What if it was about a patient? If it was a personal call, she'd have received it on her cell."

"And she went into a fugue state over a patient? I don't think—"

"You know how she is," Joy said. "She gets attached."

"Let's check her out physically before we decide. We'll take things one step at a time."

"We have to get her memories back for her."

He nodded. "We both know how tricky that can be, but brace yourself, because Weston's definitely on his way here."

Joy felt helpless against the alarm that scuttled her nerves and gave her a sick feeling in her stomach. Even though Weston had apparently made an about-face a few months ago, she continued to wait for him to change back at any time. She'd seen too much of his dark side.

***

Zack looked out the plate glass windows once more and then glanced back to the ER, put an arm around Joy and walked with her down the hallway toward his office. They turned a corner and he stopped her and pulled her into his arms. "Finally."

She buried her face into his chest. He wanted to hold her like that for the rest of the night—something that would get them both fired. Her warmth and the obvious love she had for him gave him strength he didn't always feel, especially after having a phone discussion with a man who nearly seduced her last year. He hoped his love would surround her with the reassurance she needed. "Yes, finally." This was likely what she needed to distract her from everything else.

He eased her back enough to look into her face. "We've got to stop making do with these offhand meetings," he said just before his lips covered hers.

He allowed the tingle of pleasure to heat his skin. Forget Weston for now. After a long, satisfying kiss, Joy snuggled into him, head beneath his chin, matching his faint aroma of Betadine and soap that mingled with her own natural scent, warm and delicious. All woman. A totally dedicated doctor. He dreamed of marriage to this loving, kind, fascinating woman. He needed just one more kiss. He lifted her chin.

"You're trying to distract me," she said, just before his lips caught hers and claimed them again. And again.

"Have I told you today that I love you?" he asked when they came up for air.

"I think that's what you're doing—"

He pulled her closer, claimed her mouth, her chin, her cheek, her ear. If he continued, he wouldn't be responsible for her actions. Or for his.

"Zack." She drew away.

"I know." They had so few times like this—which was probably a good thing. But Myra would be walking through those front doors any second, and they had to be prepared.

With reluctance, Zack released her. "Sorry. I've missed you so much."

"Things can't continue like this. I wish I could focus, but what you said makes me wonder. I don't understand why Myra couldn't tell me about having dates with Weston if he isn't actually a patient."

Zack nearly groaned aloud. He could use a subject change. He drew her to the inner wall, leaned against it and pulled her close. "If you were Myra would you mention to your best friend that you're having intimate dinners with the man who nearly destroyed her happiness last year?"

Joy stiffened in his arms. He'd misspoken yet again. "Intimate dinners? How intimate are we talking?"

He'd better watch his words a little more closely until she got this Weston thing out of her system. If she did. "When you think about it, a counseling session is intimate whether it's over lobster or over an office desk." Where was it he'd heard about hatred being akin to love? Was she protesting too much?

"If he's responsible for this fugue state—"

"Hey, peace on earth, remember? A minute ago you thought it might be something about a patient. I know we're having trouble with forgiveness, but it really isn't our business what Myra does with her private life, is it?" He tipped her chin up and gazed into her eyes with such love he knew she couldn't resist.

"Sorry."

"Sweetheart, it isn't as if you and Myra have a signed contract to tell each other everything. I think she tells you things you can handle, and keeps the rest to herself." He kissed the top of her head, trailed kisses down her cheek, then lowered his lips to hers, gently caressing her face, her hair, drawing her still closer. "This is becoming unbearable. I wish we were married already and you didn't have so many wedding plans. We should have gotten married this summer."

She pressed her hands against his chest, obviously resisting the urge to simply rest them there and enjoy the touch and closeness. "Sometimes you don't take things as seriously as I do. I wish I could be more like that." She slid from his arms.

He suddenly felt abandoned, and he wished Weston had never called. The man was still interfering with Zack's very vital relationship with Joy. With another lingering kiss on her cheek he gave a heavy sigh and allowed her to move away. "We should probably get back to the front. I think I heard the door open. Why don't I let you work this out with Myra once she's herself again?"

She looked up at him, eyes filled with regret. "What happened to my forgiving heart? I once thought I'd forgiven him."

"I'm having the same problem, but I'm going to try again."

"If only I could forget what he did to us."

"I know." Zack didn't want to be reminded; it would only make seeing him again that much more difficult, but the man had apologized more than once and had made amends financially to show his remorse. People did outrageous things when they were

31

broken. And Zack knew Weston was a member of the walking wounded. The big question was whether or not he could ever heal.

***

Joy sighed as she walked beside Zack to the waiting room. He was right. She was going to have to pray for a renewal of the forgiveness she thought she'd found this summer. Just how she would do that while protecting Myra, she didn't know.

She turned the corner in the hallway and saw Myra sitting next to Mom.

"I'm meeting with him tomorrow," Zack said. "I'll see what more I can find out."

Before Joy could protest Zack was walking away.

Chapter 5

Unbelievably anxious, Myra tried hard not to cling to Molly Gilbert. The smells in this hospital were familiar and she braced herself against them. Memories threatened to attack; she didn't feel strong enough to defend herself against them.

She heard footsteps and turned to see Joy walking beside a hunk of a man with sandy brown hair, golden brown eyes, and a smile that was all for Joy.

At the sight of Joy, Myra went weak with relief. It surprised her. Though she felt as if she'd only known the beautiful, dark-haired, brown-eyed woman for an hour at most, some kind of familiarity remained between them. That didn't mean Myra was getting her memories back, but it meant she could be assured she was among trustworthy people who had her best interests at heart as she endured this nightmare.

"Myra," Joy said, stepping up behind the attractive man, "meet Zachary Travis. You two know each other well in your other life."

Myra wiped her sweaty hands on the coat, then realized she was abusing someone else's outerwear. "So you're the one who broke your engagement to my best friend last year?" she said, holding her hand out to him with a forced grin.

He glanced at Molly and Joy, then winked. He took Myra's hand and smiled. "That would be me. What other horrible things has she told you about me?" He turned to lead them to a door, nodding to the secretary at the window to let them in. After it clicked, he pushed it open and held it for the three women.

"No use in talking about it now," Myra said. "I'll come to my senses pretty soon, right? Then I'm sure I'll recall everything." Not that she wanted to rush it. But she did want her mind back. The inner conflict kept her arguing with herself. Why didn't she just ask Joy to fill her in on everything she needed to remember?

"I'll need to do some testing first," the handsome doctor said.

"I understand that we can't predict these things," she said, "but familiar surroundings can be most helpful."

He gave her a look of surprise. "You're obviously retaining a good foundation of knowledge. Excellent sign. Since you seem capable of thinking clearly to a point, you can decide if you wish to preserve your privacy or if you want someone in the room with you."

"I'll be out in the waiting area," Molly said. "It hasn't been too many months since I was a patient here, and I know how much I preferred my privacy. But Myra, if you don't have to spend the night here for observation you have an open invitation to my house."

Myra nodded and gave Joy's mother what she hoped was a warm smile. All she really felt was sudden, absolute terror. What if tests revealed something physically wrong with her? A brain tumor? Something else?"

Zack spoke with a nurse who led them all to an empty curtained cubicle. Not a lot of privacy.

Myra focused on keeping her hands from shaking. "I guess you want me to get into that gown and lie down?"

Zack gave her a perfectly beautiful smile. "I'm sure you don't feel like lying down, but it'll help as we prep you for tests." He waited until she entered the cubicle and then started to pull the curtain.

She looked back at him. "Oh, by the way, you could do with a little less lipstick." She gestured to his face.

He grinned. "Thanks for the beauty advice. It's a relief to see you haven't lost your personality."

She looked at Joy, whose lipstick was practically smeared off her face. "You could use a trip to the mirror as well, girlfriend." She tried to smile but felt it falter.

Joy reached for her hand and squeezed firmly. "All you have to endure is a contrast CT, blood work for any drugs someone might have slipped to you, and peeing in a cup—always one of my favorite things to do in a public bathroom. We'll also need medication history in case you've started taking something you haven't told me about." She looked up at Zack. "And on Christmas Eve, where will we find that?"

"I've been having my private practice patients keep a medical sheet in their billfolds or purses, so you might check there," Zack said.

"I left everything in her car. I'll go check while she changes." Joy squeezed Myra's hand again, turned and rushed out.

Myra stared at the gown for a moment, then closed her eyes and muttered, "Dementia versus delirium."

"Not dementia," Zack said behind her. "Anything that comes on this quickly is likely to be from a shock or injury, drugs—"

"Or the result of a brain tumor."

"I'm pretty sure that isn't what this is."

She grasped at those words in desperation. "Why?"

"Does the name Weston Cline mean anything to you?"

It didn't. She shook her head.

"He's a friend of yours. He actually called here looking for you from Corrigan, which is a suburb of Kansas City."

As before, she felt that surge of unexpected fear.

"Don't worry," Zack said quickly. "All I'll tell you is that from my own personal experience you have a tendency to become emotionally involved with your patients. I learned from Weston tonight that it's possible you've received news that could have caused this."

She closed her eyes and reached for the bed for support. "Please, I can't go there right now. I can't—"

"It's okay." Zack caught her other arm and helped her sit on the side of the bed. He called for a tech. "I think our patient's going to need some help."

"I'll be fine." Myra gave Zack a nod. "I'll change by myself if you don't mind. Then you can run the tests you would ordinarily run."

"Call if you feel dizzy or need help." Zack pulled the curtain shut.

Myra stripped out of her clothing and pulled the flimsy garment on backward so she could more easily tie the strings that held it together.

She was settled into the bed, covered by the sheet and a light blanket when Joy called to her from the other side of the curtain.

"Myra? Need some company?"

"I sure do. Did you find anything in my purse?"

"Nope. You're young and healthy except for the obvious. All you take is a vitamin pill, and I only know that because you told me." Joy stepped between the curtains, turned to make sure the entry was securely closed, then frowned at Myra. She reached for some tissues and held them out. "Any idea why you're crying?"

Only then did Myra realize her face was wet with tears. "I have no idea. Zack suggested this fugue state might be related to one of my patients, but it was conjecture."

Joy took her hand in a quick squeeze. "It's going to be okay."

"Do you know anything about what's happened? Something you're not telling me?"

"No, but even if I did would you feel prepared to hear it?"

Myra shook her head. "I have a feeling this fugue state won't last much longer, but something terrifies me. I want to know everything right now, but at the same time, what kind of horrible shock could cause me to reach this state?"

"Why do you feel it won't last much longer?" Joy sat on the edge of the bed as the medical technician pulled a monitor, blood pressure cuff and pulse oximeter to Myra's right side.

"Why else would I be crying? It's possible the memory is surfacing from my subconscious." She looked up at the tech. "You'll find my vitals are all good."

The young woman smiled at her and shrugged. "You're probably right, but you're getting the full treatment."

Joy pressed her fingers to Myra's wrist. "Still a little elevated. Not surprising. I told Mom to drive your car to her house. When you check out of here I'll take you home with me."

For a fleeting moment Myra felt as if she clung to a cliff's edge. Something about Joy felt so familiar all of a sudden. She stared into Joy's dark eyes, the gentle contours of her concerned face, and the feeling of panic subsided. She got the impression that this woman was a source of comfort, but that could likely be from Joy's own description of their friendship.

"You live with your mom?" Myra asked.

"For now. I'm keeping an eye on her health and it didn't make sense to rent a place of my own when I'll be married in a few weeks. Or months. Or whenever all my friends and relatives decide on the best date. Don't worry, you'll remember everything when you recover."

"I like her."

"You always have."

"What about Weston Cline? Have I always liked him?"

The tech fumbled the pulse oximeter and it bounced onto the bed. She shot a surprised look at Myra.

Joy slid from the bed to the chair beside it. "Remember, Charla," she whispered to the tech. "Patient confidentiality."

The tech's eyes widened. "Not a word, Dr. Gilbert. I value my job."

Myra watched the blond-haired, blue-eyed tech, mystified as the young woman finished her job and left with a finger to her lips and a knowing look. Who was this man named Weston Cline?

***

Joy sank into the chair next to the exam bed, relieved that Myra was the one connected to the monitor right now. It wouldn't do to have two women in one curtained cubical with elevated heart rates. Joy had to focus on breathing deeply, slowly, intentionally. It was torture to see Myra like this, looking at her as if she was a stranger. Asking glibly about Weston as if he was a stranger.

She shut her eyes for a moment, willing herself to calm down. Myra might have no emotional response to the man's name, but Joy did. For over a year her experience with him had driven her from the depths of despair to surprised delight to blind fury. When he decided he wanted her last year he'd shown no conscience about doing what it took to get her.

What Weston didn't expect was that Molly Gilbert's daughter was as strong-willed as Molly. Joy had seen his surprise when he discovered he'd met his match in her. For a year, from the time he decided he would have her to the day she and Zack reunited, she'd lived in anxiety over the political and financial power Weston wielded.

But she'd also seen the brokenness beneath the charismatic exterior. Few other people had seen his vulnerable side, except perhaps for Zack and Weston's daughter, Tressa, who had a lot of depth for a sixteen-year-old.

When Joy opened her eyes she found Myra watching her. Somewhere deep in that clouded mind were memories of a man who could break down the barriers of a woman. Knowing her, however, she'd also seen that broken side.

"You look upset," Myra said.

Joy nodded. If only she knew how to measure her words. With Myra in such a fragile state she couldn't speak freely. "I'll do all I can to protect you and help you as you regain your memory. You can count on that." She laid a hand on Myra's free arm. "I need to go down the hallway for a few moments. You know to push the buzzer if you need anything." How she wished she'd asked Mom to stay. "I won't be long."

Myra hugged herself. She looked frightened. "You won't?"

"Promise. I need to make a call or two. Trust me, I'll be back soon. Try to rest." She slid between the curtains and found Zack at the u-shaped workstation in the middle of the ER.

He looked up from his computer keyboard. "How is she?"

"No memories yet." She couldn't help wondering about his state of mind. He'd just admitted he was still struggling to forgive Weston. What if it went deeper than that? "You're going to prep her for contrast CT?"

He typed a few more words and ended his patient chart. "I'm setting it up now."

"Perfect timing. I'll be back shortly." She avoided his questioning look and left the ER, bracing herself for a fight.

Chapter 6

Ice covered the first bridge Weston came to when he reached I-70, which made him question his determination to make it to Juliet tonight. Though the town was only three hours away, however, it was a little farther south, so it often missed the bad winter weather that occasionally battered Kansas City.

The chime of his cell phone echoed through the Mercedes. He looked at the caller ID and his foot came off the accelerator for a second. Had the stress of the day affected his mind?

He answered. "Joy?"

"Tell me you're not on your way here." Her familiar voice filled the car over the speakers.

He slowed down to keep from spinning out. She'd never been one to mince words, even when she'd liked and respected him—even when she'd been halfway attracted to him. A year ago he would have snapped back at her without thinking.

"I'm on my way," he told her gently.

"Stop." There was a tone of entreaty he didn't think he'd ever heard from her. "Please. Go back home. I don't know what it'll do to Myra."

He'd known when Zack didn't call back that she was there. "Is she injured? What happened? Is she okay?"

"Her body's here." There was a long pause. "She doesn't even know me." There was a break in Joy's voice.

He lost concentration and nearly drove off the road before he could recover. "How could she not know you?"

"Fugue state."

"You mean she's out of her mind?" He felt kicked in the gut.

"From what I know about fugue states it's the mind's attempt to escape something frightening or unacceptable, and her presence here likely means she's afraid of something in Kansas City, or of news she received there."

He wished he'd pressed Myra's assistant harder. In fact, he needed to call her at home and tell her what was at stake.

"Look," Joy said, "the only reason I can tell you about Myra is because I wasn't on duty tonight when Mom brought her to the ER, but when we found her she didn't even know her own name."

He focused his breathing and watched the road carefully, more afraid than he'd been all day. "Any clue about what happened?"

"I thought maybe you could tell me something."

Fear battled for control of his reflexes as he forced himself to remain focused on the highway where sleet blew across the road. "At least you found her. I was picturing her injured or worse."

"I don't know if this is worse or not. A fugue state is unpredictable."

"You're saying she might not regain her memories?"

"Myra has a strong will, so I believe she'll get them back. She told me she thought it would happen soon."

"That could be wishful thinking. She needs to be in a psychiatric facility."

"No. Just wait, okay? She's in the ER having tests done, and you're not even supposed to know about her."

He needed to pull off the road, but now he was more determined than ever to get to Myra. "I've been in contact with a psychiatrist in the recent past."

"Not yet, Weston, okay? I know you're worried about her, but she's in a safe place now and I'm not letting her out of my sight. She's retained her knowledge and education, from what I can tell, so if we need advice, strange as it seems, we can get it from her."

Weston suppressed a retort. Myra needed to be in a safe facility, locked in for her own protection. That was out of his hands, obviously.

"Zack said you've been trying to find out what happened," Joy said. "We were hoping you might have discovered something more."

"Only that some things, like vital information, cannot be bought at any price from her assistant or the phone company. I know you don't have any reason to want me there, but I think she'll need to see me."

"Are you sure about that? Or do you just you need to see

her?"

"I believe we both need to see each other. Since I wasn't there when this fugue state hit, it's apparent she wasn't attempting to escape me."

There was a long, uncomfortable silence as a big truck raced past him in the left lane, slinging icy chunks of sleet onto his windshield. He flipped on the wipers.

"How far along is this thing between you?" Joy asked.

"This 'thing' you're talking about is a friendship. She's been meeting with me for dinner for a few months now."

"Zack told me, but I'd have expected to read about that in the tabloids."

"Since when did you start reading those?"

"Is the press following you?"

"No. You know how careful I am about my privacy. She's an amazing therapist who has healed a nasty breach in my family." Not only had Myra listened and guided, she'd grown comfortable enough with him to use him as a sounding board. Somehow he didn't think Joy would appreciate hearing that.

"Don't forget that in May you were declaring your undying love for me," Joy said. "And now you're so connected to Myra you're willing to risk your life to come here and see her?"

"There have been no declarations of any kind between us." Though he was ready to make them he would hold off indefinitely.

"You can tell others that all you want but don't forget how well I know you."

No. Sadly, he could never forget. "I thought you and I had overcome that problem."

There was a pause. "So did I," she said quietly. "But that isn't what this is about."

"Are you sure?"

She remained silent for too long. He recalled how horrified he'd been when he realized how horrendously he'd behaved, even when he knew he couldn't hold onto her. He'd forced himself to face the truth about the harm he'd done to a woman he never truly loved, and to the man who'd truly loved her. Love and obsession were two entirely different things. How could he have been so greedy and heartless?

"Does 'rebound romance' ring any bells for you?" Joy asked.

He inhaled deeply and exhaled more slowly, as Myra had taught him to do when he needed to calm himself. "You and I never had a romance, did we?"

"Don't even try lying to me."

"You told me there would never be anything between us. You made it obvious in every way possible. A man would have to have been in a coma not to know your feelings."

"And I certainly knew yours."

"I don't think even I knew mine at the time."

"But you're the man who always knows what he wants and goes after it, right?"

He sighed. "Right now you're engaged to be married and I came to my senses quite some time ago. Are you telling me I can't move on with my life as well? You should ask Myra about what we have between us."

"Don't you dare joke about this, Weston."

"Joking?"

"She can't tell me anything right now."

"I mean after she recovers. She isn't a rebound romance for me."

"You admit there's romance?"

Another automobile came speeding up behind him. He braced for impact as it passed him and splashed him. Where did all the idiots come from on these stormy nights?

"Hello? Are you still there?" Joy asked.

His fingers clung to the steering wheel a little more forcefully. "I care for her, Joy. And I care about her." He said the words softly. "We became friends somewhere along the line when she was helping me put together all the broken pieces of my life."

"That's what a therapist does."

"I can't speak for her, but I can't help wanting to protect the person who's made such a difference in my life." Honesty had never happened to him before. Always he'd depended on the right words, the proper behavior—or at times improper, whatever he felt the situation called for—to convince colleagues, employees, enemies and even family members to do his bidding. Never had truth entered the equation for him unless he wanted it to.

With Myra there'd been no option. If he wanted change he knew he'd have to open his life completely to her or he would return to the old shell of Weston Cline. A shell he'd come to detest.

"Weston, if you care for her you need to understand that if you show up here and she's already fighting an attraction to you, this could send her more deeply into this fugue state. I don't know what happened but she's terrified to talk about Kansas City. You're from there."

"What if seeing me could take her out of that fugue state?"

"What if it forces something she isn't ready for?"

"Seeing me would be natural. She's been meeting with me face to face twice a week, and even though we don't always agree on everything, we're comfortable with each other."

"She's known me a lot longer than she's known you, and it's deadly painful to look into her eyes and realize she doesn't know who I am."

"I'll handle whatever happens."

"She spent months listening to me struggle when I worked for you, and now the two of you are suddenly great friends after the way you treated me?"

"I'm trying with all I have not to be that person anymore."

"Then don't be that person tonight. Think about the conflict she's going through. She's also afraid to talk about the research project last year. You're too close to this."

"So are you. I think you're grasping." He allowed a touch of iron to enter his voice. "It's obvious you still hold a grudge but I'm on my way to Juliet."

"Wow." It was a dry, sharp tone he recognized far too well. "That didn't take long did it? There's the old Weston I know."

"No it isn't. You and I obviously still have some issues to clear up. What better time than Christmas to seek peace?"

"Even if you have to stomp all over everyone to get what you want?"

He hesitated for a few seconds. "If I thought for a moment that seeing me would upset Myra I wouldn't see her."

"Why didn't Myra tell me she was seeing you?"

"Perhaps because she honors patient confidentiality," he said dryly. "You're her friend, not her business partner."

"She's far too vulnerable right now," Joy snapped. "If you show up and you're one of her first memories—"

"Then they'll be good memories," he said. Joy was behaving like a spoiled child. "Maybe she'll have a better foundation from which to examine more. I understand that because of our past you feel I'm not good enough to associate with someone like Myra, but where have you been these past months? How often did you visit? Would you rather see her slip away forever than to remember me before she remembers you?"

There was such a long silence that he wondered if they'd lost connection, or if she'd disconnected.

Joy finally gave a soft exhale. "It has nothing to do with whether or not you're good enough, it has to do with her Christian faith and your lack of it and how easily you could hurt her. If she cares as much for you as you obviously do for her she'll be too susceptible right now. That's a huge stressor. Believe me, I know."

"You do?"

"Come on, Weston, you know how it was. How we were. My belief system kept me from a lot of things, including you."

So Joy had cared for him at some point. Maybe those kisses were more than a simple distraction to her. Now he felt worse. Time to gentle his tone again. "I knew you shared her faith."

"Yes."

"Then exercise it a little. And maybe throw in some grace to smooth a few of your sharp edges. I'm on my way to Juliet."

Joy didn't reply.

That old weight of darkness seemed to surround him as he drove through the cold sleet, thinking about the one thing he could not buy. Faith in the Son of a God who had taken so much from the Cline family, as if He'd cursed them.

"You don't know the whole story, Joy. Unless God decides to shove me off the highway tonight I'll be there before midnight."

***

Joy's fingers were numb with cold by the time she disconnected from her call, frustrated and stinging from the argument. Weston Cline had never taken the time to consider any opinion besides his own. He was usually right when it came to business matters, but in matters of the heart he was out of his depth.

She spoke another name into her cell phone. "Laine Fulton."

44

Laine—one of four researchers who had worked on last year's project under the direction of Dr. Christopher Payson—had been the only one to remain in the field of research after their trials were shut down last year. Research was her passion but she was also a devoted friend, and not just because she was buried in the lab for long hours, day after day, without a lot of time to make new ones.

Myra, Laine and Joy had maintained their bond of friendship after the project ended. Though Laine worked an hour away from here in Columbia, she and Myra and Joy had maintained a special closeness as they traversed the maze of discovering new jobs, new co-workers, new challenges. Their motto was that the longer the friendship, the stronger the friendship.

Laine needed to know about Myra.

She answered on the second ring, her no-nonsense tone reflecting her approach to life. "Joy, tell me you aren't busy planning your wedding on Christmas Eve."

"I wish I was."

There was a pause. "What's wrong?"

"It's Myra." Joy felt the tears form at last. "Oh, Laine, I'm scared. She arrived tonight in Juliet in a fugue state."

There was a short moment of stunned silence. "What do you mean? How bad?" Laine's constant calm broke for a moment and Joy could hear the alarm in her voice.

"Bad fugue." She described it quickly. "To complicate matters Weston Cline's on his way here, and who knows what that could do to her. I don't know how to handle this."

"Calm down. Don't drop the phone."

"If Weston shows up—"

"Stop it." Laine's voice returned to its normal calm state. "First of all, everyone needs a good night's sleep. You know these things can resolve themselves on their own and usually do. Second, we all know you can't control Weston any more than you can control the wind. But also remember that Weston Cline is not as wicked as he appeared to be last year."

"You know what he did—"

"I know he was a rock for Myra when Dustin was ill and after he died. The man went above and beyond in an attempt to save Dustin's life."

"But if he does to Myra what he did to me—"

"Judging by what you said, Myra doesn't know him, remember? She doesn't even know herself."

"But when her memory returns—"

"Then we can hope to find she's still the same Myra we've always known, and she doesn't need a nanny. Stop worrying about what might happen and focus on getting her memory back."

"That's what I'm trying to—"

"Are you by Myra's side right now?"

"No. She'll be getting a scan soon."

"Then be there when she returns from that. If Weston's appearance there helps her regain her memories then be grateful for it and stop trying to micro-manage."

Joy digested Laine's words. The woman knew her too well.

"Wipe that scowl off your face. Are you on your way to Myra?"

Leave it to Laine to get to the point. "Okay, I get it. I'm going."

"Good. Progress. I'm not doing anything tonight. You want me to come down there?"

"It's Christmas Eve, Laine. You should be with family."

"That's why I asked."

"Oh Laine." Fresh tears filled Joy's eyes. Of course. One reason Laine and Myra had become fast friends in med school was because they'd both lost their parents too early, and Mom had welcomed them both into her tiny home for holidays. "I love you, too. But I hear the weather's getting bad tonight, so you'd better not take the risk. If anything happened to you I wouldn't know where else to turn."

"Balderdash, you're a grown woman with family all around and a fiancé who loves you to distraction. You'll be fine."

Joy barely prevented herself from rolling her eyes at Laine's manner of speaking. Who besides Laine used the word 'balderdash' anymore? "I don't want you to take any chances."

"Very well, but I expect you to keep me informed. Should I call Myra at the hospital or do you believe that will make everything more complicated?"

"It might be best for her to see you, but wait until the cold front moves through. If it doesn't affect the roads do you have any plans for tomorrow?"

"Most definitely. I have some testing I need to do or the timing will be off but I can drive down later in the evening if the roads are clear. I made my yearly fruitcake."

"Bring it!"

"Can you keep me updated?"

"I will." Listening to Laine's voice of practicality soothed something in Joy. "Thank you."

"Myra's my friend, too. We're in this together, so we'll find out what it is the same way. Together."

"Dinner at Mom's tomorrow night?"

"She still live with the menagerie?"

"Sure does."

"Count me in. I've discovered I have an allergy to cats, and so this will help me test a little experiment I've been conducting on alternative allergy treatment."

"Alternative?"

"It's promising, believe it or not. Patients are flocking to the alternative routes because they want to stay out of the nightmare of medical bureaucracy."

And the world continued to turn with Laine Fulton in it, tweaking a treatment here, testing a formula there, happy in her own little world when she wasn't working her day job.

"I'll see you if you can get here," Joy said.

"Where's Myra going to be?"

"I hope at Mom's house. I have no idea how her memory will be by then."

"Hope for the best, remember?"

"With Weston here?"

"Watch it, your claws are coming back out."

"You're right. Sorry. Dinner will be after I get off work, so sometime around eight or so. Come early so you don't have to drive in the dark. You could spend the night if—"

"If I weren't allergic to cats. Yes. I know. Hmmm, maybe it's time to pull out the stops and give it a more serious try. So. Last I recall Molly has a house the size of a thimble. Where would I sleep?"

"She built an upstairs and kept it a secret while I was working in the city, so if you trust her skills there are two extra bedrooms upstairs. She's been working on a bathroom."

"Has she walked across the Missouri River barefoot yet?" Laine's dry tone brought another smile to Joy's face.

"One thing at a time."

"A day with friends should give Myra plenty of time to come to herself and realize what caused the trouble."

"Or it could give us time to inherit more trouble."

Laine puffed into the phone. "Since when did you become more of a cynic than I?"

"You know the answer."

"Forgive, Joy."

"Harder than I thought."

"I would hazard a guess that his intentions are good."

Joy sighed. Practical Laine Fulton, who knew all about Weston's behavior, still chose to expect the best. She'd better be right or Weston would pay.

Chapter 7

Myra awakened from a light doze to find Joy scooting a chair closer to the bed and sitting down. It was a relief to see her.

"Hey." Myra stretched and yawned. "I thought you might have taken off and headed for the river."

"Of course not." Joy gave her a gentle tap on the arm. "No CT yet?"

"Someone's supposed to come get me at any moment."

"Then I'll make this quick. Remember we discussed Weston Cline."

"You mean the name that made that poor tech drop her supplies?" Myra turned as far as she could in her bed and faced Joy. "What's so special about this man, other than the fact that he has the wisdom to be a friend of mine?"

Joy got up and stepped to the curtains, poked her head out to ensure no one was nearby, then returned to her chair. "There's a medical school attached to this hospital, and in that med school is the Cline Research Wing."

There was that word again. Research. The one that made Myra feel nauseated. "Same family then?"

"His father paid for it. Weston took it to a whole new level of interest."

"So it sounds as if there's wealth involved. For some reason I don't think I find that a necessary trait in a man."

"You've never been impressed by wealth," Joy said.

"So what would I find attractive about him?"

"I didn't say you would." Joy glanced at the curtains and pressed her finger to her lips. "You need to remember the tendency small towns have for gossip."

"Believe it or not I haven't lost that knowledge, I just don't care very much."

"You will when you've regained your memory and the

tabloids get wind of your connection to Weston."

"Oh my. I'm all a-twitter," Myra teased. What a mystery that she couldn't recall anything about this friend who sat with her, but she had no trouble recalling the comforts and trials of small-town life. Another curiosity was she felt so safe with this woman that, compared to her experience in the cemetery, she felt practically giddy. She knew she was reconnecting with at least this one friendship, not consciously but emotionally.

Or was it possible that the giddiness she felt came from another source? For instance this Weston character?

"So spill about the man, my friend." For Joy's sake she spoke softly.

Joy spread her hands in surrender. "He's coming to see you."

"Here?"

"I just found out tonight that the two of you have been seeing each other in the city."

Myra heard frustration in Joy's voice. "And you're not happy about it."

"I don't trust him. Apparently he's been buying you dinner in exchange for a therapy session once or twice a week."

Myra wondered at a slim thread of disappointment that tangled in her mind. "Why not the traditional way?"

"It was apparently your idea, and since you never told me what you were doing I can't tell you. It'll have to wait until you get your memory back, so be working on that, okay?"

"Gotcha. These had better be expensive dinners if I'm spending that much time with him."

"Just be glad you haven't been caught on camera with him yet. He's a hot property for the gossip hounds."

Myra closed her eyes and leaned more deeply into her pillow. "Let me get this straight, I'm meeting with this man as his psychiatrist? In public? How odd."

Joy leaned her elbow on the edge of the bed. "Private room. He knows how to be discreet when he wants to. I'm sure he feels it's less obvious than being seen walking into your office. I can imagine the headlines about that."

"A reasonable supposition. But if I'm merely meeting with him for therapy it sounds as if he's a patient, not a friend. Why would one of my patients be driving here from the city to see me?"

"I think there's more to this relationship than simple counseling."

"Intriguing." Myra warmed to the subject again. "Tell me more."

"Not intriguing. Worrisome," Joy said. "He says and does what he wants without worrying about the consequences. And because of the power he wields there are seldom consequences for him. His picture was on magazine covers at a time when magazines were still read by millions, and he continues to make the news."

"For what?"

"Everybody loves a man with the ability to increase his family millions into billions."

Myra gave a soft whistle. "Quite the money man. However, I would say many resent a person of wealth. Envy can be a powerful deterrent. Is that why you resent him?" Myra asked.

"I wouldn't want his money." Her forehead wrinkled slightly and she shook her head. "What am I saying? I did take his money. When he hired me he paid off my school loans, and after he fired me—"

"You worked for him?"

"For a few months."

"Then he fired you?"

"Yes. I took too many pro bono cases. On hindsight, I know I was wrong to do that, but he also wanted more than a working relationship with me. Much more."

"Oh. And you were still in love with Dr. Gorgeous."

Joy smiled and rested a hand on Myra's arm. "I'll have to tell Zack you called him that. Anyway, Weston not only paid off my school loans but he also sold my house for me and gave me the profit after he fired me. Guilt money."

"The monster!"

Joy leaned back and rested her arm on the bed. "He could be on the big screen with his magnetism and good looks. Women swoon. Honestly. It made me sick to my stomach to watch when I worked for him."

Myra couldn't help smiling. "You're not nearly as cute when you're radiating animosity."

Joy made a face at her. There was no missing the frustration in those big brown eyes. "I'm doing it again. I can't believe this. I try to forgive, I think I've managed to do it, and then I just plunge right back into the bog. I called him when I slipped out a moment ago and warned him not to drive here to see you."

"What are you trying to forgive?"

Joy winced. "Who's the patient here? You're off duty."

"So are you and I'm curious. Please? It's something I can actually think about besides what might be wrong with my mind. Try me. I'm begging you. If you ever suffer a fugue state I'll do the same for you."

Joy sighed. "Laine would stuff my mouth with cotton if she was here."

"Who's Laine?"

"Our other best friend. Okay, here it is. Weston has a family heritage of early deaths. His little brother died when he was a child, then his father died, forcing Weston to take over the reins of the corporation, and then his son died and that broke up his marriage."

"No wonder he needs therapy."

"You helped him develop a better relationship with his daughter and his ex wife, but there's still a scary side to him. Last year he was observing our...research project."

"The one I don't want to talk about?" Myra glanced at the monitor, which began a faster rhythm.

"Sorry. He was dealing with the destruction of his life when he developed an uncommon interest in the engagement ring on my finger. He tried several times to convince me to go to work for him in his clinic in the city. Then the project ended and we all lost our jobs. Weston managed to convince Zack I was having an affair with him."

Myra's mouth fell open. "And I like this sorcerer?" The other voices in the ER suddenly grew silent.

Joy covered her mouth and shook her head. "All I know is that you've helped him in therapy, and he believes the two of you are good friends. If you've truly developed a closer friendship with him, Zack has convinced me that doesn't have to be a bad thing."

"I'm glad to hear you and Zack seem to have worked on your communication issues. Why did you call Weston?"

"I was afraid his presence might make things worse for you,

but would he listen? Not a chance. I shouldn't be surprised."

"Were you this animated when you spoke with him?"

"Pretty much."

Myra smiled. "Yep, still a lot of bitterness there. I could probably help you with that if I could find my right mind."

"I don't want to see you get tangled in his web the way I did."

Myra studied Joy's expression. "And now he's a spider."

"Haven't you been listening? He sees what he wants and goes after it. Spiders do that."

"I'm not a fly."

"Sorry. No, you're a strong woman who knows what she wants most of the time."

"Good, then overcoming this fugue won't be a problem for me. What else can you tell me about him since it looks as if I'll need to be prepared for a meeting?"

"You don't have to see him at all if you don't want to."

"I'll see him, if for no other reason than curiosity."

Joy's cute nose scrunched up. "Myra, he's a wild card."

"You have a great reason to dislike him. So do I but he's also a man who's trying to work on his faults. I want to know more."

Joy glanced at the curtain again, frustration in her eyes. She stood up, obviously restless. "Most of this discussion needs to wait until we get you home because you can bet that every single person in this hospital knows Weston Cline."

"You're not worried about hospital gossip, you're worried he'll do the same thing to me that he did to you, but Joy, I've never lost my connection to the Holy Spirit. Frightening as this is, I know Who holds me, and it isn't a billionaire. It sounds to me as if you're obsessed with this man yourself."

"I can't bring myself to trust him."

"Have you always trusted me?"

"Of course."

"I've managed to trust you even though I don't remember you, so do the same for me, okay?"

Joy hesitated, met Myra's gaze and nodded.

Myra sucked in a deep breath, and laid her head back onto the flat ER pillow. She was on a wild race against the loss of her personality, and she was afraid to face her past. How would this crazy ride end?

***

Weston gripped the steering wheel as the car slid on yet another bridge that hadn't yet been treated for ice. Where on earth were the road crews? Typically they were out long before a storm hit.

He took a deep breath and tried to calm himself. Focus. Must focus.

He slid to a slow crawl and eased forward until the bridge was behind him. If he could get ahead of the storm he might not hit a ditch, but he couldn't stop thinking about Joy's warning. Maybe other entities were working to slow him down. Maybe Joy was praying, and God was answering her prayer?

He shook his head. Since when did God start answering prayers? The gentle Jesus he'd learned about in Sunday school became the son of a harsh, omniscient being when he grew older and tried to read through the Bible for himself. So much war and killing. He'd barely made it through Genesis before he stopped the first time he tried.

And according to Joy, if he didn't believe, he missed out on the prize of being allowed to love Myra. He was unworthy unless he agreed with the faith they had in Christ, Who wouldn't save Keegan no matter how hard anyone prayed. If he wanted to start lying and pretending again, sure, he'd be able to fool anyone he wanted. He'd had years of practice doing that. But how long could he fool Myra? And how could he bring himself to do that to her?

No. Not something he could think about right now. He was determined to get off Interstate 70 as soon as possible, even if it meant following slick backroads all the way to Jefferson City, which was only a short drive to Juliet. A few of the big trucks didn't stop for Christmas Eve, sleet, ice or any other kind of danger to deliver their loads and pick up their pay. They raced past him as if they believed themselves to be immortal. He didn't relish the prospect of getting involved in an eighteen-wheeler pile-up.

Despite the distraction of careless drivers and their huge deadly weapons, he couldn't delete his most recent conversation from his mind. Did Joy really believe his arrival would interrupt Myra's chance to heal? Or did she simply believe that since he caused chaos in her own life, he would do the same to Myra?

Obviously, Joy didn't know anything about the real building

blocks Myra had used to help him because Myra didn't betray patient confidentiality even to her best friend.

Another car raced past, fishtailing into Weston's lane. He gently pressed the brake, becoming accustomed, sadly, to the fact that he was the only sane driver on the road tonight.

Didn't these folks realize that if they were in an accident during this season, specifically, and if they were killed, their loved ones—whom they were trying so hard to reach for Christmas celebration—would relive the nightmare of this holiday for the rest of their lives? That future Christmases would be ruined for those they left behind? The loss a family member to poor driving skills on this of all holidays would be a horrible blow.

And there it was again. Holiday. Holy day meant to celebrate the birth of Christ. Weston hadn't observed it as such for a long time, so intent had he been in purchasing the very best gifts for his family, and then, after Keegan's death, he'd tried so hard to just endure the memories on Christmas.

And then, of course, he couldn't help thinking of Myra. What would Christmas come to mean to her since she was actually suffering through a likely terrifying fugue state during this season? Or…could it be possible that Christmas pressure brought it on?

He refused to accept Joy's simplistic supposition. Seeing him wouldn't plunge Myra more deeply into her fugue state. If anything, seeing him, her confessor, on whom she had begun to depend as much as he depended on her, close beside her, supporting her and caring for her welfare, should give her a sense of comfort.

Joy's words continued to ring in his ears about his lack of faith. How he wished he'd argued with her. He didn't think of God as a fairytale character, only the supreme deity who had judged Weston and found him unworthy long ago.

Maybe it happened when he got Sylvia pregnant before marriage. But hadn't he then married her? Or maybe it was his behavior during and after the time Sylvia left him. A man couldn't blame God for punishing him for some of the things he'd done.

No, God would never be a friend to Weston Cline.

Still, he was not quite the heathen Joy thought him to be. Truly, he wasn't.

Was he?

Chapter 8

On Christmas morning, when the rest of the world was visiting family, ripping open presents and watching the children play, Weston awakened in his old bed at the research center at the Juliet School of Medicine to the fragrance of turkey and ham cooking somewhere in the huge building. How long since he'd even celebrated with an authentic Christmas dinner?

Last night when he arrived it was to find the roads dry, the air cold, and the town somehow darker than he remembered. Not as many Christmas lights as they'd once had.

He'd checked with Joy via cell phone when he arrived to find that Myra was being held for observation in the hospital, and apparently Zack was getting some shut-eye. Weston had no doubt that Joy had slept in a chair somewhere close to Myra's bed, even though she had to work today.

He sat up and inhaled the scent of coffee from the machine he'd set on a timer the night before. For a moment the spacious, exquisitely decorated apartment looked hostile to him, though he was sure Joy's confrontation yesterday continued to affect him. She'd always been able to do that to him, and even though she'd been gentler when he arrived last night, he knew she would never forget the past.

He should probably thank her for turning down his advances since he would most definitely have married her if she'd have had him, and he'd have ended up being one of the most miserable husbands in the Midwest. Though he admired a great deal about Dr. Joy Gilbert and always would, he'd learned the hard way that she was definitely not for him.

He threw the covers back and sat up, looking with distaste toward the huge suitcase he hadn't bothered to unpack last night. Strange how he'd felt when he brought his suitcase and a few bags of groceries into the suite from the car. As if he didn't belong here and never had. Though his family had donated the money for this research wing of the medical school, he felt very much detached from it right now. He felt especially detached from the Weston Cline who'd stayed here for so many months last year, deeply involved in the research, keeping his finger on the pulse of the MRSA project only to find that it grew excessive amounts of hair on the research animals—and they were hairy enough to begin with.

He also spent a great deal of time with the staff. As if recalling a particularly unpleasant movie he'd watched at some time in his distant past, he could remember too well his behavior, the rebellion that boiled inside him after Keegan's death, against Sylvia for her inability to cope. It was then that he'd latched onto Joy as if she'd been a lifeline. Her strength had enchanted him.

Before he got to know her personally, he'd heard enough about her sharp mind, her grades in med school, her great references, he'd designed a clinic in his head, and then on paper, that would utilize her skills. It was as if some other person took over his body and compelled him to establish this clinic. With her specifically in mind.

He looked out the window at the light skiff of snow that had fallen on the park-like setting of the hallowed halls of medicine. He stretched, changed into jeans and a sweater—a new style for him—and grabbed the cream from the refrigerator.

Myra. She loved her coffee the way he did, strong enough to open the sinuses, with plenty of cream and not a grain of sugar. He reached into the cupboard for a thermos and prepared some for her. If the hospital still made their coffee the way they used to she wouldn't be able to stomach it, and they certainly wouldn't provide pure cream for her.

Myra. Since his first dinner with her she'd helped him reconcile with Tressa and even get along better with Sylvia. But she was still Joy's best friend. What if Joy was right and he was still carrying out some crazy fantasy, only with a different woman?

He rejected the thought as soon as it occurred to him. He hadn't felt this confident and in control since before Keegan's death four and a half years ago. The Myra Maxwell he knew and cared for was a real person, not a fictitious dream he'd built around a woman engaged to another man.

He washed up, brushed his teeth, pulled on casual shoes with a grip that would serve him well if he encountered any ice. The walk down the hallway of research was a long one, and he decided not to lock the doors behind him when he stepped into the med school's main corridor. No one would be here on Christmas day.

He'd checked last night to see if his name was on the list of allowed visitors, and it was. That meant that either Myra was better and remembered him, or Joy had relented and told her about his arrival. He needed to see her. But he had to keep himself under control, remain respectful and professional, even if Joy did not.

***

By 8:30 Christmas morning Myra Maxwell, who still didn't feel familiar with that name, was beginning to feel like a prisoner indeed. Molly sat in the chair beside her bed eating the special breakfast the hospital had prepared for her. Being the mother of the doctor on ER duty on Christmas day obviously had its perks. Having to babysit a grown woman couldn't possibly be one of them.

Myra stared at the carefully placed containers of oatmeal, egg, ham with cranberry sauce, and picked up her coffee cup. She looked at it and put it back down.

"Try to eat," Molly said. "My diet expert, Tressa Cline, told me that if I skip breakfast my body will start to cannibalize itself and my metabolism will drop, then my weight will climb. Not a pretty thought."

With a grimace, Myra took a spoonful of oatmeal, swallowed without tasting it, cut into the ham and then put her fork down. "I don't even know what I like to eat."

"How's the oatmeal?"

"If I felt any hunger I could tell you. By the way, thanks for bringing me some of Joy's clothes. I didn't realize we wore the same size. I'm getting out of this place today, right?"

"Since the CT didn't show anything you'll be good to go as soon as the doc comes by. Joy wanted to check on you one more time but she got busy."

Myra looked out the window at the small amount of snow on the ground. "So we're waiting for the doc in charge to release me?"

"The hospitalist, yes, but I'll tell you what, if he balks, just smile and wink at him. The doc they have here today is a pushover for a pretty face."

Myra grimaced. After finally seeing her own face in the mirror of Joy's SUV last night, she wasn't convinced of Molly's observation. Sure, she had the high cheekbones of a Native American, the olive skin, black hair, but compared to the Gilbert women with their milky complexions and feminine features she felt awkward and uneasy in her own skin.

There was a knock at the open door and both women looked up. Myra saw the man in jeans and sweater, and slumped back into the bed in frustration. It wasn't the doctor who would discharge her.

But then she looked at Molly, saw her appreciative expression, and returned her attention to the visitor. Hmmm. He was movie-star handsome with stunning blue eyes and dark hair frosted with silver. He might be nearing forty, if she was any judge of age, and with that firm chin and physique he could hold sway over any audience. Except for her. Perhaps she wasn't the type of woman who was attracted to handsome men. Or perhaps ogling strangers, no matter how attractive, wasn't her idea of a good time.

He smiled at her and held up a thermos. "Real coffee just for you, Myra."

She studied him. "Real?"

"You love a lot of cream in your double espresso. This was the best I could do in my apartment." His smile lost a bit of its wattage. "I'm sorry. Let me introduce myself. I'm—"

"You're Weston Cline, known across the land for his financial genius and male model beauty."

Surprise parted his lips, and his blue eyes once again filled with light. "You remember?"

"I'm sorry, no. I only guess from what I've been told."

Though the smile remained in place, his shoulders slumped a bit. He nodded. "Give it time, Dr. Maxwell. I'm here in hopes that I might be able to help." He took three steps inside the door and gave Molly his attention.

"Merry Christmas, Weston." Molly apparently didn't share Joy's distrust of the man. Either that or like most women—according to Joy—she couldn't help being enchanted. He did have a way about him. It was something Myra decided not to trust yet, especially in light of what Joy had told her.

He leaned over and gave Molly a quick kiss on the cheek. "I appreciate your keeping in touch with Tressa. She adores you, you know. I'll never be able to thank you enough for what you've done for her." He stepped back and gave her the once-over. "You look better than ever."

"And you, as always, are the most charming man I know." The dark-haired beauty gave him a warm smile, then turned her attention to Myra with a quizzical expression. "No recognition at all, sweetie?"

"As I said, I merely guessed." Myra watched with surprise as Weston took her cup of cold coffee and poured it into the empty juice glass and replaced it with the contents of the thermos. The aroma stole her breath for a moment. She closed her eyes and inhaled. "Heavenly."

"Go ahead." He had a smooth baritone voice. "Give it a taste."

She reached for the cup and thanked him. "Joy told me about you last night and you're definitely as scrumptious as I've heard." She gave Molly a wink, and received a knowing nod in return.

When she looked back at Weston he was blushing. Not what she'd have expected from a man who was supposedly comfortable as the center of attention in the boardroom.

"Joy didn't say that. I know better."

Myra smiled. "Once your name was dropped in the ER last night it was all I heard about. Somehow word got out that you were on your way here, and I saw more than one staff member metamorphose from carefree, makeup free, to polished and painted to their hairlines. It's a shame you didn't drop in to let them give you a show."

Molly laughed. It was a light, pleasant sound that eased the sudden tension Myra felt. But why did she feel that way?

She distracted herself by sniffing the coffee, which smelled so delicious it almost made her lightheaded. What really held her attention, however, was her own behavior. Was she really a natural flirt? When was the last time she'd told a man he was "scrumptious?" What kind of a woman was she?

Of course, she'd simply gone with an instinct to tease him—

actually, even embarrass him a little, see what he was made of. She had to admit, she liked the blush. It made him seem more human.

She sniffed the coffee again and felt the room turn slowly around her. She looked at Molly. The woman was watching her closely.

"Myra?" Weston pulled a chair from the wall to the side of the bed, also focused intently on her.

She blinked at him and then quickly set the cup back onto the tray table before she could drop it. "I'm sorry. I'm feeling a little dizzy."

He was on his feet immediately, pulling the tray table away. "Should we call the doctor?"

"No." Myra met Molly's quizzical gaze, then looked up into Weston's eyes, which were wide with anxiety.

She took a deep breath and leaned back. "The sense of smell can be a powerful memory inducer. I do believe you're right, Weston. I love my coffee strong, and I was reminded of that when I smelled it."

She heard the clatter of the cup against her plate. He held it in front of her so she could breathe it again. "What does this remind you of? It should be something pleasant. Relaxing."

She took a sip, took the cup from him and allowed the rich cream latte to warm her throat as she closed her eyes to a remembered image of Weston sitting across a breakfast table from her.

She opened her eyes and looked at him. "I was told we shared dinners together. When did we have breakfast?"

"You remember that? Last week you wanted to talk to me about my daughter before we both went to work, so we met at a restaurant near your office. She's one of your patients."

"Yes." Myra held the cup to Weston. "I'm sorry, would you take it for a moment?" Her hands shook so badly she nearly spilled the contents of the cup before she could hand it off. It unnerved her to relive that moment in the past with such immediacy with all the emotions that had clamored inside her that morning. Joy was right. Weston Cline was a dangerous man. He probably didn't realize it.

"What else do you remember?" Molly asked.

"Other meals." The sudden flood of flashing recollections hit her like a tsunami. She braced herself for worse, but most of the flashes brought only glimpses of good conversation, laughter, occasionally anger, but nothing that would cause a fugue state. "I like steak and lobster and king crab." She smiled at Weston. "Obviously I'm not a cheap date."

"Only the best for my counselor." His voice was as smooth and rich as the coffee she had sipped.

Somewhere in the murky past Myra and Weston had developed a special bond, but with it came misgivings. She looked up at him and no longer saw the attractive features of a charismatic man. Instead she saw the person beneath the facade who struggled with all his might to find a core within himself that was true and right and good.

"Your daughter is Tressa, a beautiful sixteen-year-old with your eyes and her mother's facial features. She wanted me to tell you that morning that she didn't want to follow in your footsteps, but wanted to attend medical school here in Juliet." She glanced at the cup he held in his hands and he held it out to her again.

She took another sip, allowing the gentle memory to return to her as easily as if she'd just been there. "You told me you would be proud of Tressa no matter what she decided to do with her life, but she could do very well at Juliet School of Medicine."

"I meant it."

She smiled at him as a tingle of recognition spread through her, giving her an anchor at last. "Hello Weston."

He leaned forward. In his eyes was a longing so powerful he would have been embarrassed had he realized his transparency. "You do remember?"

"Patches, Weston. Only in patches. But enough to ground myself. There are still so many places in my memory that I'm obviously unable to face, but I know my name now, I know yours from memory." She glanced at Molly. "You're more familiar, but I can't put my finger on any particular scene in my mind. Same with Joy."

"Oh but honey, that's such a huge leap!" Molly stood up and stepped to the bedside.

"These flashes of recall come to me as if they were frames from a movie. I'm trying to fit them into some kind of chronological order."

"It's a beginning," Molly said. "You'll need more before you can restore order."

Weston took the cup from Myra and set it on the tray table, then took her hands in his. "A happy beginning. The rest will come. You're a strong woman and you'll make your way back."

She glanced at Molly and saw a cloud of concern in those dark eyes.

Though Myra recalled meeting with Weston for countless meals, she knew she'd set up the sessions strictly for therapy. Over the course of months they'd developed a cooperative partnership that could have transformed into something lovely and fulfilling had the circumstances been different.

If only he hadn't come here. But if he hadn't, would she have begun regaining her memories?

She looked again at Molly. "Would you mind asking if I could be released quickly?"

"Only if you'll promise to come home with me. You don't want to be alone now that your memories are beginning to return."

"I'll find the doctor," Weston said. "You'll be out of here in ten minutes." He walked from the room in search of the hospitalist.

Molly chuckled. "For the doctor's sake, let's hope he's available and willing, or there could be a price to pay."

Myra sank back into the pillows. "Oh, Molly, what have I done?"

"Exactly what you're supposed to do, my dear. You've begun to heal."

"But Weston."

Molly took Myra's hand and squeezed. "I'm not a psychiatrist, but even I can see the changes in him. What you've done is give him a second chance at life."

"But after what he did to Joy—"

"I wanted to kill him. I wanted to kill Zack when he listened to Weston and broke the engagement. But I saw a lot of growth in her after she returned. She wasn't the naïve, sheltered child any longer. She grew up and learned to listen to her own heart, not mine or Zack's but her own.

"And you?"

"I was forced to release her. I had to learn not to hold on to her so tightly. Zack discovered he wasn't as invincible and wise as everyone always told him he was. Lessons like those are good for the soul, good to help dampen the old pride."

"How did you forgive Weston?"

"Probably the same way you did. I saw the depth of his wounds."

Myra took another sip of the coffee Weston had so thoughtfully made for her. "Those dinners we shared? They lasted a lot longer than a fifty-five minute session in my office. Often I wouldn't get home until midnight. It became difficult to spend so much time with him and share so much of myself and not be drawn to him in other ways."

"But you were prepared," Molly said.

"Yes I was, Mama Molly." She sat up as another mental picture slipped into place. "I've recalled more! You drilled that into us. I always had those defenses you taught us, and I knew there'd be no romance in my future with a man who didn't share my love for Christ."

"Well then, it seems my work here is done."

"Not yet," Myra said. "I'm sure the bad memories are about to hit."

"Then find as many good ones as you can so you'll have a cushion when it gets difficult."

Myra held her gaze. If only it was that simple.

Chapter 9

Joy slumped into her work chair as the final patient of the morning walked out of the ER. She took a sip of her coffee, grimaced at the cold, congealing creamer on top, and stood to take it back to the break room for a hot refill.

She was pressing the muscles of her lower back when the secretary buzzed the door open. In walked Weston looking well rested and bent on a mission. Suppressing a groan, she turned to meet him. It had been a while since she'd seen him last. His hair was a little shorter, and he seemed to walk with a lighter step.

"Hello Joy. Thank you for putting my name on Myra's visitor list. You didn't have to do that."

She held his gaze. What would he have done if she'd left his name off?

"Would you page the hospitalist?" he asked. "Myra's suddenly in a hurry to get out of here."

Before Joy could reply, the secretary called to her. "Dr. Gilbert, your mother's on the phone." She sent the call to Joy's phone.

Joy picked up halfway through the first ring. "I know, Mom. Weston just told me she wants to be discharged."

"Honey, she's gone."

"What do you mean? Aren't you with her?"

"I went to heat up her coffee and when I returned she wasn't in her room. Neither is her tray, though, so maybe she went to see about getting more food. She wasn't hungry for the oatmeal."

"Did you look for her?"

"Of course I did. You think I'm going to let her wander around lost in a strange place? I didn't see her in the hallway, she never said a thing about taking a walk."

"Hold for a moment, will you?" Joy looked at Weston. "Did you come straight here from Myra's room?"

"Yes. What's wrong?"

"Mom left her alone for a moment and she disappeared."

"She couldn't have gone far," Weston said. "She probably just needed to stretch her legs."

"Her purse is gone," Mom said over the phone. "Her car's outside. I drove it in this morning. She just started having some major memories. What if she's remembered more?"

"What memories?"

"Weston came bearing coffee from heaven. It stirred some good memories."

"Just a moment." Joy looked up at Weston. "She remembers you?"

"Yes."

"Her keys are in her purse, and she took it. Please, would you go out to her car and make sure she doesn't try to leave?"

He nodded and rushed out.

"Joy?" Her mother's voice was tight with growing anxiety.

Joy raised the phone to her ear again. "I sent Weston out—"

"I heard. I'm walking up and down the hallways, and I've even checked some closets." The sound of a closing door came through the receiver. "The nurses are helping. A tech said she thought she saw a woman dressed in jeans and red sweater walking down the hall toward the stairway door."

"Which stairway?"

"South hall."

"You think she's headed to the med school," Joy said. It would make sense if Myra had begun to get her memories back. The school might stir more good memories as long as she avoided the research wing. "What did she remember?" Joy reached into her purse for her cell phone and pulled off her lab coat.

"Weston, honey. And a little about me. She's spent a lot of time with him in the past few months, so it makes sense that seeing him would jog something for her."

"That's a good start. She didn't appear upset?"

"Not at all, but what if she's begun to recall more?"

"I'm coming to help search. No patients in the ER right now. I'll be on my cell."

"Where will you look?"

"Med school. You keep looking through the hospital. Call me

if you find her."

"Will do."

Joy replaced the phone on its base and glanced through the windows. Weston stood in the snow guarding Myra's car out in the cold, arms crossed, shoulders hunched.

Something about seeing him like that touched Joy, and made her a little ashamed of her call to him last night. She knew he wouldn't leave the car and risk letting Myra get away when he hadn't even taken the time to get his coat.

Zack was still sleeping in the call room, so she retrieved his heavy jacket from the rack in the break room and carried it outside.

When the sliding glass door opened, Weston looked up. His expression switched from anxiety to surprise when he saw the jacket.

"What, you thought I'd let you freeze to death out here?" She walked across the crackly grass to the car and handed him the loaner. "It's Zack's."

"Thank you." He pulled it on. "Perfect fit.".

She took a few steps toward the building, then stopped and turned back. "How did you know you could jumpstart her memories?"

"I didn't. It wasn't until I arrived last night that I thought I might try stirring other senses besides sight and sound. Taste and smell can be powerful memory enhancers so I made her coffee with heavy cream this morning. She always loves that when we have dinner."

Time for Joy to swallow her pride. Weston had done the right thing. "Myra needed to get her memories back, and seeing you started the process. You know, you could stand inside and watch for her out the window."

"What if I'm distracted at the wrong moment? I won't take the chance. Since, as you say, I seem to have started this process, do you have any idea how this fugue might play out?"

"I don't think even Myra in her right mind would be able to give us an answer; these episodes are so individualized it's hard to say. Last night she was half afraid to start the recall process, but since the first ones were good she might be willing to try for more."

"You think she's searching for something on campus?"

"I would if I wanted to go back to a safer place in time."

"Except she might not find a safe place when she lands. What was her response when you mentioned the research we did last year?"

"Fear. She refused to talk."

"Then let's hope she stays away from there. Where's Molly?"

"She's helping staff search the hospital. Since the med school section is empty I'll go alone and look there."

"It's locked."

"Myra and I knew about a private passage between the hospital and the school. Last night when she couldn't sleep, I told her as much as I could about attending school here, including that passage."

"I didn't lock the research wing." He reached into the pocket of his jeans and pulled out a key. "That passage is on the third floor. This will get you through without climbing stairs"

"You know about it?"

He handed her the key. "I've always made it a point to know everything about all Cline family investments. This will get you anywhere. It's a master."

"Thanks." Joy took the key and rushed back into the building. "I'll call you if I find her." For the first time since Zack warned her about Weston's impending arrival last night she was actually glad—for just a second—that he'd come.

She stepped along the hallway that led to the hospital rooms. Now, where would Myra have gone on this campus?

***

Myra's footsteps echoed along the cavernous hallway of the med school's main building. She felt no sense of familiarity after walking the length of the third floor, where classrooms waited in the darkness for students to return. She and Joy and other friends must have spent a great many hours in those rooms, but that would have been when they were filled with other students.

What a mystery that she'd spent so many years here in this building and yet not one memory surfaced. She'd thought for sure something here would spark a recollection, but all that was familiar was the tall, curved ceiling and marbled floors of this main corridor, and that was only because Joy had described them for her last night, as she had the hidden entrance.

The gloom of gray light from the windows seemed to rush forward to meet her like ghosts attempting to frighten her away. She stared up through the panes high above, beyond which the dark clouds appeared to be gathering more snow.

Her footsteps quickened. She'd only meant to slip out for a brief look around while Molly was gone, and though she'd left a note for Molly on her food tray, she didn't want that lovely woman worrying about her. She'd thought maybe a quick trip into her past might tease a few more harmless memories to the surface, but too much time had already passed. Still, she balked at returning to the hospital wing.

Hospitals had apparently never been her favorite places, though she didn't know why, and she didn't want to. She guessed it had something to do with the deaths of her parents in such quick succession, but the recovery of knowledge didn't seem as frightening today after her encounter with Weston. If only she could be assured her other memories would be as harmless.

Okay, Weston wasn't completely harmless, but she still enjoyed the memories she carried with her of spending time with him. She felt strong when she was with him, and she hadn't felt that kind of strength since waking in this alternate universe. Last night the thought of remembering anything had become one of her worst nightmares, as if she would discover some horrible incident. For the moment this fugue state felt more manageable.

Molly would understand when she read the note. Myra needed to know more about herself, where she came from. She felt the need for more pieces of the puzzle. A lot more to help her fill in the holes and answer some of the questions she had about herself.

She stepped to a window. The patterns of lightly meandering snowfall contrasted against the sharp lines of brick that encompassed an addition to the main building. A quick thud of her heart told her that some part of her recognized this place. She felt drawn forward until she came to the double doors beneath the name Cline Research Wing stamped in bronze.

Joy had told her this was where Weston was staying, so it was possible that since the school was locked he might have left this door unlocked. She tried the door. It gave with the pressure. She slipped inside.

At once she was in a more modern hallway that didn't have the baroque décor of the main corridor. Here the walls were white instead of paneled, and floral paintings, filigreed wainscoting in light, airy colors graced the walls. Murals of birds, butterflies and greenery decorated the arched ceiling.

She caught her breath, held it, admired the beauty while acknowledging a sense of gloom that oppressed her.

Still, something drew her forward. For a moment she ignored the fact that people who cared about her might start to worry. She couldn't prevent herself from continuing down the hallway.

She peered outside and felt a stutter in her mind. She knew this place as if from a dream, where bits and pieces fell into place but others remained illusive.

As she walked she felt and smelled the emptiness of this place. Gone were the aromas of a vital and active research lab. There were no animals here now. Instead, the smell of dust teased her nostrils.

Vast windows overlooked the park-like vista of the campus grounds to her left. A windowed door to her right seemed to beckon her more deeply into the gloom of the building. It brought to her mind the electrical jolt that had shot up her arm when she placed her hand on the tall, dark monument last night.

She only saw shadows and outlines of equipment, worktables, computers, beakers, a glass-fronted refrigerator, but the view became familiar. This room was Dustin's work area. She tried the door, but of course it was locked. She pushed anyway, as if she had every right to enter, because she knew she'd had free access at one time.

With a gasp, she knew that the accident that infected Dustin Grooms with MRSA took place past this door.

Her second stream of memories for the morning struck her with a nasty jolt, the reaction so real she could see the man she loved as he bent over a vial, his lab coat brilliant white, starched to stiffness. His black, short hair contrasted sharply against a serious, bespectacled, clean-shaven face that hadn't seen sunlight often these past months. He pulled on a mask, then picked up a syringe and held it over the rubber stopper of the vial, prepared to plunge the needle into it and draw out the poison for yet another animal trial—and this animal was sure to survive.

She tensed.

They'd had good results with the serum their team had developed under the direction of Dr. Christopher Payson. They had infected their primates with increasingly strong MRSA challenge, and they'd been successful despite Dr. Payson's tendency to fire his research assistants for the least hint of infraction, forcing them to bring in probationary help and train them.

Anger rose within her as her memories returned more clearly. As if in a dream, she watched Dustin lower the needle to the stopper.

She pressed her hand against the window, slapped the pane, and he looked up. She saw a smile reach his eyes, even though a mask covered his mouth. Dustin Grooms was the most cheerful, kind person she'd ever known.

The needle slid into the rubber, but the top flipped from the vial with an explosion of fluid, bursting the vial. Shards of glass flew into Dustin's face, penetrating the mask. Myra opened her mouth to scream as she watched the fluid splash across his face. The dream image in the lab faded. Myra slapped the window again and again until agony dropped her to her knees.

She curled in on herself, eyes squeezed shut as Dustin's image flicked across her mind in dizzying speed—Dustin bleeding as he locked the door to keep everyone else out. Dustin following decontam protocol. Dustin sick in the isolation room within the research wing, built specifically for instances such as this.

Dustin in worsening stages of blood poisoning by the most resistant staph infection they had yet discovered.

The scenes switched in her mind to find herself sitting before Dr. Payson's desk, practically kneeling in supplication as she begged him to permit the use of the serum to save Dustin's life.

"It's working," she'd said. "We knew it was working. Dustin was so excited. The subjects are all well. Human trials come next. Let him be the first."

"No." There was anger in Dr. Payson's voice—anger at Dustin for being sick, at her for reminding him of it, at the whole world because this accident threatened his dream to make a name for himself in research.

"But he's dying." She scooted to the edge of the chair. "Please don't let him die!"

"Whose fault is that?" The man's voice had never been more harsh, or his angular, sixty-year-old face more filled with fury. "Who failed to follow protocol?"

"No one. I saw him myself. The vial was faulty."

"Who did I task to prevent that?"

"Does it matter now?" They both knew Laine Fulton, her coworker and friend, was in charge of quality control. Laine was fastidious in her work, so the fault had been hidden within the vial. "We shouldn't be sitting here placing blame. We must move as quickly as possible to save Dustin."

Payson slammed his hands on his desk and stood, glaring at her. "That won't happen."

"What will your financier do when he discovers you wouldn't even make a move to try? Weston Cline invested his millions to save lives."

"Cline invests his money to make more money. You think this is about helping the masses? Pharmaceuticals are about the bottom line. You'll just have to console yourself with the knowledge that your boyfriend—"

"My fiancé. My future husband," she said hotly. How had she come to work for such a despicable man?

"Whatever you want to call it. If I remember correctly, your young man was sickened by animal trials. He made pets of them, probably held funerals for them and prayed over them when they died."

The tone of the man's voice made Myra want to leap across his desk and grab him by the throat. The very look she gave him could get her fired. She didn't care, except for one thing—if Payson wouldn't seek permission to treat Dustin, and if Cline couldn't, then Myra would do what it took to save the life of the man she loved.

"If he doesn't survive," Payson said, "you can always know that he gave his life for his precious concern for those masses."

She recoiled from the realness of that memory and felt the cold tile beneath her, felt the shaking of her body as her sobs echoed down the corridor. The pain of loss was as immediate as a sharp knife in her ribs. The man who'd been her friend and confidante, who'd become her future, had been abandoned by the employer who'd once praised him for his brilliance. If only she'd known then that the serum was more deadly for humans than the bacterial infection it was created to stop.

She tasted the salty tears as that scene dissolved and another took its place.

She stood outside the isolation room, having been banished by Dustin. He'd insisted on doing the injection of the serum, himself, in order to protect her as much as possible from any fallout. What he did was illegal. Injecting himself with the serum when the animal trials weren't complete, without even special permission from the FDA, was serious enough to cost him his career, and they all knew Payson wouldn't hesitate to have him prosecuted.

As she watched the man she loved administer the serum into the IV in his arm, she prayed as she'd never prayed before. He was so weak, his face jaundiced and thin.

Even after Weston Cline made multiple calls to the FDA, begging for their permission for that special allowance, they'd been turned down. She'd been so sure the treatment would work. All of them had been sure Dustin's life would be saved.

Myra wrapped her arms around herself. The final blow came when Laine discovered the serum killed him before the MRSA could.

That scene, as well, faded from the screen of her mind, and opened to another, where she stood between Joy and Laine before the closed casket that held the shell of the man she'd loved. He was gone.

It hadn't worked. His death was a shock of horrifying proportions.

Chapter 10

Weston ran into the research wing within a minute of receiving a panicked call from Joy. Myra's sobs mingled with Joy's words of comfort along the passage, and he followed the sound of their voices to find them huddled together on the floor outside a lab door. He knew this place. His heart ached for Myra. This was where Dustin Grooms had his accident last year.

"Myra?" He dropped to his knees beside them.

She looked up at him, tears streaking her face. "I remembered."

"I'm sorry," he put his hand on her shoulder. "It must feel to you as if he died today."

Myra nodded. "I relived the whole thing in a few seconds. It was like taking blows from a sledgehammer."

Weston had never been good with women in tears and he felt helpless. He knew the pain she was experiencing; nothing could change that. He didn't think it would help to remind her of the many talks they'd had about grief. What she needed was time.

"I found her lying here," Joy said. "She doesn't seem to have hurt herself."

"I called Molly. She's on her way." He took Myra by the elbows. "Let's get you off this hard floor." She felt fragile as he lifted her. "Are you sure you should be discharged from the hospital now?"

"I need to get away from this memory," Myra said.

Joy handed her another tissue. "Let's get you to Mom's, then."

The three of them walked along the hallway as Myra dried her face.

"Why did you come here specifically?" Weston asked.

"I'm not sure." Her voice was still soft and shaky from crying. "At first all I wanted to do was walk through the school, see if anything came back to me about my years here. It wasn't until I found the research hall that I felt drawn to it. When I reached the door of the lab it was like an old-fashioned movie reel flashed past me on a huge screen."

"Next time call me," he said. "You don't have to do this alone. We were worried about you."

"I left a note for Molly on my tray."

"Which was picked up by the time she got back to the room," Joy said.

"I'm sorry. I didn't mean to upset everyone."

"Don't apologize for what you're going through." Weston almost reached for her hand, but he stopped himself. "Last year was a nightmare. We all endured a lot. We would have been here to help you through it if we'd known."

Myra slowed her steps and looked outside through the wall of windows into the lazily falling snow. "It's passing quickly."

"What is?" Joy asked.

"The memories of Dustin hit me hard just a few minutes ago. I recalled Weston begging for permission from the FDA for emergency use of the serum. Dr. Payson fought it. I remembered watching the funeral."

Oh, yes, Weston remembered it all. He only wished Myra hadn't been subjected to the ordeal again. "Payson will never get more funding for that project."

"Who knows?" Joy said. "He could find another billionaire to bilk."

"If it comes to that I'll stop him," Weston said. "You have enough to worry about. Let me handle him if it ever happens." When they reached the end of the passage he pushed the door open and held it for the women to step out into the school's main hallway.

"The memories aren't nearly as fresh now," Myra said.

"So quickly?" Joy asked.

"It's as if they're settling back into their proper time frame in my mind."

"That's a good thing, right?" Joy asked.

"She's grieved over Dustin since his death." Weston locked the door securely. "She shouldn't have to go through all of it again." If he hadn't left the door unlocked in the first place Myra would probably still be happily enjoying another cup of coffee as she waited to be discharged. "She risked everything for the man she loved."

"I also remembered that it was the serum that took his life, according to Laine's findings," Myra said. "Not the MRSA."

"Don't do that to yourself," Weston said. "Laine wasn't sure, and even if she was, the MRSA had infected his blood. The serum was a last ditch effort to save him. Dustin's sacrifice saved many others because I had good reason to pull funding."

And now his focus was on keeping the final results from Payson. So far he'd managed to do that with Laine's quiet help. Another more powerful treatment had been introduced by a pharmaceutical company on the heels of Dustin's death, which had negated the financial benefits of future research. That had given Weston a good excuse to pull his finances from the study. For now. Until that new treatment, as well, failed to kill future strains of the flesh eating bacteria.

At this moment his only concern was that despite all their best efforts, Dustin Grooms, a promising young physician who could have helped thousands of patients in a long lifetime, had died. Myra was still recovering from that discovery. He wanted to support her, but he found, to his shame, that it had been difficult to see her grieving over another man's death.

Myra dabbed at her eyes one final time and gave Weston a look of gratitude. "You were a rock for me then. I remember now so vividly. You risked a lot. I don't know how you kept us all from getting into trouble."

"I would do it all again."

"What's to keep Payson from conducting his own private studies?" Joy asked.

"Time. He would need more time and staff to help him. He's in Columbia, where you can't swing a stick without hitting a physician. Word would reach me."

Whatever desperate measures he took to save Dustin last year, it didn't blot out the memory of the manipulations he had used to disrupt Joy's relationship with Zack at the same time.

"Thank you both for being here." Myra took one of Joy's hands and one of Weston's. The warmth of her touch spread through him.

"This is turning out to be a pretty rotten Christmas for you," Joy said.

Myra shook her head. "I'm literally finding myself. It's scary and painful, but now I know my past isn't lost to me forever."

Weston didn't comment. Myra had endured too much tragedy in her life. He didn't want to see her have to relive it. While Myra recovered she would continue to be slammed by the bad memories. He hoped that the incidents farther in the past would be gentler when she faced them.

He glanced over Myra's head and caught Joy's worried look. She realized it, too. Myra had endured more loss than she knew, not counting the episode that had caused her to revert to this state in the first place. They didn't even know what that was yet.

More footsteps approached in a rush, and they looked up to find Joy's mother coming toward them.

"What happened? Is she hurt?"

"More memories," Myra said, the vulnerability gone from her voice.

"Don't worry, sweetheart, we won't leave you alone." Molly tapped her daughter's shoulder. "I just received word there's a ambulance on the way, and two patients just arrived by car, one of them with a bloody towel around her arm."

Joy groaned. "Not now."

"Don't worry," Molly told her. "Myra will be safe with us. You go do your job."

Joy hesitated. "Of all days to be on duty."

"Go," Weston said. "I'll find that hospitalist and get her discharged immediately."

"I'll call him and have him meet you in the room." Joy turned and ran down the massive corridor.

Weston touched Myra's shoulder lightly. "You're always telling me that it helps to talk. Fill Molly in."

"Protocol," Myra said.

"We'll swear her to secrecy."

Molly fell into step to Myra's right and listened as Myra's quiet voice recounted one of the worst times of her life.

Weston had no doubt that Myra would be in excellent hands at Molly's, but would that be enough? Experience had taught him that sometimes a woman needed another woman to cling to, to speak her language, and to listen without interrupting or trying to fix things.

So far Myra had regained her memories by triggers such as the coffee and seeing the place where Dustin's accident occurred. Were there triggers like that at Molly's?

Myra had helped him to communicate more completely with the youngest woman in his life, and judging by his daughter's improved attitude toward him recently, he was learning. Perhaps he could be of help today.

"Dustin wouldn't let me give him the serum," Myra was telling Molly as Weston tuned back into the conversation. "He made me leave the room and promise to never tell Payson about my involvement."

"But you couldn't cover for the missing serum," Molly said.

"Laine took care of inventory." Weston still worried about drawing the young researcher too deeply into the cover-up.

"We heard Payson practically screaming at Weston behind his closed office door," Myra said.

Molly's dark eyes flashed. "I know Christopher Payson from a former life, Weston, and I don't trust him. If he ever suspects—"

"He didn't."

"You're sure he didn't see the final files?"

"Payson doesn't know of their existence since he didn't know about the serum used. All he really screamed about was losing my funds."

"If he ever finds out he'll drag you through every court—"

"Losing financial support before the trial was completed would blackball that particular project, as was my intention. Everyone in the world of medical research knows I was his financial backer, and I know this because I've received plenty of requests since then for funding. They know I didn't run out of money, so word on the outside would be that the trials had failed. That's why Payson was so upset."

"Still, let me know if he does try to come back at you," Molly said. "I can bring him down if I have to."

Weston raised his brows. This woman never ceased to surprise him. She'd gone from an overweight recluse last spring to this delightfully vivacious, bold woman who knew how to dish out compassion and confidence. Last year he'd seen her as an angry mother trying to manipulate her daughter. She'd changed. But what did she have on Payson?

"Just trust me." She gave him an enigmatic smile.

"Don't worry about him. The project was shut down well over a year ago, and Payson's been quiet ever since. I think he's moved on." Weston would never forget the battle of wills he'd fought with Payson. But in the end, he convinced the furious doctor to back down.

When they reached the doors that connected the medical school to the hospital, Myra hesitated. "I can't go in there right now."

***

Instead of the heavy double doors, Myra caught a dream glimpse of herself stepping over the threshold from school to hospital with Laine and Joy and other classmates as they made rounds. She looked over her shoulder at the wide corridor of the school, and her mind peopled it with students. She could almost hear the chatter as they moved between classes.

This was where she'd fallen in love then fought a desperate battle with death and lost. The only reason she'd agreed to take the research position was to be closer to Dustin. A psychiatrist didn't get to practice her trade in a research lab.

Weston put a hand on her arm. "Another memory?"

She nodded, torn between two men—one was dead, the other was off limits. She would have to pray her way through this emotional minefield.

"Molly, I know you'll never breathe a word of this to anyone," Weston said.

"I'm the one who taught Joy the importance of patient confidentiality," Molly said.

Myra nodded. Still, she had a bad feeling that this issue would rise again someday. "Sorry for the wait. Let's get me checked out of this place." She tossed her sodden tissues into a bronze-topped waste receptacle at the doorway and stepped into the hospital while Weston held the door.

"Molly," she said, "I'll take you up on your offer if you don't mind. I don't want to leave town."

"As if we'd let you. I've already set up a room for you, and there's even a door, so the animals can't sleep with you if you don't want them to."

"Oh, I don't know. I think I might welcome the company." She expected to relive some good memories there, and the thought of being surrounded by affectionate furry creatures made her smile.

When they reached Myra's room the physician was there to check her out before release.

Weston stepped up behind her. "I'll be here for a few days. Molly, would you mind if I followed you out to your house later? Zack's supposed to call me when he wakes up, but I'd like to help you get Myra settled."

"Come whenever you want, but be sure to come for dinner tonight," Molly said. "If you're not allergic to cats, dogs, goats and raccoons."

His warm chuckle and the strength of his presence gave Myra a sense of peace she wouldn't have expected.

He smiled down at her, and she felt a surge of thankfulness for this man who, above all things, was her friend.

He placed a hand on her shoulder. "I'll see you when I get there, then?"

She looked up into his blue eyes and decided to treasure this friendship as long as she could. There was no way to control this high wire of emotions she would be victim to for however long it took to regain her self. She felt vulnerable and helpless. Though coming here last night in a fugue state had been a dangerous move, she'd come to the right place, where friends would care enough to guide her.

She could guess at Weston's feelings for her. She'd seen it grow in his expression, heard it in his voice, and it was evident by his trip here to find her. Before she could address anything more, however, she needed to become Myra Maxwell again. And then? He would have to learn, for once, to become a very patient man.

Chapter 11

Joy finished an intricate suture repair, treated two cases of influenza and ran a CT on a patient with a possible concussion, and when she finished the last chart it was two in the afternoon. Where had the time gone?

She looked around at the rest of the staff. Two nurses wore elf hats with bells at the ends that had been jingling all day; twice she'd almost asked them to take the hats off, but after all, it was Christmas.

The poor patients suffered the most. They'd had their special day ruined for them with illness and accidents. Someday, when she and Zack had children, maybe they would want the time off so they could celebrate, but eating at Mom's tonight would do just fine for her now. For her and Mom the holiday season had been more about thankfulness than shopping for expensive presents, decorating and parties. Being raised by a loving single mom had its peaceful qualities.

"Take a break, Dr. Gilbert," her secretary called from the front desk. "I just saw Dr. Travis head to the break room with his hair sticking out all over the place."

Joy smiled. He'd just awakened.

"I made some fresh coffee, too," the secretary said.

"Thanks, Christine." Joy circled the workstation to rush to the break room for a quick hug. She'd reached the entry when she heard him speaking with someone. Was that a little irritation she heard in his voice? Zack didn't often become irritated, so when he did she picked up on it.

"What? No. Of course I haven't told her today." He was talking on his cell phone. "You do realize it's Christmas, don't you? She's already working so everyone else can be home for their families." There was a pause, and then he said, "My relationship with her has nothing to do with it. I'm off duty, so this number is being switched off. Have a Christmas for once." He pressed his cell phone and slipped it into the pocket of his jeans with a low growl.

Joy stood in the doorway strangely disoriented. She shook her head, rehashing what she'd just heard as she watched him pour a cup of coffee into the mug she'd given him as a gift before he came on duty last night.

"Zack?"

He turned around. Typically she loved the way he looked after waking up from a night shift, not all combed down and well-groomed, but human and real. Today she didn't like the look in his eyes—hostility and frustration that morphed into suspicion when he saw her.

"Tell me you didn't eavesdrop on that call." He set the mug on the counter.

She stared at him for a moment, then backed out of the room and looked at the sign above the door. "Break Room. It says so right there." She pointed. "It isn't eavesdropping when I just happened to be on my way in to see you and catch a break in the break room."

He sighed and rubbed at his eyes. She walked over to the fridge and pulled out her stash of cream, poured a dollop into his coffee and put the cream away. Suddenly, she wasn't in the mood for another cup of coffee. She also wasn't in the mood for a hug or kiss of greeting. He'd obviously been keeping something from her as easily as he would carry a few dollar bills in his pocket. She'd picked up on nothing unusual in his demeanor when they were together. But how long had he been doing this? She set the mug on the table at the place where he usually sat.

He slumped into his chair, dragging the mug toward him until it was inches from his nose.

Joy couldn't sit down. She was suddenly wired with stress and dread. "You might as well tell me."

"Joy, can't we just relax and—"

"Too late. Tell me the secret you've been keeping with such apparent ease." She closed the door so the whole staff wouldn't be privy to this.

He pushed the mug away and straightened with a sharp look up at her. "When you came to ask for a job here, who did you ask?"

"You know who I asked. You."

"And why was that?"

"I was desperate?"

"Why me specifically?"

She reached for the chair across the table from his and gripped it to keep from saying more. She was using bad form. She pulled the chair out and sat down despite her need for movement. "I'm sorry." She forced the words out and forced herself to remain steady. "I didn't respect your position. I shouldn't talk to you like that, especially not here." Yes, he really was doing this. He was pulling rank. Visions of Weston Cline danced in her head. The old Weston Cline.

"I didn't want to be the director in the first place." Zack took a swallow of coffee, set it back down on the table with a heavy thump that nearly splashed some of the contents over the edge. "I don't throw my weight around."

"That's what you just finished doing." The words slipped out before she could stop them. Bad girl.

"But I have to maintain the respect of the position or everyone, from the techs to the nurses to the secretary and other docs, will walk all over me."

Typically she would say something to soothe him, but this wasn't one of those times. She stared at him, waiting.

"When I'm told by the governing board of the hospital to do something, I do it, whether or not I completely agree," he said.

"Oh, really? If they tell you to poison a patient, you do it? If they tell you to go kick a dog on the sidewalk, you do what they tell you, whether or not you agree?"

He scowled at her, looked down at the coffee, shoved it away. "When it comes to hospital politics I have to listen to the board."

She braced herself. So he was going to tell her what the unknown caller wanted him to say after all. "And that would concern me how?" She kept her tone lighter this time, but inside her head was a roar of outrage because she knew what was coming.

"The administrator has been receiving more than the usual complaints about ER wait times in the past few months."

Joy pressed her finger against the edge of the table and slowly drew an invisible line across the surface to the other edge, directly between herself and Zack. Yes, this was happening. "I'm being blamed."

He sighed. "Not by me."

"But you can't tell them what you think? Is your job so precarious?"

"I've talked to them, believe me."

"Have they considered that the waits are because we're getting busier, and have lost a nurse practitioner?"

He picked up his mug and looked at her. "They checked it out when I told them about it, but I lost the staring contest."

She held her hands out, palms up. "Just spill, please. It's too late to turn this conversation off now."

"The board members are putting pressure on the administrator to find another physician and cut your hours to the part-time status on your contract."

"And then, let me guess," she said, "they won't renew my contract when it expires."

His silent, sad gaze spoke volumes.

She closed her eyes as her heart pumped so hard in her chest that it hurt. She felt the pain all the way through her body, but she knew not to react in the heat of the moment. Instead, she opened her eyes and stared at that invisible line she'd drawn. If her fiancé was going to do this, so be it. He needed his job. But so did she. There wasn't enough in her savings account to even begin to think about opening her own practice, and that was her full focus right now. That, and the big wedding her grandparents were so insistent she host for the whole town. Sure, they were paying for it, but she had to plan it.

"We'll be married before this becomes a big deal," he said, as if reading her mind. "You're living with Molly until then, so you don't have to worry about money."

But the pain she felt didn't come from losing finances. Again, she had to force herself to calm down. "That isn't what's bothering me, boss," she said quietly.

"Joy, please—"

"As you have reminded me, you're my director. You can't talk to me as if I'm your employee one moment and your fiancé the next. I have to live with the fact that you're now the second person this year who is firing me."

"I'm not firing—"

"You're allowing the hospital board to call my abilities as a physician into question."

He stared into his coffee, and she realized with a jolt that she'd expected him to immediately reassure her. How much had he defended her? His silence began to dismantle the confidence she'd developed over these past months.

She knew she'd helped a lot of patients. She'd seen the patient reviews, the praises written by many she'd treated, lives she'd made better, even the lives she'd saved, but she wouldn't tell him that now, because it would appear she was begging. Or bragging. She'd gone above and beyond what was necessary to ensure their welfare.

She pushed away from the table. "I'll contact one of those agencies that constantly barrage me with calls to do temp work," she said. "I'll ask for family practice, not emergency work." And if that put a kink in the wedding plans, she was in the mood to push the date back indefinitely.

That was how she felt right now. Once she came to her senses, she'd feel differently. "I can't help wondering how long you've known about this, because I never picked up on it at all."

"I warned you three months ago that the board was pushing for shorter patient visits, fewer tests."

"And I pushed myself to do as I was asked."

"Apparently not enough."

"You could have warned me that I was actually being singled out. Maybe I could have done something more about it."

"What would you have done? You just told me you pushed yourself to do better."

She caught her breath with the pain. "You're saying I'm not capable of learning? Of changing?" Must keep her voice down. Had to. "Couldn't you have at least given me the chance? Did you have to make the decision for me by remaining silent?"

He closed his eyes and turned away with a heavy sigh. "They've forced the issue because of our relationship."

She glared at his back. He wasn't answering her question. "And that was wrong of them. Unless they can prove I'm receiving special privileges due to our engagement, I can bring them up on charges for hostile intent."

He looked over his shoulder with a glare. "That's foolish behavior for someone who wishes to become a family practice physician in this town someday. You don't want to make enemies of the hospital board."

"Juliet isn't the only town that needs physicians."

"What are you saying?"

"I think what I'm saying is that I'm officially giving you my resignation as of today." She stood up and slid the chair beneath the table. "The hospital can pay extra to bring in temp docs. You know what I mean, don't you? Real ER docs who know how to move the meat." Again, she nearly had to clamp her teeth down on her tongue to curb the bitterness spewing out.

He stepped in front of her. "I'm not a real ER doc, either, Joy."

"You're not the one being fired, so obviously they like your work just fine, and you don't know how it feels to be fired at all, so please have a little patience if I'm reacting poorly."

"I told you, I'm not firing—"

"No, you're not firing me, I just gave notice so you wouldn't have to." She winced inwardly. Part of her hated herself for doing this to him, but most of her resented him for agreeing with the hospital board, despite whatever arguments he might have presented on her behalf.

"Just think about this and give yourself time to cool down," he said. "You need this job."

"In case you haven't noticed, there's a shortage of doctors all over the country. I get calls constantly from headhunters, and I have licenses for Missouri and Kansas, so that gives me double the opportunities."

"You really want to leave home again?"

"I proved to myself I could do it." Though it had broken her heart, and though she ached at the thought of it even now. "Since I was technically hired for part time work, there's no reason for me to keep working the long hours and full-time shifts, so you can tell Wilma Rush she'd better get on the phone today and start looking for my replacement."

"Which means I'll be working more shifts."

"Not if you stand up to them for once and refuse to. They

can't legally force their director to work any more shifts than he's working now."

"How did you know Wilma Rush was—"

"The one who just called you? President of the hospital board? Of course she's the one."

Wilma Rush was the bane of this town, a woman filled with bitterness and an insatiable need for power. A dangerous combination. Power was her drug, and revenge was her food and water.

"I know she never got along with Molly," Zack said. "I never understood why."

"She hates my mother, therefore she hates me."

"But why?"

"Does it matter? She's making it personal. I'm surprised she ever agreed to hire me in the first place, but maybe she thought firing me would be more satisfying." This was Wilma's chance to get her revenge, because she still grieved the loss of her late husband, who died with Molly Gilbert's picture in his pocket— something Molly never knew about.

Joy took a glass from the cupboard and filled it from the faucet. Her hand shook so badly she could only fill the glass halfway.

Her thoughts bounced from place to place and her eyes burned with tears she refused to shed. She knew Zack must have fought for her, but how hard did he fight? He'd just told her he knew she couldn't perform better. Did he secretly agree with the hospital board? Word would be all over town by the weekend that Dr. Zachary Travis had fired his fiancé. She could hear ol' Wilma clucking about it now.

She drank the water, rinsed her glass and set it in the sink, then turned to leave. "I'm not sure I'm cut out to spend the rest of my life in Juliet. All this small-town backstabbing is pathetic."

"Joy."

The sharpness in his tone halted her. She turned to look at him, still fighting tears.

He reached for her. She stepped back. At any other time, being in such close proximity to him, she wouldn't have been able to resist wrapping her arms around him and drawing closer. She dropped her gaze.

"I hate this," he said.

"Not as much as I do."

"You weren't in those meetings."

She thought about that and tried to put herself in his place. It was impossible.

The door chimed, indicating that a patient was being brought back, but she knew how cruel it would be for her to walk out without another word to him. She couldn't blame him for the actions of others.

"I'll see you tonight." She didn't reach for him, didn't take his hand, didn't meet his gaze, but she could do no more without giving way to the tears, and she'd already shed too many of those today.

***

After a filling and nutritious lunch at Molly's kitchen table, Myra thanked her hostess, excused herself and pulled on the heavy wool coat Molly loaned her. A bracing north wind nearly took her breath away, but she caught a faint whiff of the Missouri River, probably less than a hundred yards from the house. At least she knew that nothing here would stir up bad memories. Or so she hoped. Joy had told her she loved the animals, and never minded sharing a bedroom and bathroom when she spent the night.

This morning, when she suddenly remembered Weston in that hospital room, she had also remembered Molly and Joy, but it wasn't the same. Strangely, with the aroma of the coffee, pictures of Weston had shifted through her mind in short bursts until she easily recalled their time together these past weeks. But it wasn't until she was in the research wing that she recalled Weston from last year.

She had begun to feel a sense of familiarity to Molly and Joy, but she had only a few vivid memories to back that up, and after the episode in the research wing she hoped to be finished with new memories for the day. Though snow still powdered parts of the field and the trail that led to the river, she'd borrowed a pair of Molly's boots, which fit perfectly. It was a relief to get away from the churning thoughts that had attacked her at the med school campus. If she never returned to that research wing she wouldn't miss it.

At least, that was how she felt at the moment.

Three of Molly's cats, one dog and an inquisitive raccoon had followed her down to the cliff, and the dog, Buffer Zone, trotted down the narrow walkway ahead of Myra that led to the water, as if he felt it was his duty to play host.

The pink-trimmed white house was set just high enough on a slope that those who lived there could see at least half of the river from the front porch, but no matter how much the river flooded, the Gilbert household was never in danger of floating away.

Myra wrapped Molly's scarf more completely around her neck as the damp river air blew across her face and whipped her hair in every direction. She noted that two of the cats, Worf and Trippurr, were vying for position closest to her, and the raccoon— she thought this one was named Queen—nudged her in the back of the leg, as if urging her to walk faster.

The presence of the animals gave her a sort of comfort as she brooded over the flowing water below. Existence on this earth was never static. Like the water in the mighty Missouri, the substance of life's river was new every second, and as new replaced old, the frame of this life was gradually shaped—or eroded—by a person's decisions. What kinds of decisions had she made in her past? Had those decisions—good or bad—caused the trauma that led up to this fugue state?

Joy told her she'd had to quit college for a year because of the deaths of her parents. She felt things deeply, that much she knew. Apparently, she'd inherited that depth of emotion from her mother, who'd died so soon after Dad. How powerful their connection must have been for something like that to happen.

Myra shivered at the thought of more memories to come, yet at the same time she needed those pieces of her past to find herself again. Though the memories had settled where they belonged, her response to the research lab continued to frighten her. How much more could there be? She had too many empty slots left to fill, pieces of herself to recover. She could only hope the worst was over, and the rest would settle into her mind with gentle discovery. But she braced herself for more.

Chapter 12

Weston descended Molly's porch steps amongst a furry wave of cats. They flitted around the edge of the house and sniffed beneath his car, checking out the tires, the undercarriage, watching him with curious eyes. Somewhere in this menagerie were raccoons, which he'd seen this summer. Molly had found them cowering beside the broken body of their mother after a car got her.

And of course, Molly being Molly, she'd had to raise them.

He smiled to himself, but the smile drifted away as his thoughts darkened. Right now the world seemed to hold its breath as everyone waited for Myra to remember who she was. He feared the outcome. He knew Molly stood at her front door watching him, hoping his presence was more helpful than hurtful. Of course she hadn't said that, but he knew. Joy had been bold enough to express the thoughts of everyone, and he didn't blame her. He worried, himself. He just couldn't stay away. Myra had been there for him. Now it was his turn to do whatever he needed to so she would recover safely. He was now on speed dial to one of the most eminent psychiatrists in the state, just in case he would need the man's help.

Two calicos trotted after him like puppies as he strolled toward the river, following Myra's footprints in the snow. Who would have believed, a year ago, that on Christmas day he would be trudging down a winter path with animals in his wake, wearing faded jeans, an old sweater and jacket, to offer help for a struggling friend? This had never been the Weston Cline style. Oh, sure, he did charity work for public relations, but this was not public.

When married and raising children, he and Sylvia had the perfect home, perfect décor for the holiday season, took pictures every year for Sylvia to send to relatives and friends. That seemed like such a lifetime ago.

He winced at the words. They were true. The end of his son's life had immediately blasted what remained of the Cline family into a million pieces. Those were the pieces Myra worked on so well. She'd found them and replaced them with gentle patience. Now Weston knew they would all be able to move on. They would never be a traditional family again, but he'd learned how to communicate with his daughter, and he'd learned to be more patient with Sylvia. It helped that she'd finally met a good man instead of the losers she'd become addicted to after the divorce.

He studied the cliffs that overlooked the river, where Molly had told him Myra was headed. Though he'd been concerned about Myra at the cliffs in her state of mind, Molly assured him she'd spent a great deal of time there after her parents died. He saw no sign of her yet. He wouldn't start worrying until he got there, but his pace increased.

Who would have thought he'd care so much for a friend? Last year he'd never considered Joy Gilbert to be a friend. She was a goal for him, her skills something to be utilized for financial gain, her chastity something to be conquered. He'd failed on both counts, and she'd left him wondering at the strength of conviction she held so dearly.

He wanted to hold a conviction that close to his heart. He was old enough, and had been disappointed enough by the benefits of wealth, that he knew there had to be more to life. Still, to open himself up to a God salesman, who used high pressure and guilt to force him into a specific box of obedience? No. He'd seen too many charlatans using the name of Christ to suck the lifeblood from fellow humans, promising prosperity the way a Ponzi scheme salesman promised money. The people they attracted were weak-minded, emotionally needy people who became clones of their salesmen. How many people who claimed the name of Christ in the Bible belt merely used the name for financial profit? When he saw a cross on an ad, he avoided it.

Even Joy, whose faith had secretly impressed him, had been deeply wounded by the God sales force, her church, before she left Juliet. How many Christian patients in his clinic had prayed for healing? And how many still struggled with their illnesses and pain? He rarely heard them talk about praying for anything else, just their health, perhaps money, as if they believed their "salvation" had granted them three wishes, and they couldn't understand why their first three wishes—health, wealth and happiness—didn't come true.

But here he was on Molly Gilbert's property, no less— someone he'd spent many months resenting because of the hold she had on her daughter, of the faith she'd instilled in Joy so earnestly. He didn't see Molly as a charlatan.

Judging by the modest holiday décor in her house, she held Christ in higher esteem than the exchange of gifts or following traditional Christmas protocol.

Around the first of November this year when Weston's assistants asked about any new, splashy publicity stunts he might want to try, he couldn't help thinking about the pro bono cases Joy had quietly taken when she worked for him, never calling attention to herself, never in it for the glory. He'd fired her for what he'd called "wasting their time and resources"—and for other things he was still even more ashamed to contemplate.

One of many reasons he kept seeing Myra was because he didn't want to become that man again. What concerned him was that she'd told him often she couldn't change him. What he became would come from outside either of them. All was up to Someone more powerful.

He knew there must be another way, because that Someone, whom he'd blamed and berated and hated since his son's death— maybe even since his little brother's death as a child—would not want him.

So in attempts to change—maybe even remove his image from the pedestal so many had built for him in their adulation--this year his companies remained low-key for the season. He knew his employees wondered why, but he didn't care. When he did give to a charity now, no one knew about it. Something in him was definitely changing. He wanted to be a better person, and he was stuck trying to make all those changes himself.

He thought about Joy's remark earlier, about his lack of faith compared to Myra's. It meant there would never be more between him and Myra. He knew that. Most definitely, Myra's friendship influenced him, but even before that he'd come face to face with his mortality. It had stunned him.

A little more than halfway to the riverbank he finally spotted her, the silky flow of ebony hair covering her shoulders, and he slowed his steps to catch his breath. She sat on the edge of a lower cliff surrounded by animals. An occasional cold wind took his breath, and he hoped she was warm enough. He stopped for a moment and watched her with the two cats and the raccoon—apparently the raccoon had lived around the cats for so long it thought like one of them, because traditionally they were enemies.

He recalled those three orphaned baby raccoons Molly was raising when he was here this summer. He also recalled the vineyard Molly was growing, the garden rich with vegetables, and the peace he'd glimpsed here.

Myra's hands idly fondled the cat and raccoon fur equally. He smiled at the scene. Maybe Molly had the right idea. Animals never told a person how to live one's life, never reminded one of his past sins or judged him. They didn't depend on a person for anything besides food, water and company—and the raccoons would soon be on their own completely.

Animals didn't come to a vulnerable psychiatrist with their shattered lives, expecting her to help them build their psyches back into something solid once more. He'd seen how those patients affected her when she answered their panicked calls, interrupting dinner so many times over the past months.

He'd also noted how gentle her voice was when she talked them back down from that panic.

Molly's big golden retriever mix jumped up from somewhere on the lower cliffs, covered in icy mud, and licked Myra, excited by his expedition, a huge smile on his face.

Weston chuckled to himself. The dog's name was Buffer Zone. How appropriate. That was exactly what Myra needed from the world—a buffer zone, and she needed to find a better way to do it. Fugue states weren't the answer.

***

Myra brushed freezing tears from her face as the dog nuzzled her hair and teased the cats and Queen. This was a helpful distraction. Right now she needed an emotional foothold, but she could find nothing solid to hold onto, so the company of animals would do. All she had were painful or conflicting memories to anchor her. More tears dropped down her cheeks and onto the heads of the poor little cats snuggling next to her.

They merely moved a few inches and continued to purr, which made her smile through the tears. How much easier life would be if humans could adjust so well. Humans, however, didn't often lapse into fugue states to escape.

She pulled another tissue from the pocketful Molly had sent with her.

Buffer Zone whined, perked his ears and headed back up the slope toward the house.

She heard a soft groan of the human kind, and turned to find Weston, still in his jeans, heavy sweater and old coat, bracing himself for the dog's advances. Watching his reaction, she was impressed to see a grudging smile cross his face when the filthy dog loped straight toward him.

"Down Buffer." Weston held his hand out, and the dog sat, panting, tongue lolling. "Good boy." Weston rubbed the dog's ears, and the well-trained dog sat and enjoyed the attention.

"I knew Molly Gilbert was an animal whisperer, but I didn't know that about you," Myra called to him.

He gave the dog a final pat and walked toward her, and as she watched him something squeezed in her chest. She'd known the moment she inhaled the coffee this morning that Weston Cline was a temptation for her. She also knew that she would do nothing about that. The memories of him were becoming clearer, and she heard Phantom of the Opera music playing in her head. The healthy side was so beautiful. It was the part of him that he presented to the world.

The damaged part didn't show as clearly to those who didn't know him, so he could walk around in public view without striking horror into the hearts of strangers. Still, it was there. He could be particularly dangerous for her, because she knew how he felt without his saying a word to her. He'd imprinted her onto his heart.

If only she hadn't imprinted him onto hers.

However, as he sat down beside her with enough space between them that the cats didn't have to move, she knew she needed his friendship right now. So far he was showing exceptional respect for her personal space—something he'd never done with Joy. How long that respect would last, she hadn't a clue.

"I don't know anyone but Molly who can herd cats," Weston said, rubbing his hand through Trippurr's fur. "She can tame wild animals."

Myra felt a sudden nudge in her behind and looked around to see Queen nosing beneath her for something. "She might tame them, but she hasn't managed to train this one to have good manners."

Weston chuckled, eased the raccoon away, then met her gaze. "She told me you were out here. Having more memories?"

"Only struggling with the ones I've had."

He gestured to the river and held his hand up against the wind. "There are warmer places to contemplate your life."

"Not places that will protect me from more memories."

He raised an eyebrow at her as the dog walked to his other side and plopped down next to him, leaning in close, as if for warmth. Weston wrapped his arm around the muddy coat. "I've never known you to back down from a challenge, especially after you took on my whole messed up family."

Myra could only catch vague pictures of his ex-wife and daughter in her memory files, but she did have a feeling of satisfaction. That was enough for now. "You were the tough one to crack. I think you still are, but at least it seems some of Molly's animal-whispering ways have rubbed off on you. That dog nearly knocked me off this cliff when I first sat down. I think he wanted to sit in my lap."

"Yes, but you correct people with gentle tones and logic, whereas I control people like an autocrat. Dogs can sense that."

She nodded and returned to her contemplation of the river. He remained silent, leaning against the dog, possibly lost in his own thoughts.

"Do you recall if I ever told you why I chose psychiatry?" she asked.

He grinned. "I asked you that one night when your phone rang for the second time. A patient calling for help. Again."

She shivered and hugged herself, as if bracing for the conversation. Her job was one thing that frightened her. "What did you say?"

"I asked if you were a psychiatrist or a babysitter."

She gasped. "What did I say?"

The grin died as he looked away. She marveled at the silvery sheen of his blue eyes. That typically only happened when he was perturbed about something.

"Weston?"

He studied the length of the river. "You're out here to avoid memories, right? Not stir up more."

She pulled in a slow breath. "As I told Joy last night, something that happened to me years ago shouldn't make this amnesia worse. So tell me something I don't know. Literally. I'm collecting the building blocks of my life, whether I want to or not." She was conflicted but determined. If she could recover information about safer subjects, then she would be more secure when the worse memories hit.

He turned to her. "You know why you chose your profession, but there's some reason you're suppressing it. Maybe it's a good one."

She studied the firm lines of his face, the black hair barely touched by silver, the long black lashes lying low over his eyes at the moment. She didn't recall ever having to force him to talk. In her recollections of him, he'd spoken easily with her, and he was never afraid to speak his mind. She recalled more than one debate.

What was she forgetting? Obviously, judging by his demeanor, it was something serious.

"I'll have to get past this and back to work, and I must have had a reason to choose psychiatry."

He nodded, then picked up one of the dog's paws and held it out. "Myra Maxwell, meet your best friend."

She frowned at him, shaking her head.

"Buffer Zone," he said.

The dog wiggled all over at the attention, his smile wide and toothy.

"Buffer Zone." What on earth was the man talking about?

"One of the debates we started having quite some time ago was about your tendency to always be on call, no matter what time of the day or night. If you weren't counseling a patient in the office, you were counseling over the phone."

"I don't remember."

"You gave out your calling card like candy and told every patient to contact you any time. I resented having dinner interrupted nearly every time we met together, and I let you know about it. One time you even tossed down the money for the whole bill, angry that I'd complained."

"Did I leave?"

"Not until I told you the money wasn't enough to cover the bill. Then you stormed through the restaurant in a very adorable snit, turning heads at every table."

Myra's mouth fell open, and then she laughed. It felt good. "I take it I didn't come back with more money."

"You didn't even turn around. I would have much preferred a nice, heated argument over staring at the empty chair across the table."

"Did the headlines carry the news the next day?"

"I didn't look. I'm not into tabloid rumors, and we switched restaurants often so we wouldn't be hounded by photo-hungry bloggers."

"Notice I don't have a cell phone with me. Maybe I secretly agreed with you."

"I only saw you once or twice a week, so I didn't know the whole story. You need a buffer zone. You need your time off or those people with all their problems will drive you mad."

"You mean like I am now?"

"Exactly. You need to change that practice, not only for your well-being, but for theirs. If they have you as a crutch, they'll never learn to handle life themselves."

She kicked the cliff beneath her and some snow filtered down to the next level of rock. "You were obviously right."

"That wasn't what you told me."

"Things have changed. You never told me why I went into psychiatry."

He looked down at his hands. "I don't think you'll want this memory at Christmas."

"When you're with me I feel stronger. Tell me while you're here. I can take it."

"You're sure?"

She nodded, bracing herself as she stared at a branch floating along the swift current of the river.

"Your family history contains mental illness." He said the words gently.

"And that would be...?"

He grimaced and rubbed his hands together. "I wish Joy was here right now, because you two are best friends and—"

"So are we, Weston. Tell me."

"It was depression. You once told me that a large percentage of the population suffers with depression from time to time, but for your family it was worse." He spoke slowly, succinctly, as if measuring each word. "Your maternal grandfather committed suicide."

"I don't remember."

"Your mother inherited it from him."

She looked up into Weston's compassionate blue eyes as she worked out the rest of the story for herself. The memories didn't hit her as hard as Dustin's death, but they did come, slowly as if through a fog of deep and endless grief.

"That's why my mother died six months after my father's death."

"She couldn't recover."

"Last night Joy implied that Mom died from an illness. I took for granted it was physical. Sometimes when people are extremely interconnected, especially after a long and loving marriage, once one spouse dies the other one goes downhill quickly. I thought that was what happened."

He reached into his coat pocket and pulled out some tissues. "Molly told me you might need these."

She thanked him and wiped her face. Again, she'd been crying without knowing it.

"You told me all about it," he said.

"They were both too young." She squeezed her hands into tight-fisted knots. "It wasn't as if she died of old age."

"She overdosed."

Her face crumpled.

He laid a hand on top of hers and squeezed, then released her, as always, respecting her personal space. "She left a note of apology to you, but you never understood how she could do that to her daughter. You specialized in psychiatry because you needed answers. You wanted to prevent that from happening to others." He reached for the tissue in her hand and used it to dab fresh tears from her face. "I'm so sorry."

It flooded her more clearly then, the mental pictures of Dad's funeral, Mom's flat-lined behavior, the agony of watching her slip away, as if Mom and Dad both died on the same day. Only an empty shell was left behind. Myra buried her face in her hands and her shoulders shook with the deep flow of sorrow.

She felt Weston's hand resting lightly on her shoulder, letting her know he was there for her but not intruding. She wanted a shoulder to lean into and soak with her tears, but as the memories flowed through her, from the day of Dad's death to the days and weeks afterward, the sobs eased. Time took a step backward, as if it had rushed at her like an attack, and something inside her pushed it back into place.

"She couldn't cope with eating even the simple meals I prepared for her." Myra straightened and pressed the tissue to her face as Weston removed his hand from her shoulder. "She lost weight, lived in Dad's clothing for days at a time without a shower."

"You did all you could for her."

She nodded. "It wasn't until I caught her soaking in a tub of hot water with a sharp blade beside her that I knew I had to quit school. I couldn't keep up. I had to do whatever it took to keep her alive."

"You're still doing that. It's the brokenness you live with. It's something we have in common, but for you, with each patient you have, you're trying again to save her life."

She nodded, caught another tear with her tissue, sniffed. "I tried to keep all dangerous medications out of her reach, but I underestimated her determination to follow Dad." Myra had thought she'd emptied herself of tears, but there were more, and her head ached with them. Six months after Dad's funeral she arrived home from a quick trip for groceries and found Mom laying peacefully in her bed, covered to her neck by blankets, eyes closed. She looked asleep, but her face was white paste.

"Your mother's illness was more deadly than anyone knew, and you can't keep trying to save her or you'll lose yourself."

Myra understood that, and some time in the past she'd come to terms with it, but right now she was reliving it. She looked up at him, and was struck by the tenderness in his gaze. There was no missing the compassion flowing from a man who was supposedly a financial and relationship shark. Had she ever let her guard down with him before the day she told him about Mom?

"My life is Swiss cheese right now, but I'm recalling more," she said. "For instance, after Mom's death Molly and Joy took me in here. I stayed with them for a few weeks. I spent a lot of time right here on these cliffs."

"Thus, the return of more memory," he said.

"What I remember most about that time was being surrounded by the love of two women who had strong faith and a healing love for me." She'd also been surrounded by the flitting bodies of affectionate animals who seldom left her completely alone, who covered her like a purring blanket on her worst days, and taught her how to laugh again.

"You've been trying to support all your patients the way they did. No wonder you had a meltdown. One person can't carry the whole world on her shoulders, not even a woman as strong-willed as you."

She stared down at the gray water as yet another broken tree branch floated east on its way to the Mississippi, then she looked up into the sky. "I remember the days after Mom's funeral, sitting here night after night, watching the moon grow smaller and smaller, like the head of a mature dandelion blowing away in the wind. That was how I felt about my life. Pieces of me were breaking away and disappearing. My life was falling apart. She not only killed herself, but her death nearly killed me."

"I can identify." Weston's voice also held pain.

She looked up to find him also staring out across the river. "After my brother died my mother was never the same. For the longest time I believed she blamed me."

"When did you discover differently?"

He looked at her. "After Keegan died. Then I was able to identify with my mother. I know you felt like dying after finding your mother the way you did, but you're still here."

"Emotionally damaged, perhaps."

"But you're still Myra Maxwell, who lives her life to rescue those in need."

She couldn't help responding to the gentle tone of his voice. He made her sound like some kind of heroine. If only she knew herself better. It felt so wrong to know him better than she knew herself.

"Have you ever seen a field of dandelions die off without being poisoned?" he asked. "I remember trying to keep them out of my yard. A dandelion spreads its seeds with the wind, and it continues on and on, just as you've continued using what you've learned in your past to shape your future. You're spreading your healing touch to others to make their lives better."

"I like the way you look at it."

He smiled at her. "Now you're reclaiming your memories one by one. You're reversing the process as you pursue your memories."

She shivered despite the warmth of her clothing and his nearness.

"Don't be afraid, Myra. You're in a safe place surrounded by friends, and you're rebuilding your memories like a waxing moon, not a fragile dandelion moon."

His cell phone chose that moment to buzz.

She gave him a playful shove. "Business on Christmas day? And you get mad at me for answering my phone when we're at dinner."

"Who says this call is business?"

"When do you ever get any other kind?"

"Maybe I'm beginning to." He glanced at the screen and smiled. "This isn't business, it's a friend. Or at least, someone outside my normal business arena." He answered. "Zack? You're awake?" He winked at her as he listened. "Good," he said. "I'm at Molly's." He hesitated, listening again, then sighed.

She wondered what Zack was saying.

"Yes, Myra's with me," Weston said. "We're watching the river." Again, he listened. "Fifteen minutes? I'll be there."

He disconnected and stood up, sliding the phone back into his pocket. "See how short that was?"

"Sure it was, you were talking to Zack, who's probably sleep deprived, and judging by your side of the conversation he's wondering about our friendship."

"And that's why you're a shrink. Want to walk back with me? I have a session."

"A what?" Myra frowned up at him. "What kind of session? No, nevermind. None of my business. Zack has his own practice, and he could do worse than to come to you for business advice."

"You think Zack would come to me for anything after what I've done to him? I'd do anything to help him, but I don't think it's likely he'll ask." Weston held his hand out to help her up and she took it.

"Then, um, forgive my nosiness, but what's up?"

"I thought I'd get a man's point of view about a few things for a change."

"And I thought I was the only person you confided in." She nudged the raccoon off the top of her foot.

Weston rubbed her hand in both of his and didn't reply.

She let him pull her up, then brushed the snow and leaves from her coat. "I thought you could talk to me about anything." She was going far past pushy, but his behavior had her curious.

"You've had enough patients taking up your time these past months, and right now you need to heal, yourself, not take on someone else's baggage."

She studied his expression closely. When she'd first begun working with Weston it seemed to take a mental crowbar to pry honest answers from him. Sure, he was never at a loss for words, but she didn't trust those words for a long time. As they learned to work together he improved dramatically. That's why she could tell when he was holding something back, and right now he was doing just that. But what?

Chapter 13

Myra's green eyes widened, and Weston could see the questions forming, but this was one time when complete honesty wouldn't be the best idea for either of them. He wouldn't lie to her, but he also wouldn't weigh her down with the burden of his thoughts. Before she could ask more, he distracted her by tugging the sleeves of her sweater lower to cover her hands.

He wrapped the scarf more securely around her neck, and it occurred to him he was doting on her. But since he was on a roll, he might as well give her a bit more tender direction. "You need to stay warm."

"Yes, Dad." She had the most beautiful smile. It began in her eyes and spread across her face with pure and friendly warmth. She enchanted him.

"Do you want me to teach you how to disassociate yourself emotionally from everyone around you? Because I know how to do that."

"Um, I think that's what I'm doing right now, isn't it?"

He took her arm and started walking with her. If she knew what was really going on in his mind right now she might run back and hurl herself over the cliff.

"I think you could use a few pointers when you're better," he said. "Then maybe this kind of thing won't happen again. I'm an expert at it, you know." He looked sideways at her and winked.

"That's why you needed me in the first place, remember?"

"I haven't resorted to a fugue state."

"You've lived in a semi-fugue state for years."

"So you're saying I'm almost as unhealthy as you."

She walked beside him in silence, and for the first time in his life he wished he could read minds. Hers, at least. He couldn't recall the last time he was concerned about what other people were thinking. Most of his adult life he'd had a bad tendency to believe he had all the right answers. The early successes in his life didn't teach him much humility. Now it seemed he did care more about the opinions of others. Especially Myra's.

"I think you're changing." She looked up at him thoughtfully. "You're in a state of flux, just as I am. That's what Joy told me last night."

"Great way to change the subject."

"Oh, you'll be getting a lot of that from me for a while. You started it by holding that coffee cup under my nose this morning."

"I hope it didn't do more harm than good."

"Thanks to that trick I remembered many of our dinners in great detail, and the memories became clearer as the day progressed, but they've been coming from every direction. Nothing's in order right now, so I'm tripping down rabbit trails every time I have a new thought. Did you do that coffee thing on purpose?"

"It was an attempt to engage more of your senses. You taught me that."

"Glad you remembered. And of course you remembered how much I love after-dinner espresso with cream."

He remembered a lot more than that. For instance, she loved lots of butter with her lobster, but not so much with king crab. Her steak was never complete without the hottest horseradish, and her favorite salad was seaweed.

The freezing wind hit them from behind. He instinctively drew her closer. She stiffened, and he released her.

"Sorry," he said. "I have no right to treat you as if you're my daughter, but it's getting colder."

"There's another thing that's changing about you," she said.

"What's that? I'm treating you like my daughter?"

She paused thoughtfully. "You're more tender, quicker to apologize, more caring about others."

Her words touched him more deeply than he would have expected. "Don't tell my family, okay? Clines never show vulnerability."

"And you cover your tender side with humor."

Strange that this lovely woman seemed to know him so well when she couldn't remember her own life.

"There's a vulnerability that seems to drive you," she

continued. "It gives you the sense of purpose you need to change. There's only One who can give you everything you seek."

"I know Who you're talking about. Joy told me, you've told me. Zack is likely to tell me. Give me time to consider everything. And thank you for caring."

"I'm not a Cline, so I'm allowed." She smiled up at him.

It was always her smile that weakened his defenses. Time for a subject change. "Have you had any more new memories this afternoon? For instance, the cats, the new rooms Molly built, or the fact that she painted her cottage with Pepto Bismol pink trim?"

She gave a tiny gasp. "I do remember that. Another good memory breaking through! Pink is her favorite color. Not the bright color she ended up with, but she loves pink." Her steps slowed. "Followed by another."

"Another what? What's wrong?"

"More memories."

"That's a good thing."

She sucked in a deep breath and raised her hands to her face. Fear filled her eyes. "Not now. It's black and menacing."

"Can you control it?"

She closed her eyes and reached for his arm. "I'm trying."

He took her hands. Of course she was afraid of more memories. One in particular. If only he knew what it was so he could prepare her. "I'll call Zack and cancel our meeting. I don't want to leave you here alone."

"No, you need some guy time. I understand."

"I need to make sure you're going to be okay. That's my reason for being here in the first place."

She opened her eyes and looked up at him, and he was caught in her spell as he had been so many times before. This woman drew something from him that no other woman had done.

Sylvia had become his obligation after she got pregnant, and he'd remained true to her throughout their marriage, but he would never have married her otherwise. He loved his daughter dearly, but until these past few months he'd tended to want her to simply obey his wishes. Pursuing Joy last year had been one of his worst offenses. The other women he'd kept company with for a night or two of casual and mutual comfort.

He felt connected to Myra by nothing more than conversation

as the binding agent, a sharing of thoughts, ideas, dreams, wishes. What a powerful attraction.

He watched her slowly move forward, carefully watching her steps and avoiding the dreaded Trippurr, who was a beautiful but stout cat known best for the words that made up her name.

"Last night I felt as if something evil hovered just outside my conscious thoughts. It frightens me that I might retreat even more deeply than I did yesterday."

"Is that likely to happen? You're the expert."

She looked up at him and slowly shook her head. "Hard to determine, but not likely with you here to tackle me and hold me in place."

"Try to focus on something else. Remember you once told me that in order to stop thinking about one thing, I needed to replace that thought with something else entirely. It doesn't work to try to not think about something."

She studied the ground ahead of them. "Thank you. I can do that." She looked up at him. "So tell me more about your meeting with Zack, even though it isn't my business."

Weston found himself mimicking her motions, watching his steps, matching hers. Honesty was one thing, but he was beginning to wish he'd kept his mouth shut about his meeting with Zack.

"He was concerned when I called looking for you last night."

"Got that already. Everyone was concerned."

"What I meant was that he wanted to know more about the time you and I spend together."

"Zack seems like a perfectly nice doctor with a good bedside manner, but why would he care?"

"The same reason Joy cares. I could be a bad influence on you."

"I'm not a child."

"He wanted to know why I was taking such a personal interest in your welfare."

"Why are you?"

Weston hesitated a half second too long. "Because I consider you a very good friend. When I tried to call you yesterday and you'd left without notice, I knew you had to be in trouble. I knew you still thought of Juliet as home, and with Joy here I thought you might have been in touch with her."

"And of course you couldn't call Joy because of your past history with her, but Zack was also involved in that."

"Yes, but he was at least willing to talk to me last night when I called. Zack's opinion means a lot to me, but I'll call him back right now and cancel our meeting if you want."

"Really." Her brows puckered. "I don't tell you how to live your life, and no one tells me how to live mine. If I want to remain friends with you, nothing Zack says will impact my behavior, and I believe you're man enough not to allow it to affect yours."

"I think you once mentioned to me that a wise man listens to other wise men. I can't help feeling beholden to a man who saved my life and my daughter's after everything I did to him."

"Beholden enough to let him influence our friendship?"

"I won't allow anyone to dictate my behavior, but I wouldn't mind learning from others whose ethics I admire. Blind obedience isn't the same thing as befriending a wise man."

"Even if that wise man distrusts you?"

"Even if he hates me."

"Does he?"

"That remains to be seen."

Myra shot Weston a brief glance and he still saw the fear lingering in her eyes. She returned her attention to the path on which she walked. "I've learned my lesson, and you were right. I'm changing business practices as soon as I get back. I wish I'd listened to you sooner."

"I'll try not to rub it in."

She laughed, and even though the laughter sounded more like the venting of tension it eased his tension as well.

"I can count on one hand the number of real friends I have in this world," he said. "Thank you for being one."

Myra walked with him in thought for a moment, avoiding Trippurr with a quick side-step.

"Is that why you never told Joy about our sessions?" he asked. "Because you didn't want anyone interfering with our friendship?"

"No. She asked me to take you as a patient in the first place, so I didn't expect her to protest."

"So why didn't you tell her about our arrangement?"

"Don't tell me you have your own clinic and you don't know about the necessity of patient privacy."

"If Joy referred me to you in the first place, she could get follow-up reports."

"Even though we were meeting under unusual circumstances, I still keep that privacy, and you were never her patient that I recall. Neither Joy nor Zack could have access to that information, and that's just conjecture since I don't remember."

He watched her silhouette, her upturned nose red from the cold, her cheeks flushed…and appearing to flush more deeply. Her shiny black hair blew across her face, hiding her eyes, and it looked as if she intentionally left it there.

"But as you said, we're good friends," she said. "Very good friends."

He focused on that one word. Very. He wanted to shout but refrained. He wanted to ask what she meant by it, but thought better of it.

"I don't think Joy could accept how close you and I have grown," Myra said. "She's still struggling—"

"To forgive me. I know. I called her on it last night."

"She needs to forgive you for her own sake," Myra said.

"When you consider what I did—"

Myra nudged him with her elbow. "When are you going to forgive yourself for that?"

He stumbled into Trippurr, stepped on the poor cat's foot, grimaced at the loud yowl, and scrambled to stay on his feet.

The roly-poly cat kicked up snow as she raced toward the house, shooting Weston a look of reproach over her shoulder. She didn't make it all the way to the house before she stopped to lick her foot, give him another reproachful look and then trotted back toward them.

Myra burst into laughter, and it echoed from the trees, from the pink-trimmed white house ahead of them, from the sky itself.

Weston waited, watching her, held breathless by the sound of her laughter. And then he joined her, feeling the thrill of it as his own laughter mingled with hers. Hers was a voice he could live with for the rest of his life. Her face, her smile, her personality all drew him.

But her character—the part of her that she'd used to measure the choices of her life every day—chained his heart to hers with a power he feared would never let go even though he knew there could be no future for them as things stood.

No matter what Zack said or thought, or what Joy worried about, Weston had this moment with Myra to laugh, enjoy life, to feel something he hadn't felt in a long time—a kind of lightness inside, an ability to appreciate what was around him, even the pink trim and wind-chime décor of Molly's house.

He wanted to catch this beautiful woman in his arms and hold onto her and never let go.

When Myra finally stopped laughing, tears of a pleasant kind streamed down her face. "I'm apparently a slapstick humor kind of girl."

"Yes, you are."

"Laughter therapy." She chuckled again. "I might need to add that to my list of treatments. But then maybe I already do. I have no idea."

"I think you might have fewer memories if you stop talking about your practice. Yesterday it frightened you, so maybe you could avoid it."

She stepped closer to him, shivering in the wake of another burst of cold wind. "You're right, of course. I'm still trying to recall when you suddenly got so smart."

Her words and admiration warmed him, but even as she spoke her expression changed. Her eyes filled with anxiety.

"I just realized I have no way to do my job," she said. "I don't know my patients and I'm a psyche patient, myself."

"You were planning to be off work until after the first of the year, so give yourself time to heal. The memories are returning more quickly than any of us imagined."

"And in a more harrowing way."

He gently placed a hand on her shoulder. "Myra, I said give yourself time."

"Help me slow it down." She reached for his arm with both hands. "There's something...I don't know what it is, but something keeps trying to break through—"

"If it does I'm here right now. I won't let you go, and I won't let you hurt yourself. The big mistake you made yesterday was leaving alone. You can't do that here." He took her arms and held them firmly, resisting the urge to draw her closer. "How can I help you? I'll do anything you need." She was right. Her mind was skipping from place to place in a panic and he didn't know what to do.

Her gaze met his with a sense of urgency. "Keep me distracted?"

"How?"

"Talk about anything but therapy tonight at dinner."

"I'll tell everyone there to do the same."

"You're my lifeline, Weston," she whispered. The trust in her eyes, the sound of her voice, the words of honesty mesmerized him.

She should know by now that he would do anything for her. As badly as he wanted more from her, he would respect her wishes—her needs—with all his self-control. But that was going to be much more difficult than he'd imagined.

"Because of the amount of time we've shared these past months, you're the one I feel closest to," she said.

"Even though I have a bad track record?"

"I don't care about your track record, I care about the strength your friendship gives me, and if that's selfish I'm sorry."

This was why he needed so badly to talk to Zack.

"Zack and Joy need to understand this, Weston. Tell them the truth, and make them accept how much I depend on you," she said.

"How much truth?"

She darted a glance at him. A glimmer of humor once again lit her eyes. "I wouldn't expect you to share the same kind of table talk you and I do."

He considered her words for a moment. "I also won't be sharing tastes of my food." And he wouldn't participate in the light, harmless flirting he often did with Myra—which she reciprocated in kind. "Zack doesn't need to know every detail of every conversation we've ever had. I'm telling him the truth as I see it. I'm sure I'll hear something different from him." He only hoped they didn't get into a wrestling match on the campus of the Juliet School of Medicine.

Chapter 14

Myra focused on the man walking beside her, the sun peeking through the clouds in lengthening increments, the cats running from tree to bush to house and back again. The raccoon sniffed at the leaves and snow along the tree line. She focused on anything but the sense of impending catastrophe that made her feel breathless every few moments.

Think of something else. She looked up at Weston and studied the strong shape of his face, the tufts of hair blowing in the wind. When he returned her attention she held his gaze and shrugged.

"Trying to fill my mind with other things," she said.

He smiled. He'd promised to be with her throughout this ordeal. He could be difficult, pushy, stubborn. He could also be indulgent and supportive. He'd helped her several times with business advice, even though she would never have asked. He simply offered.

"You know, you might make better headway with Zack if you offer some business suggestions. You do that so well."

Weston took a few steps in silence, rubbing his hands together as if to stir up some warmth. "Not something a man appreciates without asking first. Would you stop stressing over this? If you truly remember our time together as well as you said you do, you'll recall that I've spent my adult life and some of my teen years facing down bullies and bureaucrats."

"I don't think Zack is either." She stopped walking and turned to Weston, touching his hand. Distraction was key, and right now she was desperate. "I'm sorry to put you on the spot, but I have to say this and get it out there. I believe there's definitely more than simple friendship between us. Much more."

Weston's hands clenched, and she glanced at them as a pleasant warmth spread through her. He couldn't clamp down on his emotions that easily.

She had no desire to lead him on, but she'd had Weston to herself all these months, and it bothered her more than she could say to have others interfering with that. "I'm afraid you're going to tell Zack you're in love with me." She braced herself for his reaction.

He took a deep breath, and she watched the fog form in the air as he exhaled. He held his hands out in front of him, flipped them from side to side. "Interesting that I don't look so transparent."

"You drove down here in the sleet last night on the off chance that a mere casual friend might be here, needing your help, when other friends were available? That isn't the Weston Cline I know. If even Zack can see through that, you don't think I can?"

She watched the color deepen in his face, and she smiled to herself. She'd been right. There was more to this relationship for her, as well. Interesting that she didn't recall that he'd ever mentioned anything so private—nothing past the teasing, the occasional moments spent gazing into one another's eyes a little too long for a casual friendship. All this time, in the memories she could string together, he'd been respectful, forthright, he had matched her flirtatiousness with his own, and he was occasionally irascible, but never had he attempted to take their dinners to a more intimate level.

"I feel the same way, Weston Cline," she said softly. "Why avoid speaking about the truth?" She wanted to clamp a hand over her mouth, but just this one time she felt the necessity to say the words. "We both know it, so it might as well be said."

"Except for a huge chasm between us, you're correct."

She knew what he meant, but she had to ask. "Chasm?"

"I might not have mentioned it in our talks together, but I know I'm a goat."

Her mouth flew open and she gasped, trying hard not to laugh at his choice of words. "A what?"

"I think Molly has one around here somewhere if you want to see what they look like."

"Um...." She pressed her lips together. Too late, she caught the glint of humor in his clear blue eyes.

The humor was forced, she could tell, and then it disappeared altogether. "Remember the division of the sheep from the goats in the Bible?" he asked.

"Yes." And it was no laughing matter. "You've read that, have you? And you think you're a goat? So you're saying that you don't believe in Christ?"

"Belief in someone and becoming one with someone are two different things. I believe all I'd have to do would be bow my head and say a prayer and behave in a way that would convince everyone I was a new man and you and I could have a future together, because I've never loved anyone the way I love you."

She held her breath, afraid to say anything more. She'd started this conversation. "But you can't do that without meaning it."

"I won't do it, no matter what I stand to lose."

"I asked you when you could forgive yourself, but if you believe there is a God, you must believe He's more powerful than any of us. He can do what we can't. He can soften the hardest heart, and He can love the unlovable."

"From what I've read He also demands righteousness."

"He demands faith in His Son, the Righteous One. You've known all this time you can't do enough to make up for your past, but Christ already has. The payment's been made."

"I know. You've told me this before."

"Okay, then I won't push. This is between you and Him."

"According to the Bible those who don't believe in Him are infidels," Weston said. "Meaning they have no fidelity to Christ, and in the end will be separated from His sheep."

"You've been thinking on this for some time, then?" She recognized an ache inside, something she'd experienced at other times today.

"I think the question should be worded differently."

She stood facing him and waited, listening to the shuffle of the leaves in the wind.

"I've known for several years that God hates me."

She swallowed. How quickly she could go from laughter to sorrow with this man. "I'm so sorry you believe that, because it's a lie."

His eyes widened, his handsome features caught in a moment of vulnerability that made her hands sweat.

Myra shrugged. "God created you, and He loves His creation. Can you imagine hating Tressa?"

"That's different."

"Yes, that's true. God being God, He's able to love much more perfectly than even the best human could love his child."

His attention didn't waver. "But if someone intentionally hurt my child, as I did to Joy and Zack, I would nail them to a brick wall."

"How about a cross?"

"Another difference between God and me. I would never nail my own son to a cross."

"That's why you aren't God. What if the children you loved were fighting? You don't stop loving one because he's picking on the other. You might discipline him, but you wouldn't hate him. We are all God's creation."

He took her arm and starting walking beside her in silence, stepping around Trippurr when she stopped and blocked the path yet again.

Myra needed to explain more, but she was pretty sure he knew what she was talking about. He obviously knew something of the Bible, and the most important part was that of Christ taking the pain for the sins of the world.

"I've just had another memory," she said.

He slowed his steps and gave her a quick glance, as if braced for the worst.

"A good memory," she assured him. "The best." It hit her with a rush of such peace that she knew why Molly had brought her out to the house. "I told you about how Molly and Joy took me in after my mother committed suicide. Their actions taught me that I mean more to God than I could mean to anyone else on earth."

"How?"

"Through their humility, mostly. If I remarked on their hospitality, or Molly's caring nature or Joy's solid friendship, they didn't take credit for it. Without being all ultra-holy and pious, they turned the compliment back on me, as if my disruptive presence could possibly bless them. They showed me that no one but God is capable of perfect love, and they pointed out their imperfections. I realized if they could love me like that, then the God of the universe had the power to love me so much more."

"I'm glad you were able to grasp that peace, Myra. You deserve it."

"I grasped it and accepted it right here in this place. I don't deserve it any more than you."

"Remember how difficult it is for a rich man to get into heaven."

So he did know the Bible more than she'd realized. "But with God, all things are possible. You can't take the verses out of context. When you've walked with Him, gotten to know Him, you'll learn for yourself."

"You're saying this as if you believe it's a foregone conclusion."

"I've known for a long time that nothing besides friendship could happen between you and me without the Holy Spirit being a part of that, and so yes, I believe in someday because I believe I'm where God wants me right now. Don't worry that I'll keep trying to shove God down your throat. He has to draw you. I simply believe I was drawn to you for a reason, and I've learned to trust His guidance."

***

Weston was so stunned by Myra's declaration that when Trippurr slunk between his feet he had to do another quick and silly dance to keep from squishing her. The woman he was falling in love with had just told him she was also falling in love. Wasn't that what she'd said? But hadn't she also told him, barely a few moments ago, that she needed him to be her friend?

"I'm confused," he said.

"So am I. I can't remember what I ate for breakfast yesterday morning."

"You told me you needed a solid friendship you could depend on. And yet you see something more between us. Mixed signals."

She looked up at him. "When God says wait, I know I have to wait, and don't ask me how I know that. It's just something I know, like I still know my job even though I don't recall getting my degree."

"So we're waiting on God even though I believe He hates me. You don't think He's playing a cruel joke on both of us?"

"I only know I'm waiting, and that God isn't cruel," she said. "I don't know how long He intends for me to wait, and I don't know what's going to happen next, but I do recall that last night I didn't even remember my own name, and now I know it. I made up my mind that I would wait this out and see what happened. So maybe I'm a little more prepared than you are. You're a person who makes a decision and carries it out. Now you have to learn patience."

"Not one of my stronger qualities."

"We all have to learn things." She looked up at him, eyes wide. Did he detect a hint of hope there? Or maybe it was his own apprehension mirrored in her face. He slowed down as they drew closer to the house; he wanted to prolong this time with Myra.

"The assignment you gave me to practice honesty was a good one."

"Why?" She matched her steps to his, and he noticed she didn't put much distance between them.

"The intention was to force me to consider the impact of my words on others. I realized I tended to give orders instead of stating my thoughts, and that didn't work with my daughter."

"Why do you tend to give orders?"

"Tell me you haven't lost a memory again. My father—"

"Yes, your father developed liver cancer and handed you the reins to the family empire a year before you received your business degree. He never saw you graduate with your master's in business administration—at the top of your class, no less. He told you then that no one would take you seriously unless you stood up to the older directors, toe-to-toe."

"Wow, you did listen."

"And I remember that conversation vividly. I know you've endured a lot of heartache in your life, as I have. Maybe that's why we've been able to help each other. You did quite well with your family holdings."

"If money matters, yes, I did well with it. I'd been trained from infancy, so I should know how to handle money."

"And remember you didn't lose a single director while you felt your way through the business."

"True. So at some point I learned to exercise tact." Unfortunately, that was more of a business strategy than a personal one until he started seeing Myra. He would always be grateful to her for that, no matter what happened between them.

She stumbled against Trippur, glared down at the cat and

picked her up. "Let's put this thing back in the house before one of us breaks something."

He took the cat from her. "Poor girl. All you want is a little attention, right?"

Trippur nuzzled against his neck.

"Since I've decided to change strategies on the job front, I believe you need to stop considering our dinners counseling sessions."

"I'm not sure I ever did," he said.

"Good, then we're officially dating. Molly will freak. She always told me never to date a man I wouldn't consider marrying."

"And you just said you're waiting on God. So keep waiting."

She quietly caught her breath.

"Instead of meeting you for dinner, I could pick you up at your house so you wouldn't have to drive out in the dark. And then I could take you home. A real date. Even a movie."

"Exactly." She caught his gaze, then buried her fingers into Trippurr's thick fur as she held Weston with her alluring green eyes, giving him her complete, enchanting attention.

For a second he forgot himself and allowed his attention to focus for only a second on her shapely lips. It was too much temptation. He turned toward the house. "Let's get you inside before you develop frostbite." He definitely wanted to continue this friendship—this very good, very strong, very compatible friendship—for as long as he had breath.

How he wished he hadn't involved Zack in this whole thing.

"You know, we wouldn't have to keep doing dinner," Myra said.

"You're tired of steak and seafood?"

"I've been putting on a little weight. Maybe we should focus more on healthy pursuits. You know, like walking one of the local trails after work in the evening. Ever thought of biking the KATY Trail across the state? Wouldn't that be a nice change of pace? A vacation. It would take several days."

He held his breath, studying her to see if she might be teasing. But Myra didn't typically tease about things like this. He played along. "It's true that you would be safer with a male escort who is a friend. We would have to book two rooms for each night, but think about the possibilities."

117

"I could do an intensive, multi-day counseling session."

"I thought we weren't going to talk about that."

"Just pretend."

"I'd be a new man by the time we reached St. Charles. You could report your findings to a state board of some kind, write up my case." He was kidding, and he hoped she knew it. Except for the separate rooms.

"And I could be famous." Her smile widened.

"I would be thrilled to help you make a name for yourself."

She slid on a pile of leaves and grabbed his arm to catch herself. He dropped the cat and steadied her, then tried to release her, but she clung to his arm.

"Myra?"

She clung more tightly and looked up into the sky. A beam of sunlight peeped from between the clouds. "I felt...for a moment there it seemed as if a black cloud was lowering over us."

"I think I need to get you back to the hospital."

She shook her head. "I know what it is."

"Memories returning."

"I don't want them to."

"I know how strong-willed you are, but honey, you might not have a choice." He let the endearment slip out and ignored the surprise in her eyes. "It seems to be getting worse. Ride with me to the ER. You can hang out with Joy or come with Zack and me. Either way Molly won't have total responsibility to keep watch over you every moment."

She hesitated. "Zack ran all those tests on me last night."

"Joy Gilbert happens to be one of the most intuitive physicians I've ever known, and she's your best friend. She might notice something no one else would notice. As a favor to me, would you please come? What if this time it turns out to be something physical?"

"But Joy was with me during those tests last night. She would have spoken up if there was any other test to run."

"Joy was distracted last night, first by your amnesia, and second by Zack's presence. She can't keep her eyes off the man."

"Nothing's changed."

"Come with me and we'll work things out when we get there. I don't want to leave you and Molly alone out here."

Myra closed her eyes with a heavy sigh. "You win. Let's warn poor Molly. But I don't think medical science can help me right now."

"I just want medical science to watch your back."

Chapter 15

There was more. Myra sat in the passenger seat watching the occasional glimpses of the Missouri River as Weston drove the mile to town. She couldn't escape that black cloud she'd run from since yesterday. No medical test would help her, but Weston was right. While Molly kept busy preparing Christmas dinner, Myra needed to stay with others. If only there was some way she could keep Weston nearby without getting caught in a clash between him and Joy. Or Zack. The discomfort of these messy relationships certainly put a strain on everyone.

Unfortunately, as soon as they pulled into the parking lot, she saw Zack walking toward them with a scowl on his face. She supposed working as many nights and weekends as he'd been covering would make anyone grumpy, but she wished the guys could put off this "man talk" until Zack was in a better mood. This whole thing gave her an edgy feeling. Did he dislike Weston that much? This did not bode well.

Weston jumped from the car as soon as he parked. He stepped over to say something to Zack and was circling the car toward the passenger door when Myra got out.

"I don't need to be escorted inside," she said. "You guys go on with your stroll, or whatever you're going to do."

Weston took her arm and strolled with her across the grass to the sidewalk and through the sliding doors of the waiting room. Zack nodded to her in greeting and followed them in silence.

She paused and looked back at him. "Everything okay, Zack?"

He gave her a friendly nod. "Long night." There was no smile in those golden brown eyes. She also noted that he didn't look toward the inner sanctum of the emergency department, where Joy stood waiting at the reception window.

Even more surprising, Joy didn't look at Zack when she

personally pushed the unlock button so Myra could enter from the waiting room.

Myra pushed open the door, then hesitated. "Don't I have to check in first?"

"Not today. You're off the books." Joy nodded to Weston. "Thanks for the call."

Myra didn't move. "What call?"

"Go on in," Weston said gently. "Everything's okay. I called to see how busy this place was while you were in the house explaining the situation to Molly."

Myra looked from him to Zack. Even though she knew her friends were rallying 'round to protect her, she didn't like needing a guard. Still, she softened when she recognized the worry in Weston's eyes. "You know this isn't necessary."

"I believe it is," Joy said from behind her. "Since we don't have the inestimable Myra Maxwell in full control of her faculties, we're going to have to wing it on this one."

"Got a straightjacket around anywhere?" she asked.

Joy stepped up behind Myra and pulled at the door. "Come on back."

Myra swallowed. Calm down. If only she could trust herself. That nightmare memory continued to hover just past her consciousness. "I've already proven that anything's likely to happen at any time."

"And that's why you're here with me today. We need to have a talk." Joy's attention switched briefly to Zack, who retreated to the waiting room entrance, looking anywhere but at Joy.

Interesting. Myra followed Joy into the ER proper. "What's up with your fiancé?"

"That's for a later conversation." Joy waved her hand around the interior of the emergency department. "You've got me all to yourself for at least the next few seconds."

"You can't guarantee it'll stay this way."

"The staff's taking a much-needed break, and Weston can duke it out with Zack for however long they can stand each other."

Myra blinked at Joy, surprised by the intensity of her voice.

Weston seemed in no hurry to join Zack. He stood at the front window watching Myra, as if, with the least amount of encouragement, he would stay with her.

Myra studied Joy's deep brown eyes, and saw that they held unaccustomed secrets. From somewhere in her mind, Myra knew she had the ability to gain access to those secrets if she focused hard enough. But of course, Weston had told her to stop practicing her vocation when she wasn't at work.

"Zack doesn't seem to be in the mood for guy time with Weston." Myra wandered around the U-shaped staff work desk, casting another glance toward Weston. She nodded for him to join Zack.

"Who knows? They could become best friends." Joy shot a glare through the window in Zack's direction.

"This is different," Myra whispered. "You and Zack fighting? You never fight."

"That's where your memory's fried."

"Sorry, I just assumed."

"Hello? Breakup last year? We fight."

"Are you going to tell me what's going on?"

"I've discovered those two have more in common than I would ever have dreamed possible," Joy said.

"And which of Weston's social skills has Zack mimicked?"

Weston gave Myra a shrug from the doorway, held up his cell phone to remind her she could call any time, and joined Zack with a look of exaggerated desperation, as if he'd just been told he was headed to the gallows. She appreciated his attempt at humor.

Maybe she should call him in a few minutes in case things didn't go well with Zack.

She turned to say something to Joy, but the words she was going to speak slid from her mind. What on earth would Weston's reaction be if she called to get him out of an uncomfortable situation? It would be like a mommy following after her little boy with a napkin, attempting to wipe mustard from his mouth.

Weston could handle himself in pretty much any situation. He didn't need rescuing.

For a few seconds, the room spun and darkness descended. She closed her eyes and gripped the edge of the central desk. No. This couldn't happen. Not now. Distraction.

"Is Zack spoiling for a fight?" she asked Joy, forcing herself to take a deep breath and focus on something else.

"If only."

Myra frowned at the tart clip of Joy's voice. "Let's just suppose he's in a bad mood about something. Do you think he'll take it out on Weston?"

"I'm obviously not the person to ask about that." Again that bitter thread.

Myra noted Joy's red, swollen eyes. She'd done a poor job on makeup repair, and some of her mascara was still smudged. She'd tied her hair back in a sloppy ponytail, and her nose was red—likely not from the cold.

"You've been crying." How could she have missed that?

"Never could fool you." Sarcasm deepened Joy's slightly southern accent.

Already, Myra was breaking her word, but her friend obviously needed help. "Joy, time to focus on you for a minute. You and Zack are barely suppressing hostility. What's going on?"

Joy picked up a file and led the way toward the back. "Since when does a patient come to the ER to counsel the doctor?" She presented an empty room with sound-suppressing sides and a door, unlike the curtained enclosure Zack had led her to last night.

Myra wondered if last night the staff was hungry for some gossip, and they knew they could get something through a thin curtain.

"Maybe I should be in a lockdown unit in a mental ward," she told Joy.

Joy looked over her shoulder and rolled her eyes. "That was Weston's suggestion when I talked to him last night."

"What I want right now is a distraction to put off thinking about myself, because when I do that the memories start to come. I've had more since I went to Molly's."

"Let me guess, after Weston arrived there."

"The good memories, yes. Only one bad experience. I want it to stay that way."

"Good memories?" Joy shot her a quick look of interest. "With Weston?"

"He did help me recall the time I stayed with you and Molly."

"That wasn't a good memory for you."

"Mom's suicide was horrible, but staying with you showed me what true Christian love was all about."

"You've been hit pretty hard today. I wish I could give you

something to make you sleep, and when you wake up you'll be yourself again."

"So do I. If I don't recover any more bad scenes from my life until after Christmas I'll be happy."

Joy closed the door behind them, but opened the shades of the observation window. "I don't know how you're handling this so well, honey."

"I'm not. At all. I jump at every uncommon sound, and right now every sound is uncommon. Everyone around me is uncommon. I have no idea what to expect from one moment to the next. I'm glad Weston came to Juliet, because he's the one who's been with me face-to-face more than anyone else. He listens to me as much as he talks and I can feel comfortable with him."

Joy stared out the window for a few seconds. "So the dinners—"

"They've metamorphosed into something…different."

"And I didn't ease any tension by warning you about Weston last night."

"I didn't even know him until he showed up this morning. Thanks to your warning, when I did remember this morning, I wasn't shocked. Over these past months he and I have discussed everything he's done in great detail, and I recall our times together better than most anything else. He owns what he did and he regrets it, but as I've pointed out to him several times, he has to move forward. But then, so do you."

"I'm trying."

Myra stared at Joy's stiff shoulders. "Don't take this wrong, but please keep in mind that even though you and Zack are in league against my friendship with Weston, when it comes to physical presence, he's the closest friend I have right now."

Joy turned around, lips parted in alarm. "First of all, Zack and I aren't in league about anything right now. In fact, we aren't even speaking at the moment, as you can see. Second, why shouldn't you remember me as well as you do Weston? We've been as close as sisters for decades. We talk on the phone several times a week."

"You're too far away. That makes a huge difference, at least in my case. Patients in the fugue state can recover their memories in different ways, and this happens to be mine."

Joy sat beside her. "I'm sorry. That makes sense. People can have their Internet friends and they can Skype and talk on the phone, but nothing compares to spending honest time one-on-one."

Myra nudged her friend with her elbow. "Don't worry, I'm getting my memories of you, too. I just want it all to stop right there for now."

"I wish I'd never said anything to you about taking him on as a patient."

"What is it you're so afraid of, Joy? You were wise enough not to have a relationship with Weston when he pressed for one, even after Zack broke your engagement the first time—"

"Hold it. I didn't say we've broken the engagement again."

"Good. But what makes you think I'm going to rush into some kind of wild romantic fling with Weston?"

"Because you're vulnerable right now, you said it yourself. None of us knows what to expect."

Myra acknowledged those words in silence, feeling the hovering, unwanted memory. She closed her eyes, but an image reflected against her lids. Something familiar and haunting. Okay, no more closing her eyes to escape reality. Everything was drawing closer. She wasn't going to make it past Christmas.

"Myra?" Joy touched her arm.

"Unless I have some kind of extremely rare physical condition that's doing this to my mind, there's some knowledge waiting to pounce on me and quite possibly do the same thing it did yesterday. I can't predict what my reaction will be."

Joy slid from the bed and paced across the cramped room. "This time you're surrounded by long-time friends. That's why Weston wanted you here with me this afternoon, so he could be nearby."

"I'm surprised you agreed to it."

Joy hesitated for a moment, then sighed. "I don't hate him."

"But you don't forgive him."

Joy looked away. "I might still be struggling with some resentment, but maybe that's just my mood lately."

"Back to Zack, then. I noticed he was a little grumpy. I don't want him to take it out on Weston." And now she was trying to play mommy again? Was it an obsession of hers?

"Weston's a big boy," Joy said. "As for me, I admit it's taking longer than I expected to forgive him, but he was able to fool me last year, and trusting him landed me in a huge mess."

"If I remember correctly, Weston bailed you out of all your debt, paid your school loans, sold your overpriced mansion in the city and gave you the surplus. So he took away that mess."

"He didn't erase the year I lost with Zack."

"No, he's not God, but maybe Zack needed to get his head on straight and find out the hard way that you were trustworthy."

Joy stopped pacing. "Hold it. Are these memories from last year you're talking about?"

"Sorry. No. They're memories of my talks with Weston and Molly." Myra studied her friend, who circled through the small exam room like a lioness in a cage meant for a kitten. "Can't we at least talk about what's going on with you and Zack? Because it looks to me as if you resent him even more than you do Weston right now, and that's just scary."

"I know, but if I talk about it I'll start crying again."

"Better here with me than out in the real world with a real patient. What on earth happened between you two since I last saw you this morning?"

Joy returned to the window and glanced into the empty ER. "We're not doing this. I'm here to help you, not use you as my counselor. You're off duty."

"I'm not off duty as your friend, I see no reason why you can't assuage my curiosity, especially since I need distraction. So let me have it."

Joy stood at the window for so long Myra wondered if she would refuse to discuss it. Then she sighed and turned from the window. "I think you might be right about the broken engagement. The wedding might be off."

Chapter 16

Weston trudged after Zack with burning lungs from the freezing air. "You know, maybe we should go somewhere for coffee. It's cold out here. I have a nice coffeemaker in my apartment."

Zack didn't miss a step. "Not thirsty. Not cold."

"Would you like to put this off for another time?"

"Please tell me you aren't staying in town that long."

Ah, yes, a friendly, comfortable conversation with a good buddy. Exactly what he'd been hoping for. "Cocoa, perhaps? Something to sweeten a sour disposition?"

Zack stopped so suddenly Weston nearly stumbled into him. He slid on the snowy sidewalk, and was glad for the traction of his shoes, which kept the two of them from landing together in a heap.

"This was your idea," Zack said. "You wanted to talk, so talk."

"I was sort of hoping for a more friendly conversation. You know, two sided? If all I wanted to do was listen to the sound of my voice I could have saved myself the effort and used my recorder."

Zack stood glaring at him for a long moment, but Weston quickly realized he wasn't so much looking at him as he was looking through him. It didn't take a therapist to realize something had changed since their discussion on the phone last night.

So Weston stared back and waited. He'd seen that expression in the mirror enough times to guess at the pain Zachary Travis was in. He didn't know why, but he could get close to a guess.

"Zack, you know Joy remained true to you. She never loved me. She had nothing to do with—"

"Shut up."

"You said to talk. Make up your mind."

The man gave an impatient jerk of his head. "If you apologize to me about that one more time I'll—"

"You'll do what, punch it out like a 'real man'? I'm not apologizing, but something's got you in an unholy rage, and for once I didn't cause it."

Zack shook his head, eyes closed. A thick plume of fog escaped his mouth as he released a pent-up sigh. "Not everything's about you and your past sins."

"No joke? And here I thought I was the center of everyone's universe."

Zack finally met his gaze. "First you're worried about Myra, next, you want to talk to me. Why, I have no idea."

"My primary reason for coming was to help Myra. She was alone in the city and she needed a friend."

"That's what you're calling yourself?"

Weston's fingers clenched and unclenched. "I had thought I might be able to discuss that with you, but apparently not. It isn't as if I'm encroaching on your territory this time."

"I didn't say—"

"If you were such good friends with Myra, why doesn't she remember you yet? Why did I jumpstart her first memories instead of Joy or Molly? I'm glad I came here for her, because she needed to start remembering herself, so don't expect me to apologize, and don't expect me to get lost any time soon."

Zack held his gaze with a glare.

Weston shook his head. "You know what? Forget it. I didn't come here to wrestle with an angry bear." He turned back toward the hospital. He could take Myra back out to Molly's for the rest of the day.

"Wait." It was more of a growl than an entreaty, and Weston took a few more steps, wishing he'd kept his mouth shut last night about meeting with this cranky man with a huge chip on his shoulder.

"Would you just stop?" Zack called.

Weston looked over his shoulder and returned glare for glare. "Any reason why I should?"

The fire in Zack's golden brown eyes—typically friendly eyes, actually—slowly dissipated. His stiff shoulders fell into a slump. Weston recognized that posture from his own reflection in his window last night, but he was afraid if he opened his mouth about it Zack might punch a few teeth out. Still, this mood appeared to be from another source.

"If you drove all the way down here to finagle some kind of blessing from me so you could seduce Myra, you wasted time and gasoline," Zack said.

It was Weston's turn to slump. The doctor wasn't nearly as insightful or kind as he'd once seemed. "I don't think Christmas is a good time for a brawl on the front lawn." He turned back toward the hospital. "I shouldn't have called in the first place." So much for his hope for forgiveness. Or friendship.

***

Joy peered through the viewing window and barely caught sight of Weston in the distance. He'd turned away from Zack and was making quick work of reaching the hospital's front doors. "I thought the men were going to take a walk."

"They were, but if Zack's on a rampage I doubt Weston will hang around. Do you blame him?"

"Zack told me Weston wanted to discuss something with him."

"That subject would be me, I believe," Myra said. "I'm apparently a helpless ninny who doesn't know her own mind so the menfolk have to decide for me what is and isn't good for me."

Joy winced. "Sorry they're making you feel that way. Weston told you that?"

"Not quite. I get the feeling he's reaching out to make a friend. It isn't something he's done often, and Zack's obviously a very bad choice today."

"Agreed."

Myra paused and caught Joy's gaze. Joy had to look away first.

"I also think he's hoping to talk to Zack about the most honorable way for us to continue our friendship," Myra said. "Because we most definitely are friends, and that isn't going to change. Since I barely remember Zack I don't care what he thinks, and I don't understand why Weston holds Zack's opinion in such high esteem."

"Neither do I," Joy muttered. She did, however, care about Myra. "Weston brought you into town with him today because of this memory that's trying to push its way through?"

"I think he was afraid that if I had another bad reaction Molly wouldn't be able to keep me from taking off again, and there are more people here, apparently waiting around for someone to treat." Myra slid from the bed and walked to the window. She stood beside Joy, who watched the staff meander to their workstations. "You going to tell me, or do I have to start guessing, Joy?"

She sighed and closed the blinds, unable to meet Myra's gaze. How could a woman who had lost most of her personal memories read so much from the tone of someone else's voice? "I guess you've noticed how attractive my mother is."

Myra's eyebrows drew together as if she'd just discovered Joy was the one who'd lost her mind. "Who could miss it? Inside and out. You look a lot like her. What on earth does that have to do with you and Zack?"

"More than you can imagine, but it's a long story."

Myra leaned on the exam bed. "Oh, believe me, I could use a long story. Just tell me the fight wasn't about Weston."

"It wasn't. Not directly, anyway. I almost wish it had been, because then I'd have something to blame him for."

"You need more? And are you going to tell me what your mother's looks have to do with this fight?"

"I'll explain it all. Just know that Molly Gilbert has dealt with jealousy a lot in her life, not only because of her looks but because of her intelligence and abilities. Sometimes people take their petty jealousies out on me, as well." Joy sank onto the visitor chair with a soft groan. "I'm stuck in the past, Myra. And you're stuck without a complete past. I think you and I need to balance each other out."

"It's Christmas. Let's just enjoy the day without any changes."

"Easy for you to say."

"Oh, yeah, it's so much fun not knowing who I am."

"But you're getting your memories back."

"You'll get unstuck from the past. I think maybe it's a God thing, though. He might have to help you through it."

Joy closed her eyes. "Sometimes I wonder if He even cares. Or maybe I'm being punished."

"For what?"

"For blaming Him for something a group of church members

did last year."

"Refresh my memory."

Joy hesitated. Myra had already experienced the memories of Dustin's death this morning, and though it turned out to be a painful ordeal, she'd recovered quickly as that piece of her history slid into the proper place in her mind. This was probably safe ground. "Some members of my church saw me spending a lot of time with Weston last year because of Dustin's illness. Word spread that I was having an affair with Weston, and though now I know Weston was responsible for that debacle, at the time I was so disgusted with the rumors in the church that I had them remove my name from church membership."

Myra shrugged. "So?"

"Some of them told Mom I was in rebellion."

Myra rolled her eyes. "You think God's punishing you for that? I'd think He'd applaud the decision, since they were obviously engaging in unbiblical behavior."

"That was the church I grew up in and I've never found another."

"Punishing you for that still doesn't sound like the behavior of the God you and Molly introduced to me after my mother died. He'd be more focused on wooing you back. In fact, it's interesting that you maintained course throughout everything. Someone in rebellion wouldn't have remained so focused and...um...chaste."

Joy looked down at her foot, which bounced against the floor. "So you do remember that?"

"I do. The memories are less vivid, but they're settling in."

Myra's words swept away a lot of rust and corrosion that seemed to have built up over Joy's heart this past year. She felt a sudden longing to feel closer to God again, and it was a good feeling, as if she could somehow turn and He'd be right there waiting with open arms. When was the last time she'd experienced that welcome by God?

Especially now, worried about Zack, she needed to realize that his opinion of her didn't matter nearly as much as the One she'd loved and served all her life.

"My concern is that you left the church for the same reason Weston avoids God—Christians can't show forgiveness even after Weston apologized."

Joy felt those words like a punch in the gut. She blinked at Myra in surprise. She thought about her call to him last night, arguing with him over the phone, putting up a wall to keep him away. "I can't forget."

"Of course you can't," Myra said gently. "It's part of your life, and you need to remember so you can learn and grow. But forgiveness is part of that growth, and just as you haven't forgiven the church that hurt you, you haven't truly forgiven Weston. You think he can't see that? Refusing to release old hurts is like refusing to be all God wants you to be. It means you stop growing, and that's obvious with the increasing number of people you can't forgive. That can turn into bitterness."

At first Joy wanted to protest, but the truth of those words hit home far too hard. Myra was ripping too many layers away from her at once.

"You and Zack can't even forgive each other right now," Myra said. "How does that appear to a man who's seeking some kind of truth in his life? So now Zack's out there taking out his frustration on a man who was hoping for some spiritual guidance. Whether he realizes it or not, Weston's testing those who call themselves Christians to see if the Holy Spirit he saw in you when you worked for him is going to show Himself through you and Zack now. I think you planted a seed, but between you and Zack you're about to kill it before it can sprout." Still, Myra's voice was gentle, even pleading.

How could Myra, in her confused and frightened state, be so solid and sure about the very thing that had eaten at Joy this past year?

"Now. What's going on between you and Zack?" Myra asked.

Time to relent. Myra needed distraction, she'd get it, and suddenly Joy was more than ready to change the subject. "Beginning of story. My mother's good looks have always made things difficult for her. Being an unwed mother, she had to put up with a lot of comments at church, 'loving words of wisdom' from some of the older busybodies. Worst, though, were irreverent men in town who jumped to the wrong conclusions about her. They even made moves on her. Often. Married men. And almost as often, if their wives found out they blamed Mom."

"You're upset with Zack and Weston, and you're blaming that

on your mother's good looks?"

"Don't interrupt. I'm getting to it."

"Just trying to make sense of the story."

"Fine, I'll shorten the story. The president of the hospital governing board manipulated her way to her position. Her husband was one of the worst offenders when it came to Mom, and when he died his wife went through his hidden drawers. She discovered how obsessed he was with Mom. I mean, Wilma's been jealous of Mom since long before Mr. Rush died, but now she's turned revenge into a higher art form."

"And she's taking it out on you?" Myra straightened from the bed. "And Zack's allowing this?"

"He told me he disagreed with them, but they didn't listen." Joy hazarded a glance at Myra. "What worries me is that I don't know how hard he tried. I got the impression that he believes I shouldn't be working ER."

"Did he say that?"

"No."

"Then why don't you focus on what you know and stop jumping to conclusions? We can't control anyone else's thoughts, only our own."

"I quit today before he had a chance to fire me."

Myra sighed. "Oh, Joy, no. You need the income from this job."

"I can do locum tenens work with one of a dozen headhunters."

"And hide from the situation with Zack for another year or so? Or for the rest of your life?"

"As I said, I'm rethinking the wedding plans. He accepted my resignation quickly enough."

"He did?"

She thought back to their argument. "Okay, maybe he just didn't fight hard enough to keep me." And she was being so immature.

"Maybe because he was reacting on his emotions, as well."

Joy considered that for a moment. How hard had Zack fought for her job? She couldn't shake the feeling that he doubted her abilities. Maybe he didn't even want her working with him at the clinic.

"I think I'm overreacting," she said. "Probably because I was already fired once this year. My first clinic position and I'm fired in less than a year?"

Myra stepped over and rested an arm over Joy's shoulder, and the hug comforted her. "Do you think we'd have worked through the trials of med school if we'd known we'd still have to struggle once we graduated?"

Joy nodded. "Mom would have dragged us both to class each day if we'd tried to quit, but I never wanted to be an ER doc in the first place. I never wanted to be a pain specialist."

"But Weston says you're a great physician."

Joy spread her hands. "Listen to me whine. I'm spilling my heart out to a patient." Time to draw this depressing conversation to an end.

"To a friend."

"To someone who needs me to be the strong one for once."

"Or maybe I need you to treat me like I'm a normal person, not someone who's too fragile to confide in," Myra said gently.

Once again, Joy fought tears. This Christmas was a nightmare.

Chapter 17

Weston walked across the salted sidewalk, feeling the grit beneath his shoes, listening to the crackle of it as he battled disappointment. That same hard grit churned somewhere in his gut. The glass door slid open and he was about to walk through when he heard the sound of a footstep behind him.

"I never knew Weston Cline to run away from a fight." The voice was gruff, maybe tinged with a whiff of disappointment.

Weston glanced behind him and gave Zack a level look. "You don't know me at all. I don't brawl like a junkyard dog. If you're spoiling for a fight, find another dog."

"Junkyard dog, angry bear. What am I, an entire zoo?"

Weston turned again to enter the hospital.

"Why don't you try to do the psychology thing with me?" Zack called after him. "Isn't that what you're learning with those meetings with Myra? How to manipulate people with more…finesse?"

Weston frowned. Obviously, the man had to get this testosterone hostility out of his system, but something was eating him, and by now Weston knew for sure he wasn't the object of Zack's irritation. Before he could enter the hospital and retreat from the icy chill of the air and the company, he gave in to curiosity.

He pivoted and returned Zack's cold gaze. "Interesting that until now you've implied I've been trying to use my time with Myra to seduce her. So which is it?"

Zack looked away, and the wind-whipped red of his face deepened a shade. Weston couldn't tell if it was anger or shame, and he decided to quit trying to figure this man out. "I'm getting in out of the cold. This is a waste of my time."

"Wait. Weston, hold on a minute."

With a sigh of impatience, Weston turned back. "What? I've

been seeing Myra to help me learn to be a better person, among other things—not that it's any of your business. You can jump to any conclusions you wish. It's not my problem. Your antagonism isn't my problem, it's yours."

"You're right."

"Then stop using me as a punching bag. I'm perfectly aware that you consider me unworthy of your time or energy. Besides, you obviously have your own problems, and I don't think I caused them this time."

"You didn't."

The quick honesty surprised him.

"In fact," Zack said, "maybe the great Weston Cline could teach me a thing or two." It was said as a challenge. But it was also, if Weston wasn't mistaken, something more. "For instance, how does one fire an employee and manage to remain friends?"

Weston stepped away from the door so it would close, and faced the cold air once more. "What makes you think I know anything about that? Obviously I didn't remain friends with Joy. She hates me as much as you do."

"I don't hate you. Neither of us—"

"How many employees have *you* fired?"

Zack studied the face of the hospital, looking suddenly defeated.

"Tell me you didn't fire Joy," Weston said.

"That isn't how it happened."

"You've got to be kidding me. A man doesn't fire his fiancé. It's just not done. It would be better to quit, yourself, than to—"

"I said I didn't fire her."

"So what happened? I thought you'd earned a reputation for working well with people." Though he hadn't displayed that capability yet today.

"The reputation lost some major points this afternoon." Zack's voice held a growl of frustration.

"No kidding," Weston allowed the sarcasm to bleed through his voice.

Zack turned from the building and ambled away. Though reluctant to face the cold air and the cold shoulder again, Weston followed. "If you're talking about a relationship, I'm not the person you need to ask about that, obviously. I'm the one who can tell you what not to do, but since you've already done it I'm not going to be any help."

"You think you know the kind of help I need?" It was a challenge.

Weston listened to the crunch of their footsteps. "You're asking a businessman how to handle business?"

Zack shrugged. "I think that's what I'm doing."

"The first thing I learned recently was not to mix business with personal life."

"Too late."

"Obviously. The second thing I learned was not to fire a good employee simply because she doesn't always agree with you."

Zack looked around at him. "How many times do I have to tell you I didn't—"

"Fire Joy. I heard, but she's somehow disconnecting from the hospital, and you probably had a hand in it."

"She quit."

"What did you say to make her do that?"

Zack glared and turned away.

"Knowing Joy, I think she might have acted in the heat of anger. If you could manage to calm down and come to some kind of truce with her you might get it worked out. But that's more of a personal thing, so not something I'm good at."

Zack slowed his steps. "Sometimes a man can talk things out with another man without having to worry about saying the wrong thing. Thanks."

Weston's right foot nearly slid out from under him, and his left one nearly followed. "Hold on. I think I'll need to make a memo of this. Mind if I go grab my recorder?"

If he wasn't mistaken, he caught a glimpse of a grudging smile on Zack's face. "I'm not repeating myself for posterity."

"You have your own business. I can help you with that if you want, but I'm clueless when it comes to Joy."

"Interesting that your employees seem loyal."

"How would you know that?"

"I read an article about you once. Your companies are in the 90th percentile for employee retention among the Forbes 500 companies."

Weston recalled hearing that a year or so ago. "I pay well."

"I don't have control over pay. All I can offer is praise for a job well done."

"Have you praised Joy lately?"

"There's the rub. I don't check her work because I trust her, but what can I say when I hear complaints from the board?"

"You keep them to yourself. I can afford to grumble when something doesn't suit me, you can't. And you can't trust the reports you're getting about Joy unless you check them out yourself."

"I read a complaint from a patient who had to wait."

"Obviously the patient didn't die," Weston said. "What was the emergency?"

"Didn't say."

"Then ignore it. It isn't as if an ER takes appointments. A piece of business advice? My father taught me that I was going to hear a lot more complaints than praises. Angry people let their feelings be known to the whole world. Those who are satisfied take excellent service as their due and never say a kind word. This system the hospital sets up for patients to air their complaints, the Press-Gainey scores? Horrible idea. I put an end to that not long after I fired Joy."

"Did you praise Joy?"

Weston shook his head and sighed. "No, and look what I lost. I fired her without taking into consideration the need she had to help those who couldn't always pay."

"You had a business to run."

"I'm thinking you might need to do some groveling. It didn't work for me, but she actually likes you."

"Not so much right now."

"Wouldn't hurt to try. All I can teach you is how to win the heart of a woman who's engaged to another man," Weston said. "There's a fine quality to have."

Zack scowled at him.

Weston needed to quit baiting the poor man, but he made it too easy. "Really? You're going to believe me again? Don't you believe in the woman you love? I never won her heart."

"You got her to move to Kansas City."

"I offered her a job she couldn't refuse because she'd just lost her job and her fiancé," Weston said. "She took a job she didn't want because you let her go. I'd advise you do whatever it takes to keep her this time. Listening to the complaints about Joy from the hospital board is just as stupid as listening to my lies about a fictitious affair she and I had last year."

Zack slowed his steps. "If I'd been on my game you'd have never gotten away with it in the first place."

"If you let Joy get away a second time you're not the man I thought you were. Doesn't the Bible say something about God giving wisdom to those who ask?"

Zack stopped and looked at Weston. "He also works in mysterious ways, like talking through a donkey."

"Glad you don't read the King James Version."

Zack closed his eyes with a soft exhalation. "Thanks for reminding me about what I should be doing."

"You mean loving your future wife more than you love the hospital board?"

Zack glanced back toward the ER entrance. "Exactly."

"Good," Weston said. "I came to Juliet with the intention of asking a strong, wise man of God about how to handle my own life. This wasn't what I expected."

"I'm just an irritable man walking through a mine field. Don't look to me if you're trying to find God right now. Humans will let you down every time."

"I think this is the perfect time to look to you. I'm interested in seeing if there's a difference between the way Christians handle their challenges, and how the rest of the world handles them. I haven't seen much difference."

Zack turned to look at Weston more closely. "You're serious?"

"I'm dead serious."

Zack seemed to deflate a little. "I hope you don't think everything's supposed to be all roses and bluebirds for Christians. In fact, sometimes it feels as if the opposite's the case." The fight had obviously gone out of him.

"That's how you talk people into becoming Christians?"

"The truth sometimes hurts, but I don't set people up for disappointment. Still, I can't imagine how I could have made it through the tough times without Him."

***

Myra watched Joy's jerky movements as she jumped up from the visitor chair, walked to the window and looked out, then returned to the chair. She obviously wanted out of here, but no patients had come in to distract her from the tension that cut through the room like razor wire through human skin. Myra guessed that what she really wanted was to talk to Zack.

"You never liked babysitting when you were a kid, did you?" Myra smiled with affection.

"What makes you say that?"

"You're about to explode."

Joy took her hair from the elastic, shook out the long, dark brown waves of silk and slipped the band around her wrist. "Rough day."

"Is there a way you can make it better?"

Joy sighed and held up a finger. "I can figure out a way to forgive Weston." She looked at Myra. "That's what you want, right?"

"This isn't about me."

"It's all about you right now."

"Not from where I'm sitting."

"Good, then first I'll get an apology from Zack so I can forgive him. I'll work on Weston later."

"You don't need an apology to forgive. Just deal with it. Remember we'll all be at your mom's for Christmas dinner. It would be nice to speak civilly to one another around the dinner table."

Joy scowled. "You're not giving me a lot of time."

"You've had time and opportunity. Make your move."

Joy shoved her hair away from her face with a jerk of impatience. "I'm curious about what the guys are saying out there."

"At first I thought they were discussing whether or not Zack approves of Weston dating me, but now I think it's probably about the two of you. It's good to be out of the limelight for a change."

Joy rubbed the diamond engagement ring on her left hand. "I was right, wasn't I? The man can make a woman sit up and take notice. And you noticed."

Myra focused on a slow inhale. "This fugue state no longer disconnects my emotions from Weston since I've regained most of my memories of him. But he doesn't take precedence in my heart. God does."

"Some people might ask why you would enter a fugue state at all if your faith in Christ is so strong."

Myra shot Joy a look.

"I'm not one of those people." Joy spread her hands. "I've just had too much experience with the jerks who would ask. It's why I work so many Sundays. It keeps me from being judged by the masses."

"Persecution complex."

"Paranoia." Joy smiled. "You remember that old exercise we used to do when you were in residency."

"Just now." Myra smiled, relieved that she knew Joy better by the second. This business with amnesia was torture, especially when she could feel a memory forcing its way to the surface that she could no longer suppress. And now she was even afraid to close her eyes for more than a half-second.

"It's true I'm feeling more like my old self." She would give anything to step back a few hours into the past, because her heart rate was increasing and she felt a buildup of anxiety in her chest. "Weston has convinced me to slow down. I'm no longer going to take calls after hours."

"Then maybe I have good reason to forgive the man." Joy spun the engagement ring on her finger again.

"Not fitting too well?" Myra asked.

"Nothing's fitting."

"I know how that feels." Myra focused on the ring as well. "Everything's changing on an hourly basis, like a circus I never paid to attend."

Joy looked up at her. "Hence, the reason you're here."

"I believe there's a reason Weston's here, too. I think maybe you and Zack are being given a chance to get to see how he's changed since last year. And maybe he's also here to see how you and Zack are living out your faith." It wouldn't hurt to give the warning more than once.

Joy grimaced. "Don't you ever have a fight with someone?"

"Sure do. Weston and I had a tough one two nights ago about all the calls I was taking. It took this awful experience to convince me he was right and I was wrong. He was paying for my dinner, after all. I need to have some down time in my life."

"Did he make you question your ability to do your job?"

"That's exactly what he did. It made me furious. It turns out he wasn't questioning my ability to help others, but my tendency to carry everything on my own shoulders. I'm trying to save my mother over and over again."

"I hate to admit he's right."

"How about Zack? Do you hate to admit he might be partially right, too?"

"He's right to make me doubt myself?"

"Do you think he meant to do that?"

Joy closed her eyes. The muscles along her jawline flexed.

"Talk to him," Myra said. "You're a great physician, but as I discovered, there are always things that can be improved. Just forgive Zack. Shadows from the past will continue to stalk you in the present if you can't forgive."

"The question is, can I?"

Chapter 18

Zack turned to walk across the crunchy, frozen grass to the sidewalk. He turned left on the path that meandered around the building and campus, past trees and metal benches built for casual conversations, though not in this weather.

Weston watched him for a moment, then shrugged and followed. "You know, I can't handle a woman any better than you can, but the problem is that we attempt to 'handle' them in the first place, rather than treat them as equals and grant them the respect they deserve."

"I've always treated Joy as an equal. We were classmates together. She was better than I was in anatomy lab. It isn't so simple when you're the boss."

"You're not the boss, you're middle-management."

"I'm a physician who got stuck here because no one else would do the job."

"A man can always say no. So when a man disagrees with a decision from upper management, especially one this significant, he puts a stop to the mistake about to be made."

"I was trying when Joy overheard the conversation."

"Typical of her to jump to the wrong conclusion."

"And typical of me not to react well."

"I'd never have survived middle management," Weston said.

Zack stopped walking until Weston caught up with him, then they continued along the salted path side by side at last. "I asked her to get the patients through faster. She did. I noticed, but the board didn't."

"Would it hurt your male ego if I spoke to the board?"

"Yes."

"Then I suggest you tell Joy you have no intention of firing her, and if the board wants her gone, you'll be leaving, too. And then I suggest you tell the board the same thing. Joy quit today?"

"This afternoon."

"Then you have plenty of time to undo the damage," Weston said. "And what better day than Christmas to put the bad stuff behind you and start fresh? Take it from someone who's made that mistake, don't let your pride get in the way. I'm serious, get counseling with Joy before you blow it again."

Zack stopped walking and turned to Weston. "I'm supposed to listen to you why?"

"Who better to tell you what not to do than the man who's done everything wrong?"

Zack glanced back toward the ER entrance.

"I've done a few things right, like getting a therapist," Weston said. "Find someone to help you work it out together, and let her know that you know she's an excellent physician."

Zack hesitated a second too long.

Weston groaned. "She's got to be sensing your doubt in her. The wrong person has been allowed too much power in this hospital. When you lose a good doctor you've lost a lot of business, and the administrator needs to realize that."

Zack grunted. "Our administrator would be fine if she didn't listen to the board."

"Wilma Rush, hospital board president? I can get rid of that troublemaker."

"If I can't handle this situation myself I have no right to be the director."

"When will you and Joy start your own private practice together?"

"I've been waiting for mine to grow so I can bring her on board. Now she's threatening to leave Juliet."

"Then we need to get back inside now. You need to make sure she knows you're not in league with the devil in the power seat. You're the director. Man up. Handle it."

Zack stopped walking. He turned to Weston, eyes narrowed against a stray beam of sunshine forcing its way through the clouds. Then he smiled. It was a smile of warmth. Maybe even a touch of friendship.

"I don't think you're going to need the hot cocoa after all," Weston said.

Zack reached a hand out, and Weston grasped it. "You're

right. All I needed was a friend to help me get my footing again."

***

Joy peered out the observation window again.

"Tell me Zack and Weston aren't brawling out in front of the hospital," Myra said.

Joy shook her head, then met Myra's gaze over her shoulder. "I just caught sight of them in the distance, walking side-by-side." She turned around. "I was worried that you wouldn't be the Myra I knew when you started recalling your past—and I was worried you might not recall it—but you're beginning to sound like my best friend again."

"You mean your bossy friend."

Joy rolled her eyes. "The bossy friend who's usually right."

"Weston and I have decided to stop calling our dinners counseling sessions. I hope you don't feel betrayed because I've welcomed his friendship."

"I felt betrayed initially because you didn't tell me you were seeing him, especially since I suggested it in the first place."

"You didn't suggest I start having dinner with him." Myra chuckled. "That's it, isn't it? I didn't do it your way."

"I never expected a romance between my best friend and the man who felt like my worst enemy once upon a time." Joy slid a glance toward Myra and met her gaze. "And you have to admit it was pretty romantic for him to drive down here in a storm on a hunch that you might be here, to come to your rescue."

"Now that you mention it."

"Dangerous to fall in love."

"You think I haven't thought of that?" Myra closed her eyes, and an image of a blond-haired woman stared at her. She blinked and stiffened, catching her breath as memories flooded her.

"Myra?"

"No. Joy, it's happening."

"What is?"

"I'm remembering everything. All at once. Our first meeting in high school, our sleepovers, playing with all the animals you and Molly rescued over the years."

She was all at once exhilarated and terrified. The memories came too quickly. "College. My decision to become a psychiatrist after Mom's suicide. Med school, residency, all of it's coming at a rush and I can't stop it. Joy, help me slow things down."

"I'm right here." Joy rushed to her side and took her hand. "Did you ever notice how the worst times in our lives can bring about changes that might not have otherwise occurred. For instance, you lost your parents, but that shock brought you to your knees before Christ."

"Not without you and Molly." She felt breathless as the visions of her past swept around her from every direction. "I'm afraid my patients have been searching for something I can't give them. I failed my own mother."

"You weren't trained then."

"I was her daughter and I couldn't convince her to stay alive for me. Why should I expect to help others?"

"Because you already have," Joy said. "Look at Weston, at his family. You did that. Slow down and breathe."

"I can't slow down. I counseled so many married couples who clashed. I tried so hard to be on my guard with Weston because of that, but we grew closer anyway. I knew I would never get past friendship with him and yet I still met with him, and I wanted more."

"There you go. Now you're slowing down a little, but wow. You really are recalling everything, aren't you?"

"I am." And she didn't like it happening so quickly.

"Talk to me." Joy touched her shoulder. "Look at me. The problem with married couples? That's why I was so worried about you seeing Weston. I don't want that for you."

Weston. Myra took a slow, deep breath and focused on her memories of the handsome, black-haired man with silver barely frosting the temples. She pictured those blue eyes so often lit with laughter or mischief—not the man she'd known last year when he worked with their research team.

"I couldn't help seeing what a good team Weston and I made together. I watched him heal and grow. I shared my history, my heart, my dreams with him, and he listened."

"And you fell."

"This morning I remembered Dustin's death. I also remembered our engagement and how much I loved him. I've been meeting with Weston as a friend as much as a patient because I needed a friend connected to my memories here, and I believed I could help him recover from his son's death. We grew closer over the months, and I admit to more than casual feelings for him." She closed her eyes and nodded. "Much more than casual. Dustin was my safety net. When I started seeing Weston there hadn't been enough time to recover from losing Dustin."

"But you did lose him. I know it isn't the same, but I lost Zack when he broke our engagement, and Weston was right there—obviously—to offer me another chance. It could have happened to me, too, Myra."

"It didn't. You saw through him. He's more transparent than he knows, and though he might have the rest of the world fooled, those who know him can see what he is. He's learning to dial back the charm and dial forward more honesty."

"Let's hope he can dial back that honesty with Zack or I might be getting my next two patients any minute." Joy looked more closely at Myra and frowned. "Honey, you're crying."

As Joy spoke the words, Myra became aware of the warm tears trickling down her cheeks. And then she became less aware of the ER, the staff chattering lazily outside the door. The room spun around her, and she grabbed the bed as darkness hovered over her like a fog.

Gentle hands guided her as she fell onto the mattress. She battled nausea. "Emesis basin."

"Got it."

Just in time, Joy had the basin in place as Myra retched. Her head thrummed with the rhythm of a bass drum, not with pain, but with the sound of blood rushing through her. She was turning inward, unable to focus on the world around her.

"Myra, you're fighting the memory. Stop fighting it or you could lose all your memories again. You're in a safe place." The words came to her as if through a pipe over a long distance.

Couldn't stop it from coming. Even as she closed her eyes against the world, a picture crashed through her consciousness that she could not push away no matter how hard she tried. She cried out in agony as the face and form of a dark-haired woman reposed in the bed she'd shared for forty years with her beloved husband. An empty bottle of medicine had fallen to its side on the bedside stand.

"Stop," she said aloud. "Stop this."

Her mother disappeared only to be replaced by a young woman, pale of face and hair.

Myra could hear nothing, could see only the woman, so sad, so damaged and terrified. Someone shouted in the distance, but Myra couldn't make out the words, she only knew it wasn't the voice of the patient who regarded her with sadness. Beautiful, vulnerable Sarah Miller.

***

Weston walked beside Zack toward the hospital entrance in somewhat companionable silence for maybe thirty seconds.

"You never told me exactly why you were so insistent on talking to me face-to-face," Zack said.

Since last night, Weston had thought it was Myra he wanted to discuss, but he didn't need Zack to tell him not to push a relationship with her right now. Any fool would know better. So why?

"You've apologized," Zack said. "You've helped Joy, you've befriended her mother, and you've thanked me more times than I can count for helping you."

"How often does a man thank someone for saving his life? I didn't realize there was a social protocol for that."

"I think you've managed to reach your quota."

"I'll stop if it's annoying," Weston said.

"Nope. Adulation's a good thing," Zack said with a grin. "Somehow I don't think that's why you wanted to meet with me in the first place."

"Then I'll just say one more time how important my daughter is to me; you and Joy made my time with her possible."

"It feels good to be able to do that. I know she kind of got lost from you for a while after your son's death. But you didn't come here to talk to me about Tressa, did you? She's doing okay physically, isn't she?"

"She's a happy kid." Weston walked in silence for a moment. "She's making new friends. I didn't realize how much Keegan's death impacted her, but for the longest time I never saw her with friends her own age. For a while I think Joy was the only real friend she had. I was afraid she was following in my footsteps."

"I'd think a man like you must be surrounded by friends."

Weston laughed, but he knew it wasn't a happy sound. "A man like me? You mean the kind of man who steals another man's fiancé?"

"I've never been a billionaire businessman adored by millions."

"Those millions don't know me. Sure, they wish they *were* me, and if they could get close enough to me they probably think they could get something from me, but that's not friendship."

"Cynic, huh?"

"Realist. Try finding a genuine friend in the crowd of people viewing your picture on a magazine cover, or listening to the newshounds stalking your home or the money worshipers groveling at your feet. Impossible to find a potential friend in a mess like that. My father taught me not to trust anyone, and I learned the lesson well."

"So you look for the one person who's been making a concerted effort to avoid you, and that's who you choose to befriend."

Weston shrugged. "Who said I wanted to be friends?"

"I know it sounds funny, but I don't get any sense of intentional betrayal this time. I don't think you're after my fiancé."

"It wasn't exactly a logical choice when I called you last night. I really was looking for Myra, but then coming here made sense to me."

"Driving down in the sleet and ice made sense to you," Zack said dryly.

"I don't blame you and Joy for avoiding me. What still mystifies me after all this time is why you both risked your careers to rescue Tressa and me from my bad judgment. I wasn't cooperative, if you'll recall."

"We're doctors. We're accustomed to that."

"I could have paid someone enough money to have your licenses yanked."

"And yet you didn't," Zack said. "Interesting."

"Most doctors I know would have allowed me to contact my specialist cronies and risk my life with what you knew to be a wrong diagnosis."

"Maybe you don't know the right doctors. Anyway, my pride

wouldn't allow that."

"And Joy's pride, as well?"

Zack stared the frozen ground. "Tressa couldn't die. Neither could you. I couldn't have lived with myself, and I knew Joy felt the same. I knew you thought we were overstepping our bounds, but—"

"Why me? I was your nemesis."

Zack cleared his throat. "This is going to sound hypocritical after the way I've behaved today, but I do take my faith seriously. Because of Tressa's symptoms and history Joy and I knew what was wrong with you, and neither of us could allow you to choose a physician who might make the wrong diagnosis."

"You were pretty sure of yourself."

"I tend to get my diagnoses right. I don't think I'm being cocky, just confident. I didn't know your spiritual connection to God, but judging by your behavior my guess was frightening. I couldn't take that chance with your eternity."

"So if you'd believed I was a Christian you'd have let me die?"

Zack laughed. "No." He glanced at Weston. "Joy and I have both behaved like suspicious idiots since you arrived in town, and I apologize. This summer we not only believed your life was in danger, we believed your soul was in danger."

Weston slowed his steps and looked at Zack. Today he'd learned something new. People who called themselves Christians were most assuredly not perfect. They lost their temper, couldn't get along with one another, they could become downright hostile at times, but down deep something about a few of them remained solid. He didn't believe that was the case with everyone who claimed the title, but now he knew a few he might be able to trust.

"No matter how heinous a man's behavior," Zack said, "God's love can cover it."

"If God is the all-knowing being you Christians say He is, how could He want someone like me in heaven?"

"You've seen my behavior today, right?"

Weston nodded.

"And you've certainly seen Joy at her worst. Why would God want us? There isn't a single person on this earth who is perfect. You either belong to Him or you reject His physical sacrifice that paid the price for all. With all your billions, you can't buy your way into heaven, but if you accept His payment and ask to be His, give up the lordship over your own life, you're His. Just like that."

"It's that simple." The cynic was back.

"You've seen today that it's never simple. You told me today not to let pride mess up my relationship with Joy. So you know how pride can be a problem. Humility can be a grand thing."

They had just reached the ER entrance when Joy came running out, her eyes too wide, her face a mask of fear. "Myra's in trouble. She's blacked out and I can't wake her."

Chapter 19

Myra tried to reach for the image of her patient, but she couldn't move. She watched in horror as Sarah Miller swallowed a handful of pills with a glass of water.

No! This couldn't happen. It mustn't!

But Myra couldn't stop her because Myra had no body of her own. She was there in spirit only. Hiding somewhere in her mind again. Watching Sarah's suicide.

Sarah swallowed a different pill, and then another.

Myra wanted to scream.

"You asked too much of me, Dr. Maxwell." Sarah's soft, southern drawl sounded too real.

Myra tried to speak, but she had no mouth. It was as if she was watching a scene from a remote location.

"You can't make the whole world better," Sarah said. "Some of us can't be fixed."

No. This couldn't be. Not after all the progress they'd made together. Myra had worked with Sarah long enough and utilized the right meds that she thought they were making some progress. A lot of progress. How could she have been so wrong? The young woman had stopped exhibiting physical symptoms of the PTSD. She'd begun to own her emotional issues in a healthier way.

Before her eyes, Sarah's image blurred.

"Myra." This voice was different, and it came from far away. It was a man.

Sarah's image faded.

Myra struggled to cry out, to stop her. She had to save her!

"Myra?" Again the man called to her. It was a familiar voice. One she trusted.

Sarah disappeared. Myra wanted to scream at the injustice of this death. So helpless, Sarah had placed her trust in Myra. She should have been fine. Why did she do this to herself?

The night-dark images burst like a black balloon. Myra was in the exam room, the brilliance of light nearly blinding her. Blood pumped like hot metal through her arteries. She cried out and looked up to find Weston standing over her, watching her with his gentle blue eyes.

"It's okay," he said. "We're here with you."

"It isn't okay. Weston, it's a nightmare."

Joy appeared at the bedside next to Weston. "What is it? Are you getting more memories?"

"I got *the* memory." The faces blurred in front of her. She sat up on the bed, feeling sick again as tears dripped down her face. "I received a call from Sarah's boss yesterday. He wanted to inform me about Sarah's death."

Shock spread across Joy's face. "Not Sarah Miller."

Myra closed her eyes. "Her boss went to check on her when she didn't show up for work yesterday morning. He knows her situation and has a key to her apartment. It appears she committed suicide."

"No!" Joy cried.

Zack stepped up behind Joy and wrapped his arms around her. She leaned back against him as if desperate for his support. As if the events of the day paled to this.

"He called the police and then he called me. Last night she went out to eat and then to the company party, just as she'd planned. But her boss found her lying dead on her kitchen floor this morning. Her pill bottles were open and her bottle of alprazolam was half empty, but the date showed she'd refilled it just last week." Myra battled the nausea that attacked her again.

It wasn't until Weston's shocked grip tightened on her hands that she knew he'd been holding them. She saw the horror of Sarah's loss in his eyes. Tears gathered in them.

Joy cried softly, stiffly, as if she was trying hard not to lose control in Myra's presence.

"I'm so sorry," Weston said.

Myra shook her head in a daze of shock and bewilderment. Those words had no meaning. Of course everyone would be sorry, but that didn't bring Sarah back.

When she closed her eyes to shut out the stunned faces in the exam room, Sarah was there, burned into her mind. Then the hair color darkened until she found herself looking into her mother's eyes.

She gasped, eyes wide open. The room began to spin once more.

Weston's grip on her arms was all that kept her from losing consciousness again. "Myra? What are you remembering?"

"The meds I gave her should have been safe. There's always a chance that when a depressed person begins a new drug regimen, they might have thoughts of suicide. That's why I watched her closely for a long time. It doesn't make sense that she would have done this now."

Joy gave Myra more tissues. "Are you sure she took an overdose?"

"Her boss told me her medicine bottles were open and half empty, though one was a new refill. That makes it sound as if she did take an overdose, but there's been no autopsy yet."

"Then don't jump to conclusions until you can get that autopsy report," Weston said. "I should be able to get it for you. She was still legally a patient of my clinic."

"Weston's right," Zack said. "All you really know is that Sarah died while taking her meds. Did her boss tell you how she was dressed?"

Myra had no trouble recalling the conversation. "The same clothes she wore to the office party last night. When I took her out on a practice run, she told me she only had one nice dress, and she'd purchased a pair of heels from the Salvation Army store."

"So she'd just come back home," Joy said. "That should have felt like a triumph to her. She was following through with her plan. That doesn't sound like someone preparing to kill herself, it sounds like someone determined to get on with her life."

Myra no longer knew what to think. When it came to suicide, she felt suddenly untrained and helpless. Nothing these friends said to her could make her feel better.

"You said her boss called you soon after he called the police. And you've been out of things ever since. You can't know anything for sure," Weston said.

"Except that it appears she took at least half a bottle of the alprazolam I'd prescribed for her stress." The bitterness burned Myra's throat. "Her boss was convinced, and apparently so were the police."

"Wouldn't you be the one to know best?" Weston asked. "You're the one who worked with her. You felt she was ready to go out to dinner by herself."

Myra shook her head. "I helped her with her physical symptoms, and she was doing better, but apparently I pushed too far too fast."

"You didn't cause this," Joy said. "You gave her hope for the first time in years."

"False hope."

Frustration etched itself across Weston's handsome features. "Myra, you can't do this to yourself. How can you believe for a moment this was—"

"I didn't help her heal, I rushed her." And right now Myra knew she was a failure. All this time she'd believed she was bringing new hope into Sarah's soft, pale eyes.

Weston gripped her hands more tightly. "You're not thinking straight."

"I don't know what else to think right now. I did this to her."

Weston took her in his arms and drew her close. "It's okay to cry, Myra. You once told me it was an act of healing."

"What right do I have to heal?" And yet Weston's arms around her felt firm, strong, safe.

Myra shook her head. "Sarah was making such good progress."

"Tell us about that." Weston said. "How was she progressing?"

"Little things at first. For instance, she started greeting customers at work instead of hiding in the back doing the accounts. She started shopping for a few new pieces of clothing instead of wearing the old ones that hung on her like old sacks, and she went to the grocery store to buy groceries instead of ordering delivery online."

"Then your treatments were working."

She pushed away from him and looked up into his eyes. "How is it progress? She's dead."

Joy sniffed and wiped her eyes. "Stop doing this to yourself."

Zack continued to hold Joy. She covered his hands with hers, then turned and buried her face in against his chest.

Myra excused herself and slid from the bed. Her tears had dripped in a stream that dampened Weston's sweater. "Sorry. I've made a mess of everything. It's time to stop with the self pity."

Joy reached out and grabbed Myra. "You did everything in your power to keep that from happening. You're not a failure."

Myra couldn't speak. She clung to her friend as if holding onto a solid piece of sanity, just as she'd done all those years ago after finding that she wasn't strong enough to keep her mother alive.

***

Weston felt as if he was falling backward, attempting to observe a tragedy from a distance, and yet he couldn't place that distance where he needed it to be.

Zack tapped him on the shoulder and nodded toward the door. "They'll have a few things to talk about. Let's give them some time."

Weston followed him out the door and closed it behind him.

"This was obviously a favorite patient of Myra's," Zack said. "What's the connection with Joy?"

"Sarah was one of her pro bono cases." Weston saw various staff members glancing his way. He kept his voice soft. "We fought about her until Joy told me her story."

Zack clapped a hand over Weston's shoulder. "Why don't we go to another room and talk about it? There's no one else around who needs us right now and I've called for the night shift to come in early." Zack led Weston to another exam room and closed the door. "Maybe no more patients will come in until he arrives. This thing's hit you pretty hard, too."

"I'm just as responsible. Can you give Myra something to relax her?"

"I could, but if I'm not mistaken she's on the verge of devolving to her fugue state again. I think we need to wait and let her come to grips with it completely, without medicines that might to risk letting her forget it."

"It looks as if she needs to forget."

"I know it sounds harsh, but I'm afraid if she backtracks now she might lose this memory along with everything else. She doesn't need to go through this ordeal again. I'm hoping all of her memories will return if we let her recover naturally."

"The memories won't necessarily be good ones," Weston warned.

"Nothing could be as bad as this."

"Night before last was the anniversary of her mother's suicide."

Zack bowed his head with a groan.

"I took her to dinner to distract her, but I don't think it worked. We had a fight."

"People are more emotional on anniversaries, whether they realize it at the time or not."

"You sound like Myra." Weston shrugged. "The fighting was nothing new. Her focus has always been on helping as many people as she could. I had my own agenda."

"Don't tell me the great Weston Cline has yet another secret agenda," Zack said dryly.

"Maybe I was being selfish. I tried to convince her again two nights ago to stop leaving her cell phone on for any call at any time. I told her she was killing herself, and that I would appreciate it if she didn't drag me down with her. This fugue state proved me right, and I've never felt more like a monster."

"Why?"

"Because if I hadn't put so much pressure on her, maybe she'd have been in a better state of mind yesterday. Because when I fought with Joy about taking Sarah pro bono she told me Sarah's backstory. It was such an awful story I tried to separate Joy from it, as well. That was the day I fired her. How low can a man get?"

"Sit down," Zack said.

Weston sank onto the padded vinyl chair behind him.

"What's Sarah's story?"

Weston leaned forward and rested his forehead against his hands. "Three freaks high on drugs broke into the honeymoon cabin where Sarah and her new husband were spending their wedding night. The freaks killed her husband and raped her."

"On their wedding night." Zack's voice filled with horror.

"She started having physical symptoms of PTSD, and she came to our clinic for help. That's the person I allowed to walk from our clinic. I wouldn't allow Joy to go after her."

Silence filled the room. He didn't want to see Zack's reaction, but he deserved to see the worst.

When he raised his head, though, Zack was pulling the rolling chair from across the room. He sat down beside Weston with a heavy sigh. "It's almost as if Sarah had her mind set on dying and no one could do anything about it."

"It's what Myra's mother did."

"You don't have the power over life and death any more than Myra does. You're both stepping into God's territory."

He was right and Weston knew it. He closed his eyes. "Thank you. I think the shock has gotten to all of us. Tomorrow I'm going to make some calls and find out more about Sarah's death. Myra needs some answers."

"Good idea. Use whatever means you have available to find out for sure."

"You know, for a grumpy bear, you aren't bad with this counseling stuff. I never figured out why you didn't try to tear me from limb to limb."

"Because I've forgiven you, and I should have done it sooner for my own sake. Tell me more about Sarah."

"She was young, a tiny, frightened mouse terrified of every pain or sensation she experienced. She had herself convinced that something was going to kill her. She didn't even know what PTSD was. Joy had to dig into Sarah's past by looking through old newspaper records. That's how she found out the tragedy and realized what was happening to Sarah."

"That's what makes Joy such a good doctor."

"It's also probably what makes her times in ER slower, and got her into trouble when she worked for me."

"Which is why I'm following your advice."

"I'm glad." Weston tried to peer through the ER and catch a glimpse of Myra, but a nurse stood talking to a tech, cutting off his view. "Myra and Joy probably need you. I should slither back to my apartment."

"No, you should be there for Myra."

"She has you and Joy."

"You're the one she remembers most vividly. That's important right now. She needs to keep those memories coming."

Weston closed his eyes. "You know I love her."

"Heard it in your voice the moment you called last night."

"People are always more inclined to become attached to each other when they share an upheaval in their lives, which is why this isn't a good time for me to be with her."

"You're both adults. You can't change your emotions, but you can control your reactions to them, and I think you've learned the hard way what happens when you don't control it."

"Joy can help break Myra's fall."

"Joy's falling, herself, and she can't handle this. Remember what you told me earlier. Man up. You can maintain your distance when necessary, or so I've heard from my virgin fiancé."

Weston turned and eyed him closely. So Joy had assured him of their chaste months together, despite the pressure Weston placed on her, all the way to the bitter, humiliating end.

Zack glanced out the observation window and stood up. "I think the girls have some much needed company."

Weston followed Zack's line of sight to find the door to Myra's exam room closed.

"Let's go see." Zack eased past Weston and opened the door. "If my eyes aren't deceiving me, we might have a reunion at Molly's tonight."

The men returned to Myra's room to find auburn-haired Laine Fulton hugging her two friends. Myra's face and eyes were red from crying, but to Weston's relief there was a flicker of recognition in her eyes. For now she was retaining her memories, and was apparently recovering more.

***

Myra remembered much about Laine. It felt as if more of the puzzle pieces were finding their niches. Not all, but most. Laine's arrival was helping them fit together more completely. Grief and relief, despair and fulfillment mingled together in a twisted mess in her mind, but Laine's soft, low voice relayed words of encouragement as Joy explained Myra's most recent recollection.

The door opened again and the room became crowded as Weston and Zack entered to greet Laine. Myra focused on breathing and relaxing within her group of friends. She was safe here, and the distraction of the others helped her mind focus elsewhere, providing relief from her worst memories.

Laine's long hair had grown to her waist since the last time

Myra saw her, and she held it back with braids around the front. Her round glasses, her long black skirt and purple corduroy coat managed to retain the lines of her slender frame. There was an uncanny intelligence behind those hazy gray eyes. She was the only one of them who continued to utilize her sharp mind in the world of research.

"I came early, and it appears that's a good thing," Laine said. "Joy, do you think Molly needs some help in the kitchen out at the farm?"

"Not if I know Mom."

"She's been preparing for this for days," Zack said. "So as soon as our replacement doc arrives, we can all drive out."

Joy wrapped an arm around Myra. "I doubt you're going to be in the mood to celebrate, are you?"

Weston stepped up behind Joy. "I think the celebration of the birth of a savior is more vital now than at any other time, especially knowing that Sarah is with Him now."

Silence hovered in the room. The others turned their attention to the one person who had never laid claim to a savior.

"I'm talking about Sarah's savior," Weston said. "It's that birth that gives you hope that she's no longer fighting the effects of PTSD, isn't it?"

Myra cleared her throat. "You're saying you have hope for her?"

"I'm saying that your hope should be that she's no longer afraid of the crowd that's around her right now, and she is, in fact, happy again after so many years of suffering." He looked at the others as they considered him in diverse levels of bemusement. "Isn't that what you believe?"

"How do you know this about her?" Zack asked.

"I read the report in Sarah's file after Joy returned here to Juliet. Sarah and her husband were married in the church where they met and attended regularly."

"Of course. I remember," Joy said.

"Now, I know you Christians are never convinced of a person's afterlife without certain words being said and certain prayers being prayed," Weston said. "I believe a certain water cleansing is expected, depending on the denomination, but if the report was to be believed, Sarah was a chaste young woman held in high esteem in her non-denominational church."

"Hold it," Joy said. "You read the whole report?"

"Every page. It wasn't until she started missing church due to the symptoms of PTSD that the members began to question her faith."

"You realize you're breaking HIPAA privacy law," Joy said.

"Sarah doesn't care anything about that now, does she?" Weston asked.

"Complaints of her sporadic attendance was one of her concerns," Joy said. "One I could identify with."

"I'm not talking about the questions of the church roll-takers," Weston said. "I'm talking about Sarah's faith. The report makes Sarah sound like a believer, doesn't it?"

Myra's throat tightened with suppressed tears. She swallowed and nodded. "Thank you. I needed to be reminded of that."

"So what you're saying is that Sarah Miller is celebrating Christmas in real style today," Zack said.

"I agree," Laine said. "That's something Myra and Joy can continue to remind themselves in the next few weeks. Her life hasn't ended, only the pain in her life."

Myra wanted so badly to take that knowledge to heart.

"I brought fruitcake," Laine said, obviously attempting to break the gloom in the overcrowded exam room. "Extra for Myra."

Even Laine's luscious fruitcake slices, dipped in dark, milk and white chocolate, held no appeal to Myra, and that was a first for her. Nothing sounded appetizing. Maybe she should stay away from tonight's festivities at Molly's, because she didn't want to depress everyone.

"Myra." Laine slid to her side. "Don't worry, you'll be able to recover, and you have friends to help you. You know you aren't alone."

Laine was right. As Myra looked into the faces of her friends she knew she could recover. Returning to practice was another story. She'd failed Sarah. Who else would she fail if she returned to work? But she couldn't say that aloud. She knew they would all disagree with her, but it didn't matter.

"I could sure use a nap," she said.

The others in the room seemed to release a collective breath. She'd always been a good actress.

"I'll take you out to Molly's," Laine said. "I'm eager to try my hypoallergenic spray with all those cats." She looked at Joy. "Can she be released?"

"She was never admitted," Joy said.

"And I'll be here until Dr. McCoy shows up," Zack said. "So the three of you drive on out. Weston and I will see you soon."

Myra forced a smile as she walked out with Joy and Laine. Why ruin their Christmas with more drama? Her memories would continue to surface. She knew there was more. Somehow she knew she was missing something vital, but what?

Chapter 20

The aroma of a Gilbert family traditional Christmas dinner filled the house with warmth and comfort as Zack offered up a heartfelt prayer of thanks. Joy sat across from her mother at the far end of the beautifully carved oak dining room table that Zack and Weston had resurrected from several months of storage.

She held Mom's questioning gaze above the carved turkey, mashed potatoes, salad, yams, several kinds of healthy salad, plus chocolate meringue, coconut meringue and pumpkin pies, and dressing with gravy, buttered rolls, and on and on. Mom had gone all-out.

"Heavy on the pies and salads, aren't we, Molly?" Zack asked.

"You have a problem with my weight loss program?" Molly winked at him.

"I have no problem with your weight at all, but if you want some help, I'll take the pies off your hands." He reached for the coconut meringue, but Laine tapped on his hand with the back of her fork. "Not the whole thing, thank you very much. She cooked this one for me, isn't that right, Molly?"

"Joy put your order in last night," Molly said. "I'll trade you half the coconut for half your batch of fruitcake."

"Dark chocolate, milk chocolate or white chocolate dipped?" Laine asked.

"Some of each?"

"Deal."

"But only if you'll keep me from the dressing, the rolls and the potatoes and gravy. I can't avoid the pumpkin pie, and I must have the fruitcake, of course. It's gluten free again this year, right?"

"Absolutely. My own special recipe just for you, measured up in my own little lab, and no one could taste the difference."

"It's fruitcake," Zack said. "No one can taste the difference because no one eats it."

Laine raised an eyebrow at him, then looked at Molly, where Zack sat to her right and Weston to her left. She looked like a queen accompanied by two appreciative suitors.

Molly nodded and picked up a small piece of white-chocolate-dipped fruitcake.

"Open your mouth," she told Zack.

He eyed her with skepticism.

"You like white chocolate, right?"

He nodded.

"Taste."

He reluctantly opened his mouth and took the small piece of cake. He began to chew, suspicious at first. Then his eyes shot open wide.

"Now tell us you know anyone who wouldn't eat Laine's fruitcake," Myra said.

Zack raised his hands in surrender. "This is what I've been missing all these years?"

"It's your own fault," Laine said. "I gave you a gift of it every year and you always regifted it."

"Sorry."

Molly indicated that everyone should begin passing around the food. The men piled their plates with turkey, rolls, potatoes and dressing. Zack took another piece of fruitcake.

That bird would be gone by the end of the dinner, no doubt about it. Joy had seen both men pack it in.

She sat back and watched her friends begin to recover from the shock of the memories Myra had lost and then regained. Joy knew of few heartaches that couldn't be eased by a gathering of close friends, at least for a little while. Later, Myra would struggle to come to terms with her experiences since yesterday, but to Joy's surprise Weston had come through with the perfect words at the right time this afternoon.

She glanced at him, and knew from the way he watched out for Myra, seeing to it that she received everything she needed, grabbing her an extra napkin, he had it bad for her, more than he'd ever had it for anyone.

And Myra felt it was a good thing?

His words about Sarah's faith taking her to a place of peace still resonated. What was going on with this man?

She risked a glance at Zack, who just happened to be watching her at the moment. He winked at her. She wanted to respond, but the best she could do was nod, frustrated by the distance that still lingered between them. Or was that all in her mind? They needed to talk and clear the air, but after their experiences today she realized she knew his heart. That should be the only thing that counted. So why was she still struggling?

Because she suspected that he doubted her skills. That stung, but she wouldn't give in to the stress of the day.

She turned her attention to her mother, who was also watching her. Mom nodded toward the Christmas tree, totally decorated with animal figurines. Tucked deep between the branches was a brightly wrapped gift that Joy knew was for her.

This being Christmas day, she once again prepared herself to show appreciation for whatever gift her mother had given her. From the time she was a little girl, she'd felt the expectation from Mom for her to rip her presents open with abandon—the more excitement she showed the wider grew her mother's smile.

For Joy, the exchange of gifts had never been about the presents. Watching the pride and happiness in Mom's eyes had always meant the most to Joy. That was what Christmas was all about—accepting gifts with graciousness and appreciation, out of love, the same way a person was to accept a gift from God.

She almost always received a piece of medical equipment such as last year's stethoscope, another year's embroidered lab coat or other medical object she would need in a private practice. Mom knew what she wanted.

"How many times have I told the story about how I decided to name Joy?" Mom's voice rose above the others, and they slowly fell silent.

"Only about a hundred," Myra said. Her green eyes glowed with one of her first real smiles of the evening.

"The very day I discovered I was having a girl, I knew her name would be Joy because I knew she would be the joy of my life."

"Don't forget to tell them you discovered I was a girl on Christmas Eve," Joy said. "So that had something to do with it."

"And despite the hardships I knew I was going to face because of the circumstances in my life at the time—"

"You loved that little life inside your body with all your heart," Myra and Laine finished for her.

The others laughed.

"You might also say that it's because of Joy that I found my way to Christ," Mom said. "I feared from the beginning that I would never be enough to take the place of father and mother. Though I lived with my parents when she was an infant, I needed to make a little family of my own. Knowing I couldn't do that forced me to my knees, and that's where I found a resting place. I might never have truly turned to Jesus without knowing I would have that tiny life totally dependent on me."

Weston raised his glass of cranberry juice to Molly. "To a wise and wonderful mother."

Joy raised her glass, as well, again glancing at Weston, then at Myra, who watched Weston with an expression of wide-eyed expectation. For that moment she resembled a younger Myra Maxwell, whose parents were still alive, and who loved playing with the animals at the Gilbert household.

Joy prayed silently that this day would bring healing for her best friend.

***

For the first time in his life, Weston found himself enjoying cranberry juice. It had to be the company, because he would typically prefer a nice, smooth pinot noir with a dark, fruity finish. For a woman who spent the majority of her life working in a vineyard, attending every available college course, rescuing animals and building a second story onto her small house, Molly had done quite an amazing job cooking this turkey. Was there anything she couldn't do? She'd also been one of the first of Weston's new friends to forgive him wholeheartedly.

Never in a million years would he have expected to find himself sitting at this table, sharing a Christmas meal with these particular people, three of whom he'd hurt deeply—he knew how badly Joy's departure last year had hurt Molly.

"Did I tell you how I got my hot Mustang?" Myra asked Molly.

Weston groaned. "Oh no, please. Have mercy."

Of course, the whole group fell silent at once. He wanted to slide beneath the table. The moment he arrived here last night he'd lost all sense of dignity, and it appeared that experience would continue.

"Let me guess," Joy said. "Weston bought it for you."

Weston sat staring at the food on his plate. "Maybe we could drop the subject?"

"You didn't!" Zack exclaimed. "Weston, a man doesn't buy a woman something that costs more than an engagement ring unless—"

"It was a stupid thing to do, I know that now, but it was simply a gift for a friend whose car kept breaking down and she refused to buy herself a new one. I was afraid it might break down at the wrong place and the wrong time."

"What a kind and thoughtful gesture," Molly said.

To Weston's relief, everyone at the table suddenly turned their attention to their hostess.

Molly rolled her eyes. "With Weston's money, giving a friend a car would be comparable to most men giving a friend a kitchen utensil. Besides, I'm sure Myra reimbursed him. I think I taught her that much."

Myra nodded. "I kept the car and paid him back. He was making a point. I got it. I was reluctant to let go of my mother's old car, but she wouldn't have wanted me to put myself at risk out of sentiment."

Weston smiled at her. It had been a bold move, and he'd known it. At first he was afraid he'd offended her and so had apologized. He caught Joy watching him in wonder from time to time, as if she didn't really know him at all. And he hoped he wasn't the same man she'd loathed.

Myra nudged Weston, nearly causing him to spill his drink. She met his gaze and gave him a tender smile. He could tell she was still struggling to move forward.

He recalled her reaction to the gift of the car, and it touched him. "You've probably been trained since childhood that your money was your most attractive asset," she said, as she had the night she repaid him. "It wouldn't matter to me if you owned the whole world, because you don't own me. I appreciate you for your friendship, not your money."

Weston suspected he'd fallen head over heels the first time she said those words. "I've known for a long time that friendship isn't about money," he said, "but sometimes, when a friend is in need, why not use my money to help?"

Zack regarded him with a glimmer of approval in his gaze. "You mean like the school loans you paid for Joy?"

Weston didn't argue. Why bother?

"I get that you feel the need to pay for past actions," Zack said. "Your attempts to make up for them are admirable."

"My problem is that remuneration doesn't wipe a slate clean." Weston took comfort in Myra's look of understanding.

"There's only one payment that does," Zack said. "We're celebrating it."

"Should I brace myself for the pitch?" Weston tried to lighten the mood with a smile.

"Do you want the 'pitch'?"

"Earlier today you were dragging me out into the freezing weather—"

"That was your idea."

"But I didn't know if you were planning to shoot me or freeze me to death or give me what you Christians call your personal testimony. The pitch." And now the man was sitting here, joining Weston as they stuffed their faces. "The peace at this table is a gift, not something I expected."

"It's also a sort of testimony, wouldn't you say?" Zack asked.

Weston leaned back in his chair. "You were right. I couldn't make up for my past actions with all the money in the Cline empire.

"Then you understand that what you want, you can't do on your own?"

"You mean become a better man?" Weston asked him. "Myra said the same thing."

"There's a gift more valuable than your fortune."

Weston wished they hadn't begun this conversation. He needed time to think. He might even pray if the mood hit him, but not here and now. He had come to the conclusion that what Zack told him this afternoon had a powerful ring of truth. And then when he'd mentioned Sarah being with her savior, and everyone looked at him with eyes wide with hope, well, he knew everyone wanted that for him. It touched him more deeply than he could ever have imagined. But he had to be sure.

Maybe this spiritual regeneration they were talking about was a life-changer, but he'd seen a lot of financial offers in his lifetime that sounded too good to be true; after checking further he discovered them to be pyramid schemes or worse.

He accepted a slice of pumpkin pie from Molly. "Gluten free crust, right?"

She smiled and nodded. "You wouldn't have known if I hadn't told you."

He picked up his dessert fork and took a bite. He would never mention this, of course, but he couldn't figure out how Molly kept the house clean of cat hair.

He should stop trying to distract himself. After today's experiences, and after his experiences this past year, he now knew what these people meant when they used the term savior. Was it possible that Savior was watching over him? Had He sent Zack and Joy, Myra and Molly into his life when he was seeking someone larger than himself?

Everything he'd seen with these people boiled down to character. Someone famous had once made the statement that keeping one's character was much easier than rebuilding it once it's lost. He could testify that it was the truth.

Molly started cutting the meringue pies. "Who wants chocolate cream?"

"I do," Myra said.

"You do realize this was made with pudding from a box and a store-bought piecrust."

"Hasn't it always been?"

"How about more of that fruitcake, Laine?" Zack asked. "You've made a believer out of me."

The talk and laughter continued, and Weston watched as Zack and Joy exchanged several glances across the table. Good thing that neither of them had to work tomorrow. He got the impression, from those glances, that they had already managed to come to terms with their disagreement without a word being spoken.

He would watch and wait. The proof of God's love might show itself here tonight with these people.

Chapter 21

Joy had barely swallowed her a final bite of coconut meringue pie when Myra handed her a heavy coat and a scarf and nodded toward Zack. "Take a walk, you two. Doctor's orders."

"You think frostbite is a healthy treatment plan?" Joy asked.

Zack wrapped the scarf around her neck and handed her some gloves.

"What about cleanup?" She gestured to the table of dirty plates and empty serving dishes.

"I just happen to know from previous conversations that Weston isn't helpless in the kitchen," Myra said. "So go. Sit in the car if it's too cold, but you two need some time alone together."

Joy sighed. To do what? Fight? What if they couldn't work out this snag between them?

While she pulled on her gloves Zack grabbed his heavy suede coat—the one she'd loaned to Weston this morning when he was freezing outside during their search for Myra. She grabbed the woolen scarf she'd given Zack for his birthday and handed it to him.

While Molly pulled out a plate of fudge, Myra leaned forward to speak in Joy's ear. "Stop looking as if you're going to the firing squad," she whispered. "This is Zack. Just talk. You know you can trust him."

"Let's just hope he's walked off all his anger while he was with Weston today." Here they'd been talking quite directly about the love and forgiveness of Christ, and she didn't want to be the one to cause Weston to doubt what they'd been so earnest to discuss.

As soon as they stepped out onto the front porch, where the wind chimes had fallen silent and the air felt somewhat warmer than earlier in the day, Zack took her hand. "No matter what, we're in this together."

She looked up at him and wished they didn't have this ugly issue keeping them so formal with each other. She'd allowed it to happen. It had taken her the whole afternoon to realize that. "Did Weston coach you about what to say to me?"

"Not what to say. What to do. He nearly kicked me into next week for being so—um, what's the word? Insensitive? No, that's a girly word. He wouldn't say that since we were both trying to be so strong and macho and duke it out like real men, only with words instead of fists."

"I'm relieved fists didn't become necessary."

"It would have felt good a couple of times, believe me, but dang if he didn't have a point. Insensitive was pretty much the message I got."

"You weren't the only one." Joy loosened the scarf around her neck. The air was definitely not as cold now. Or maybe being alone with him was heating things up.

"I thought Joy Gilbert never made mistakes."

She scowled up at him. "If you're going to start out like that I'll go back inside where it's comfortable." She reached for the door.

He grabbed her arm. "Oops. Sorry. What am I saying? It must be my leftover competitive spirit from med school, forcing myself to study harder, work longer, dig more deeply with you nipping at my heels all the way for the number one—"

She stood on her toes and kissed him to shut him up.

He caught her in his arms and drew her against him. This time they kissed with enough fervor to make her forget what they argued about today. Or that they'd even argued. Now they were getting somewhere.

And yet. And yet, something was missing. Oh, he returned the kiss, engulfed her in his arms and definitely returned kiss for kiss, as if he was still competing to show who could win this particular competition.

She withdrew first, but only because she sensed he was holding something back. But what?

"It wasn't my idea to invite Weston here tonight," she said.

"I know, but I'm glad he came."

Hmmm. So that wasn't the problem. "Mind telling me what's bothering you, then?" Might as well get this over with.

Zack pressed his gloved fingers against her lips. "Relax. We have some talking to do, that's all, and the temptation to use physical communication instead of verbal right now is too strong."

"Noticed that, did you?"

"This might not be the time or place to talk."

She wasn't sure she wanted to hear this, but she didn't want the tension between them to continue. "Maybe not, but out with it anyway."

He nodded and reached out to wrap the scarf back to its snug spot around her neck. He had the most beautiful smile. And eyes. And spirit.

She took a tiny step backward. "Talking, right? You realize that when you're touching me I can't think straight."

"Sorry. Couldn't help myself. Before you locked lips with me I was going to apologize for this morning. I allowed that miserable phone call to take everything out of me, and I took it out on you."

"And I took my anger with Wilma out on you when you were only doing your job."

Zack's smile remained in place, his eyes, visible in the porch light, shining with love if she wasn't mistaken. It made her want to shut him up with her mouth again. She refrained.

"You're quite a vision of beauty when riled," he said.

"I looked like a cat with mange after last night."

"You'll need to give me a few breaks. I've never done this job before, and I'm new at it, never wanted it to begin with, so be patient."

"No problem."

He leaned down and peered into her face, then reached up and touched her hair. "Looks like the woman I love, feels like her, but you're saying you can be patient?"

She reached for the door again, and again he stopped her.

"You're the one who tried to get through pre-med in three years, just to show me up," he said.

"Just to show you up? You're being ridiculous. I'm not the competitive one. I was in a hurry," she said. "The sooner I graduated the sooner I could start paying back my loans. I hate debt, and you know it."

"Admit it, you're as competitive as I am."

"Absolutely not." She turned and noted that Mom, Myra,

Weston and Laine were all within the square of the window, watching them unabashedly.

She frowned at them and they scrambled away, returning to their work.

"We were discussing patience, right?" she asked. "When I love someone I can be patient. Can you?"

"I know what I'll lose if I can't."

"Better remember that, then."

"Aren't you afraid of what you might lose?"

She wished this conversation was over and they could get on with the rest of their lives. She peered through the window to make sure the others were still otherwise engaged. Only Myra and Laine were watching. She glared at them and they returned to the table.

"What are you looking at?" Zack followed her line of vision. "Supervising the cleanup committee?"

"They were watching us. Good thing Mom installed double panes or they'd hear every word we've said. So this is the big talk you're supposed to have with me, right? You have to chew me out for being a bad employee, and I have to sign a warning slip agreeing that if I blow it again I'll be terminated."

He held his hands out. "Do you see me carrying a piece of paper at any time?"

She crossed her arms, though with the thickness of her coat sleeves that proved to be more difficult than she'd expected. "Talk, Zack."

He nibbled on his lower lip. "Right. So here we go." He closed his eyes and sighed, opened them again. "You and I decided early on in med school not to automatically pigeonhole symptoms into the commonly accepted diagnoses—"

"We're talking about our school days now?" If she didn't know better she might suspect Mom of spiking the cranberry juice with wine. She'd have to blame that on the kisses, because the effects of kissing Zack after this awful day were making her high despite the unpleasant conversation. She needed to get serious.

"No, I'm using our past decision to segue," he said. "I've decided not to accept every order from a supervisor, the same way we decided to think for ourselves and use logic instead of blindly swallowing every med school rule and every piece of Big Pharma propaganda."

She stepped down from the porch and turned to look up at him. "You couldn't have gotten this advice from Weston."

"I do have a thought of my own on occasion, but the man knows business, and I started thinking like a businessman instead of a blind sheep."

"He fired me because—"

"He regretted firing you. Maybe he's one of the few people who actually learn from their mistakes."

She chuckled. "Wow. You've had a change of heart. Earlier I was afraid you were going to attack him on the front lawn."

"Did you hear me? Weston regretted firing you."

Obviously it was time to get serious. "I know he did, but he had every right to."

Zack stepped down to join her. "He admired what you were doing."

"What's admirable about doing free work using someone else's time and resources? If I was going to open a free clinic I should have gone through proper channels, not taken his clinic for granted."

He linked his arm through hers and walked beside her across the lawn. "You've forgiven him."

"Tonight I feel as if I've forgiven him, but I've felt that way before. All I'm saying is that I was definitely wrong to do what I did. Just because he has more money than me doesn't mean I had the right to use his wealth, even if it was to help others."

"Interesting he didn't seem to see it that way."

She had decided months ago never to discuss with Zack the extra after-hours time she'd spent with Weston. Now she wondered about that decision. What about sharing with openness and trust for the rest of their lives?

She cleared her throat. "You knew he and I spent time together after hours when I lived in Corrigan."

Zack went silent beside her.

"It's how I met Tressa," she said.

"That wasn't difficult to figure out. It wasn't something I ever wanted to talk about. Still don't."

"Bear with me. He wasn't handling visitation times well with Tressa. I started inviting them both to my place when he had nights or weekends with her. That's when she and I became friends."

"But that wasn't the only time you spent with him," Zack said softly.

"No." She stared into the darkness, choosing her words carefully. "When I first moved away from here I was so devastated after our breakup that having what other women might consider a 'catch' show an interest in me stroked my ego." There. She'd finally told him. It didn't feel any better. In fact, in his place she knew she'd have felt as he did—she wouldn't want to talk about it.

"I deserved that. I'm the one who listened to him in the first place and broke the engagement."

"He took me to dinner a few times, put the moves on me, but it wasn't real."

"What does that mean?"

She didn't like the quiet sound of Zack's voice. She looked up at him. "I mean, he wasn't you, and I didn't love him. I was still in love with you. I realized that anything I allowed with him would be meaningless. I slowly, carefully pulled away. It was uncomfortable because I worked for him, but I had no choice."

Zack exhaled, as if he'd been holding his breath. "He said the same thing. And you've told me before that you remained chaste."

"But I did spend after-hours time with him and Tressa, so I convinced myself that since I was working on my time for his benefit, I should be able to take a few pro bono cases during my regular work shift. I know now that was wrong. I volunteered my time with Tressa because I loved her." There. She'd told him everything barring a description of the kisses, and that would never reach his ears. "Maybe Weston isn't the only one who can learn from their mistakes."

Zack walked beside her in silence for a moment, and she could tell by his movements, the tilt of his head, that he had something more on his mind. Would he ask more about Weston? Would this discussion stir up all the old pain?

"I guess forgiving the hospital board won't be as easy," he said.

She looked up at him when his words soaked in. "Not when Wilma Rush is on a personal vendetta to hurt Mom through me."

"Forgiving is something you do—"

"I know the cliché; I need to do it for myself, not for Wilma."

"Maybe it's a cliché because it's truth. Let it go, even while the woman's still trying to hurt you."

"Not as simple as is sounds, and it might be easier if I didn't know she's trying to hurt my mother through me."

"Especially not when your prospective husband might be taking the heat with you."

She stopped walking. "What do you mean?"

"I'm saying that if you go, I go."

"Oh no you don't. That's not right either." The air was brisker away from the protection of the house.

"And you think it would be right to enable Wilma to misuse her authority? It would damage our hospital. Losing you would hurt our hospital. The others need to realize what she's doing, and if I have to leave for them to see it, that's what I'll do."

"That woman has been around for years. Everyone who knows her can see the kind of person she is. If they allow her to have the power, I don't see how we can change it."

He took her arm and started walking again. "I have to say this once as your boss because I agreed to, and then I'm finished. You and I have a moral and ethical obligation to provide the best care we possibly can."

"I sense a 'but' coming."

"Because your practice style is so much like mine, I can help you make the changes you need to make to satisfy the board and keep Wilma from getting the upper hand."

"I've been trying to work faster."

"You're a great doctor. Never forget that. I know you; I've seen you learn right along beside me. You care and your patients love you. But you have the highest percentage of patients leaving without being seen, and that isn't something I can change on a report to the hospital board. It's on paper."

No matter how much she'd prepared herself for this she wasn't ready to hear it; the words plunged into her heart like knives. "You've seen a report?" More patients were leaving because of her? "Did the report say who was leaving?" She wouldn't put it past Wilma to doctor those reports.

"I saw them. They were legit. I also did a little more digging and discovered those were days you didn't have a mid-level provider, so you were on your own. You had some difficult cases, some major suture repairs, cases that take extra time. Any other doctor would have had the same trouble, but in the past few months the bad days just happened to fall on you more than anyone else."

"Did you tell the board about that?"

"Sure did. Wilma outshouted me."

"Then why bother? If they're going to allow her to railroad me out of the hospital, we can't stop her."

"I had the same problem last year. I had to fight for my job, too."

"Don't tell me you got into trouble with the board."

"No, with the presiding director last year." He stopped and turned her to look at him. The moon had come out, and she studied the serious planes of his face, smelled the wood-smoke from a neighbor's fireplace. She wanted to snuggle into his chest and forget about this conversation.

"I should've recorded my arguments last year," he said. "Then you wouldn't have to repeat them tonight. Further digging convinced me that you still need to pick up the speed with the simpler cases. Time is everything."

She appreciated what he said, but this was all so difficult. The hospital could afford to hire more help. "I work as fast as I can, but how can I speed up and meet standard of care when I'm buried?"

"I can see those times when you're busy, but this is emergency medicine, Joy. When you're in practice you can take care of the whole patient, but in the emergency department we have to take care of the emergency and turf them out ASAP."

"So you're saying we have to 'move the meat.' You know I hate that term."

"Patients don't like to be kept waiting."

"They don't know if they're getting good care or not, they just don't want to have to wait so the person ahead of them gets good care, too."

He sighed, put his arms around her and drew her close. "That's what the director told me last year. Cover the emergency and get on to the next patient. We can't be a family practice in ER even if that's what the patients want. We're there for emergencies only."

"Yes, but since we're required by law to take every patient who claims an emergency, a runny nose is an emergency."

"One you can treat in three minutes," he said.

"So I can quote standard of care until I'm hoarse, but I'll still lose my job if I continue as I have been."

He kissed her on the forehead. "If you go I go."

She leaned away. "Have I mentioned how much I love you?" She threw her arms around him, thick coats and all, and met his face with a hearty kiss, missing his mouth by mere centimeters.

He held her close and kissed her cheek, her neck, her hair. "I love you back."

"I can't let you lose your job," she said.

"You mean quit my job." He chuckled, his arms warming her in so many ways. She felt his strength and she knew his steadfast heart. This was where she belonged. Why had she been so out of sorts today?

Oh, yeah, yesterday had ended in disaster and this morning had begun the same way. She didn't do well without sleep, and she especially didn't do well with the woman who had been Mom's bane of existence for so many years.

"From now on I treat patients as if I'm doing a disaster triage."

"At least when you're busy."

"Anything else?"

"Only that I'd like you to step up the speed on one more thing."

She suppressed a sigh of exasperation. "What would that be?"

"I thought you said you could be patient."

"Sorry." She cleared her throat. "What else, Boss?"

"You don't have the date set in stone for the wedding yet, do you?"

She smiled. This was a good change of subject. "Family conflicts. My grandfather wants me to have it before trout season begins, but my cousin Dawn wants to wait for a spring wedding because she thinks it'll be luckier."

"What does luck have to do with it?"

Joy shrugged and snuggled closer to his warmth. "Everyone wants to be there, but we have too many time conflicts, and I'm afraid I don't have time to deal with everything right now."

"Then don't."

She pulled back and looked up at him. "What do you mean?"

He turned her back toward the house. "Let's give everyone a Christmas gift. Why don't we ask our friends to help us do a phone tree? Get Molly's old fashioned address book out and call family and friends, tell them we're celebrating our wedding on the first day of the year."

She gasped. "New Year's Day? That's a week away!"

"No frills, just wedding."

"Most people have plans already."

"Isn't it a Gilbert family tradition to gather at your grandparents' place for that?"

"Yes, but the games—"

"We'll have the wedding between ballgames. You already said my pastor could perform the ceremony, and you wanted no fuss. My mom and siblings are coming to visit next week, and the football games will distract enough people we won't have to stay around long for the reception afterward. You and I have three days and nights off the first of the year, and I know this quaint little cottage in Augusta that would be a great honeymoon getaway."

She slowed down to catch her breath. Married in a week? "Could we do it?"

"We're mature adults. We can do whatever we want."

"Then yes! I agree. I love you, Zachary Travis!"

He chuckled and drew her closer, and for a long, lovely moment they held each other the way it was always meant to be.

Chapter 22

In the early morning hours the day after Christmas Weston wandered the campus of the Juliet School of Medicine, Bluetooth in his ear as he waited for the ME's office to return to the line. Maybe he was reverting to his former ways, pulling strings, using his name and even financial resources to get what he needed, but he wasn't doing it for himself. Not entirely.

Myra had most of her memories back, but the devastation of Sarah's death had cast a pall on her; the holiday season did nothing to lift her spirits, especially since her mother died so close to Christmas. He'd stayed late at Molly's last night making calls about the wedding and finally drawing Myra to a private corner of the house as she unburdened herself about seeing her mother when she'd lost consciousness yesterday.

A young man's voice came back on the line. "I'm sorry to keep you waiting, Mr. Cline. Dr. Trumble's been assigned to Sarah Miller's case, but he hasn't come in yet." He sounded nervous, eager to please. Exactly what Weston needed.

"Then have the body assigned to a doctor who's on duty today." He used his most authoritative voice.

"But we can't—"

"Tell your boss this comes as a special request from me. Sarah was a patient at my clinic, so it's bound to become a high profile case. As soon as the press gets wind of the rumors of her suicide they'll trample each other to see who can reach the papers and blog sites first. Has anyone even run a tox screen on her?"

"No, I'm sorry, we haven't had time—"

"I suggest you make time. The ME's office could suffer unnecessary embarrassment should the diagnosis of suicide change at a later date—and I don't believe this was a suicide. I don't care what the police said. I knew that young woman."

Without waiting for a reply, he disconnected.

It would do no good to call the police. He knew from past experience that in their line of work they had to take everything at face value. They didn't take the time to dig; since they found a half empty bottle of alprazolam on her kitchen table, they wouldn't look further. But he knew Myra, and if she didn't believe Sarah took those pills, he needed to know what really happened so he could pull her out of her grief and self-doubt.

He spoke his daughter's name, "Tressa Cline." As the phone rang he turned to see two cars pulling out of the ER patient parking area.

"Hi Dad." Tressa was her cheery self, obviously wide awake. "Did you have a good day yesterday?"

"The best. I made peace with Zack and Joy, and you're right about Molly. She's a—"

"Wait. What are you talking about? You're not in the city?"

He wouldn't worry her about Myra. Not something a sixteen-year-old needed to hear the day after Christmas. "I decided to drive to Juliet and try to make amends with some people here as a holiday gesture."

"You mean Joy and Zack?"

"Yes, among others. Myra's here for the holidays, as well."

The ensuing silence made him smile. Tressa had been encouraging him to become better friends with Myra, which was why he hadn't told her how often they'd been seeing each other lately. She wouldn't understand about the wall that continued to separate him from Myra. Tressa didn't need to be disappointed.

"I have a question for you, sweetheart," he said. "Do you still write in that journal you're always hiding from your mom and me?"

"Every day. Has Myra asked you to start writing too?"

"She suggested it a couple of times."

"It helps. Really. I can go back over the notes I wrote a few months ago and see how far I've come. You should try it."

"That might be a good idea. Myra asks everyone to journal, doesn't she?"

"I don't know, I just know she wanted Mom and me to do it." There was a pause. "I know you never like to write things down that can be found and publicized, but even if you write it down and burn it, you'll get stuff out of your system."

He closed his eyes and sat on a bench beneath a huge oak tree bare of leaves. The sun warmed his face though the slight breeze from the river chilled him. "If I wanted to start a journal and not burn the pages, where do you think I should put it where no one, especially not the press, could ever get to it?"

"Not on a computer, that's for sure. You'd have to write in one the old fashioned way, by hand. And then put it inside an old book or maybe slide it inside your pillow—not just the pillowcase, but the pillow, itself. I can think of tons of hiding places if you want to start journaling. Are you going to, Dad?"

"One never knows. We'll see. Did Joy call you last night about the wedding?"

"Yes! Mom and I are attending. I can't wait. We're going shopping for something to wear, and Mom's going to make reservations for us to spend the night in Hermann on New Year's Eve."

"Good, then I'll look forward to seeing you here next week."

Tressa gasped. "You're attending their wedding?"

He smiled to himself. Tressa was becoming more animated, more like a teenaged girl as she healed. "I told you I came here to make amends. Molly was kind enough to invite me to Christmas dinner at her place last night. I've had several talks with Zack, and though I don't expect them to consider me as one of their best friends, we're on better terms now."

"Dad, I'm so happy."

Hearing her say those words meant everything to him. "It's a relief to have fewer enemies."

"They were never your enemies."

"And now they know I'm not theirs. Enjoy more time with your grandparents, and tell your mother I won't be back until after the wedding, so no need to rush back into Corrigan for visitation. I'll see you at the wedding."

"Wait, you're staying there?"

"Unless you need me for something. If you do I'll drive back—"

"No, Mom just mentioned last night she wished we could spend more time with Grandpa and Grandma."

"Then tell her Merry Christmas from me."

For a moment she didn't reply. "You're not setting up for

another research project, are you? When you did that last year you were gone for months."

"And I learned some painful lessons. The research wing is for use by scientists, physicians and other people who have nothing in common with me. I will neither fund another project, nor will I be present for one. Don't worry, everything is going to be fine. I love you, sweetheart. I'll see you soon."

After they disconnected he remained seated on the bench and stared at the opposite bank of the river. When had he begun to tell Tressa he loved her?

Oh, yes, it was after their surgeries, when he thought he would lose her. He hadn't been raised in a demonstrative family, so at first the words had come with difficulty, but they'd finally come. Lately he'd learned to reveal the more tender side of his personality while attempting to tone down the choleric part of his nature. Being more laid back in his life, and even in business, wouldn't necessarily be good for business, but right now he didn't care.

Staying in this town for a week appealed to him. He would stay close to his apartment and keep out of trouble, but the thought of spending a few days away from the city felt good. He would have time to slow down to a steadier, less hectic pace.

One of the most depressing experiences he'd had in a while was last night after Zack and Joy came back inside, hand in hand. More than anything, that had shown him what he was missing, and it made him want Myra in his life the way Joy was in Zack's. He still refused to fake Christianity for the sake of winning Myra's heart. If he lied about faith, it meant he would lie about anything, and then he wouldn't be the man Myra thought he was.

Still, it was increasingly difficult to spend time with Myra knowing they couldn't be more than the friends they were now. Since it was painful for him, it was likely to be the same for her. He would have to be the one to make the break and stop seeing her. Just not this week.

***

Myra sat on Joy's bed watching Molly and Laine straighten the wedding dress as Joy pulled it on over her head.

"It isn't white," Laine said. "I thought a white dress denoted purity, and I know you're pure, Joy Gilbert."

Molly zipped up the back and settled the long sleeves and draped the dress of eggshell silk around her daughter's slender figure. "That's a myth."

At any other time Myra would have burst into laughter at the sudden surprise on the faces of her friends. Today she merely smiled. "I don't think Molly's talking about Joy's purity. She's talking about the dress color."

Molly's face turned pink. "Off-white is the color of purity. White means joy. At least, that's what I read once."

Myra stretched sideways across the bed with a sigh.

"Your day will come, sweetheart," Molly said, glancing at Myra briefly.

"Will it?"

Molly shared a silent exchange of looks with her, then gestured to Laine. "Come help me see if I'm going to have to take up my dress. Myra can help Joy change."

"You could stop losing weight until after the holidays," Myra called after Molly as she and Laine left the room.

"I'd rather wear a baggy dress," Molly called back as they retreated down the hallway.

Joy turned to Myra. "I know you're still upset about Sarah. So am I."

"We're planning your wedding. I need to focus on being happy for you."

"Give it time. You know you can't recover from everything overnight."

"I'm still missing some memories, and for some reason I feel they're important."

"Be patient until they come," Joy said. "I'm trying this patience thing, myself. It isn't easy."

"Weston called me this morning to see how I was feeling."

Joy slowly lowered herself to the hope chest across from Myra, her dark eyes filled with trepidation. "What are you going to do about him?"

"I wait. What else can I do?"

Joy shrugged. "I don't know, maybe drag him down the aisle and force him to his knees and make him repeat the prayer of repentance after you?"

Myra closed her eyes. "Don't think I haven't considered that very thing. I feel I'm supposed to be where I am right now. I've felt that way for a long time, and I believe this is a nudge from God."

"You're sure?"

"I've tested Him with a fleece several times. For instance, during the months I was seeing Weston I'd be praying before a dinner with him about whether or not I should cancel that night. I knew I was becoming emotionally involved. Then almost as if from God's ear to your heart, you'd call me within minutes and urge me to get out and enjoy myself that night."

"So you're telling me I was your motivation for seeing Weston?"

"I didn't intend to fall in love, and I even wondered if I was simply too vulnerable because I was still grieving Dustin. Weston and I both shared our grief, and it drew us closer."

"I don't understand why this is happening," Joy said.

"I know I can't move forward with him. Maybe this whole relationship was meant to get him here so you and Zack could reconcile with him. I still feel God has control, and I'll just have to wait."

"I've never seen Weston behave this way with any other woman."

"Not even you?"

"I know now that he didn't love me. Last night I saw how he was with you. He was never that solicitous with anyone else."

"He's changed."

"I believe he's a seeker. A serious seeker. It's why he wanted to talk to Zack; it's why he said what he did about Sarah's place in heaven. He's been listening and learning." Joy moaned and planted her face in her hands. "What a rotten example I've turned out to be."

"You're wrinkling the dress. Stop it. Let's pull that thing off before you get something on it."

Joy stood in obedience and Myra unzipped her, helped her slide out of the beaded, beautiful garment and placed it back on its padded hanger. "Mom held onto this for over a year. She really wanted to see Zack and me married."

"And now one of her dreams is coming true. Don't worry, I

think her other dream will happen, too. You'll have your own practice." Myra sank back on the bed while Joy pulled off her slip and dressed in her jeans and sweater. "You're right about Weston. He's a seeker, and I've never tried to push my faith on him, though I've explained it and we've discussed it, which might be another reason I chose to see him in a more casual setting. It's considered unethical to attempt to proselytize patients."

Joy stepped into her boots. "You don't have to push your faith on him. You live your faith. He couldn't help seeing it."

"I think it was the same with you. Your determination to maintain your chastity had to grab his attention."

"That didn't seem to impress him much at the time."

Myra smiled. "Oh, he might not have thought so but it was a good way to grab his attention. Anyway, I have to wait. And I'm feeling impatient. Last week I was good with it. I knew how I felt, of course, but I could see so many changes in him, so much yearning, that I felt sure that there would be a permanent change in his life soon, and we would both share the same faith, and we could both move forward together after I finished grieving Dustin."

"I believe you're in love with a different man from the one you went to work for last year."

Myra plumped a pillow and laid her head back on it. "As I said, when I pray about it, my answer has been 'wait.' It's possible the only reason God wants me in Weston's life is to shine a light for him. I have no assurances that he and I will be anything more than friends."

"Do you think the stress of your situation with Weston complicated everything when you received news about Sarah?"

Myra nodded. She remembered the anxiety of that day when she'd rehashed the fight she'd had with Weston the night before, wondering if he was right. Then when the call came about Sarah she'd felt as if she'd plunged into deep water, unable to hear, to see, to breathe. Too much pressed down on her at once. "I discovered I couldn't save the world."

"That still doesn't mean Sarah swallowed those pills."

"I can think of no other scenario."

Joy picked up the veil her mother had given her as a Christmas gift last night. She ran the sapphire-encrusted comb through her luxurious hair, being careful to protect the veil the comb anchored. Myra watched as Joy's hair got tangled.

"Hold it. Stop before you tear the veil." Myra jumped up and gently helped her get the tangles out.

"Did you hear Mom tell me last night that this would have been her bridal veil?" Joy asked.

Myra shook her head, cautiously pulling a regular comb through Joy's hair.

"She saved for it and purchased it herself before leaving for college," Joy said. "So now I have something old and blue. Tradition." She pulled the front half of the translucent, beaded material over her face.

"Even if you don't like tradition, it suits you."

"My grandfather insisted on this wedding, you know."

"I know. But is it something you want?"

"I just want to be married."

"I've been telling you for years that you try too hard to make your relatives happy."

Joy handed Myra the veil. "I'm sure I'm going to tear this thing if I keep playing with it. I know I try too hard. I think it's something I started doing as a child because Mom never tried to please anyone. For her, we were a family and she didn't have anything to prove to anyone, so I followed along and tried to soothe hurt feelings when I should have been more like Mom. I never dreamed of a fancy wedding, just marriage."

"Well, you're getting both whether you like it or not," Myra said. "Weston told me last night he's going to stay in town until after the wedding."

"Good. It'll give Zack and me some time to get to know this new Weston Cline. If you can, stop worrying about Weston, stop worrying about your memories. They'll return sooner if you stop trying so hard."

"I'm glad the clinic's closed this week. I need the time."

"I suppose you'll keep seeing Weston this week."

Myra sighed, leaning her head against the flat of her hand. "You know we've never kissed? And yet when I see you and Zack together, I can't help wondering what it would be like."

"You've been good for him. I can see that. The two men are totally different, though."

"You're wondering if he could ever be good for me."

Joy stood up from the bed, touching the veil with a look of reverence, which belied her hints that she didn't care about the wedding. "Stop worrying about that, too. You don't have to please me any more than I have to please every relative and acquaintance in Juliet. We have less than a week to get this wedding planned, and until then worry is a thing of fiction. Give it time."

Chapter 23

Weston got up from the outdoor campus bench and walked toward the ER entrance, where he was surprised to see Zack's car in the lot. He glanced over his shoulder toward the Cline Research Wing of the school. What incentive did his family have over the years to make such generous gestures? Were those gifts simply to gain favor in business? Was it possible his father, his grandfather and other family members actually meant to reach out and help others out of the goodness of their hearts?

He was pretty sure his motives had always been business—the bottom line for most of his life. Sure, people in need had those needs met by a generous donation here, a well-publicized gift there, but shouldn't those contributions have come from somewhere in the heart?

He turned away from the building.

"You look like a man with a lot on your mind," a familiar voice called to him from outside the ER entrance. It was Zack, wearing scrubs with a thin sweater underneath, and no coat.

Weston made his way in that direction along the winding sidewalk. The day was warm enough for a long walk with a heavy coat, but not in scrubs. "You look cold. I thought you were off today."

"Got called in. Three-car pile-up out on the highway."

"Injuries?"

"Not life-threatening. It could've been a lot worse."

"How about that mug of cocoa I suggested yesterday?" Weston asked. "I've got some in the fridge all mixed and ready to hit the stove in my apartment."

"Sounds good," Zack turned and followed Weston, and Weston couldn't help comparing the hostile reception he'd received yesterday to Zack's behavior today. What had changed?

"I suppose the ladies are in overdrive to complete the wedding plans," Weston said.

"Yep, but at least I've talked them out of a rehearsal dinner," Zack said. "I told Joy to make this fun for us, not just everyone else. A few quick directions from my pastor just before the ceremony will be fine." He cast a sideways frown at Weston. "Next week would you keep watch on my car and make sure no one decorates it?"

"Isn't that the best man's job?"

Zack gave a snort. "My brother's the most likely to do the decorating. He's at that age."

"You think you can trust me?" Of course, as Myra might say, doing anything to prevent a smooth getaway would be considered hostile, since Weston was the one who prevented this from happening last year.

Zack chuckled and rubbed his unshaved face. "I'll take whatever help I can get. You had an awfully serious expression on your face back there. Something up?"

"I'm thinking about Sarah Miller and worried about Myra." Weston gestured toward the far door of the research wing.

Zack quick-stepped toward the door. "I thought it was warming up. Guess not. You have another theory about Sarah's death?"

Weston tapped his Bluetooth and spoke Myra's name into it. As it connected he said, "Myra has her patients journal their recovery. She wanted me to do it, but it felt too much like more work."

"Darn right." Zack gave a fake growl. "Real men don't journal."

Weston grinned. "Okay, I was being a Neanderthal about it, but it occurred to me that Sarah might have done as she was asked. Myra mentioned last night that she still doesn't have all her memories back, so maybe Sarah's journaling is one of them. I'm calling Myra now."

He unlocked his door and stepped inside. "Joy doesn't have you tasting cakes and helping decide on décor?" He went to the fridge and pulled out the premixed cocoa as the Bluetooth buzzed in his ear.

"Joy knows what I like. She knows my favorite cake, my favorite punch, my favorite colors. The ladies will have it all worked out."

"What about a tux?"

"Tux?"

"She'll be wearing a wedding gown, not a gunny sack. You can't attend your own wedding in scrubs. And you'll need a new pair of shoes. What size do you wear?"

"Eleven narrow."

"Good, then if you need to you can get by with my eleven regulars." Weston cut an amused glance at Zack.

Myra answered at last, and he turned away to speak with her. "Hi. Hope you slept well with the cats last night."

"I did. They kept me warm. And I'm proud to announce that Laine's experiment is working well so far. Not a single sneeze or hive."

"Tell me Joy's planning to order a tux for Zack."

"She already called in the order."

Weston frowned and shot a quick glance at Zack. "Shouldn't he be measured?"

"She measured him last year."

Weston eyed Zack's dimensions. "You're sure he hasn't lost weight or started working out or something?"

"Hey!" Zack called over his shoulder, stirring the pot of cocoa over the burner. "I haven't lost weight, and who has time to work out? I'm a solid 180, 6'2"."

Weston shrugged. "Apparently that's solid," he told Myra. "I just spoke to Tressa, and she assured me that I'm not the only one you asked to journal about my recovery. Do you do that with all your patients?"

There was a short silence, and then Myra sucked in her breath. "Weston, that's key! I always have my patients write in a journal. Sometimes they take notes during sessions, sometimes they prefer to use their journals like diaries and keep them private, even from me."

"How did Sarah do hers?"

"Diary. I never saw it."

"Then we need to find that journal. Any idea where she kept it?"

"No, but maybe I can find something in my notes. They're cloud based. I wish I'd thought of this sooner."

"So it could be safe to say she kept it in her apartment or somewhere in her car, right?"

"Yes."

"If the police don't have the apartment taped off as a crime scene, we could call the landlord and get inside," Weston said.

"It's unlikely they consider it a crime scene, since Sarah's boss overheard them calling it suicide."

"Then all I have to do is call the landlord."

"Please Weston, let me call. I need to know."

"Do you have the number?"

"Yes. He's an elderly man who lives in the house. Sarah rented his only apartment. She thought of him as a friend. I'll call him now."

"Let me know what you find?"

"Of course." She paused. "Weston, God sent you to us on Christmas Eve. Thank you."

For a moment, Weston couldn't reply. No one had ever told him that before. "Thank you." Her words left him unprepared for the emotion they stirred in him—and he couldn't even tell what emotion it was. Amazement? Joy? Hope?

"If the landlord can find the journal he can to read it to me over the phone," Myra said. "Sarah had excellent penmanship. I can't tell you how much this means."

"I think you just did." His voice sounded hoarse to his ears.

After they disconnected, Weston turned to find Zack placing filled mugs on the table. Both men pulled out chairs and sank into them.

"Troubling news?" Zack asked. "You look a little punchy."

"Eavesdropping on my conversations?"

"You bet."

Weston shook his head, bemused. So this was what friendship was like. He picked up his mug. "Myra told me she believed God brought me here."

Zack nodded and took a sip of his cocoa. "So she feels the same way."

Weston raised his eyebrows.

"As I do," Zack said. "I have no doubt the Holy Spirit brought you here."

"What makes you think God could draw me? I'm not a

believer."

"This might sound trite, but you don't have to believe in Him for Him to believe in you, or do whatever He wants to do in your life. He's God."

"But why—"

"Why do I believe He led you here? Because of the way you've helped us, and the way you're seeking answers. Joy's finally learning to forgive, not just you, but others. I already forgave you and believe we're going to be friends."

Weston took a big gulp of cocoa and burned the roof of his mouth.

"God also used your time with Joy to show you our faith through our behavior." Zack grimaced. "Not that we did a great job of that, but sometimes God works in spite of us."

"I wish you'd told Joy about that the night I was on the road."

"You've continued to ask questions and talk about Him, even if your opinions are occasionally negative. That's the work of God's Holy Spirit."

For the first time Weston didn't feel uncomfortable talking about the source of faith for these people. "God the Spirit didn't induce me to break up your engagement."

"He did use it to prove to me that Joy won't be untrue to me, even though it appeared that was what she was doing when she left. After the actions of my own father, that was a huge issue for me."

Weston recalled the very few moments when he thought Joy might succumb to his attempts to charm her, and she never did. "I did see how a believer behaves even when she's out of her element in a strange place."

"You saw how deeply she cared for her patients, and for your daughter. Money was never her reason for getting into medicine," Zack said.

"She stayed late at night working on patient charts in her efforts to figure out how to help those who needed her."

Weston got up and pulled a bag of tiny marshmallows from the cabinet. He offered some to Zack, who declined. "I guess real men don't put marshmallows in their cocoa." He sprinkled the top of his drink with them.

"Only if they don't care about maintaining their girlish

figures."

"Then you'd better watch it until after the wedding."

*****

Myra sat cross-legged on her bed at Molly's house, holding the cell phone to her ear and praying Roger Hawkins would answer. She agonized over what she might discover, but she needed to know for sure.

The others were downstairs waiting silently, as concerned as she was. One of Molly's calico cats jumped onto the bed and started to purr as she crawled into Myra's lap. Myra took comfort in her presence.

A man answered the phone. "Yeah?" He sounded tired, as if he'd just had the stuffing beaten out of him.

"Hello, is this Roger Hawkins?"

"Yes?"

"My name is Dr. Myra Maxwell."

"Maxwell. Hmm. Yeah, I know that name. You were Sarah's psychiatrist." The brokenness in his voice told her how close he and Sarah must have been. Sarah had mentioned that he doted on her.

"I was."

"We were going to share a quiet Christmas dinner yesterday, just her and my dog and me."

"I know this whole situation is a horrible shock to you. It was to me."

"But I thought she was getting past all that," Mr. Hawkins said. "It didn't make sense."

"That's why I'm calling. It doesn't make sense to me, either, and I could use your help. Did the police place crime scene tape around her apartment?"

"No. They didn't think there was any crime," he said bitterly. "Just another holiday suicide, I heard one of them say."

"Then would you be willing to help me investigate her death?"

"How could I do that? They took the bottle for those pills they said she swallowed, though they didn't bother to take that pile of herbal supplements she kept in her kitchen cupboard."

Myra frowned. "Supplements?"

"She said those were harmless. She even had me trying some of them, thinking they might help me when I started slowing down a few weeks ago."

Myra sat up straighter. "Do you recall the names of the supplements?" Sarah had never told her about any supplements she was taking, even though the secretary always gave her a form where she was to list everything she took.

"Well, I know one of them was something like a wart, because I took it for a while."

"You mean St. John's Wort?"

"That's the stuff, and she gave me some other pills she said would help my sleep cycle. She said they work for her."

Oh, no. "Melatonin?"

"Yeah, that's it. You put her on that stuff?"

"No. I would never have allowed her to take those." Not when she was taking an antidepressant at the same time. An SSRI antidepressant combined with either of those supplements would cause serotonin syndrome, and Sarah was small in stature and not strong. It might have affected her far too quickly. "Mr. Hawkins, do you know of any other supplements she took?"

"Only something with the number 5 in it."

No. No. This couldn't be. "5HTP?"

"That's the stuff. She was always reading about herbal supplements, and you know how badly she wanted to get better."

"Did she say anything about how she was feeling physically in the past week or so?"

"Not good. She was cold a lot. Or at least I saw her shivering. I thought she might be getting the flu, but she promised me she was going to see you next week, so she'd wait until then."

Myra closed her eyes. Shivering didn't necessarily mean she was cold. It could easily have been a symptom, considering the medicines she was taking. "Mr. Hawkins, when Sarah started seeing me as a patient I gave her a journal to write in. Hers was purple, if I remember correctly. She never shared this journal with anyone that I know of, but she would have kept it someplace private where no one would find it."

"I think I know where it might be. A few weeks ago she asked me to nail a wooden, open-ended box underneath her kitchen table. Well, actually, it was my table, but I did it for her anyway. You think that might be where she put the journal?"

"It might be. Would you look?"

"Can I call you back?"

"Yes." She gave him her number and said goodbye, then immediately called Weston.

Chapter 24

Weston's cell phone rang before he finished his drink. He pressed the Bluetooth in his ear and answered.

"Did I hear Zack's voice when you called me a minute ago?" It was Myra.

"Yes, he's here."

"Would you place your cell on speaker? I need another physician's opinion."

He did as she asked and placed his cell phone on the table between them. "You're on."

"Zack, I have Joy with me and we need a consult. I reached Sarah's landlord, who told me about supplements Sarah had been taking along with the meds I gave her.

"Let me guess, you didn't know about the supplements."

"Absolutely not. I had Sarah on paroxetine for her generalized anxiety, as well as alprazolam for especially bad spells. I just found out from Mr. Hawkins that Sarah's also been taking the supplements St. John's Wort, 5HTP and Melatonin."

Zack let out a low whistle of alarm. "Nasty way to give herself serotonin syndrome. That's a disaster."

"Especially since she was bound to become extremely anxious, which would cause her to take more alprazolam."

"But a nearly full bottle?"

"That's what I'm trying to figure out. It still doesn't make sense, and I don't believe she was suicidal," Myra said. "She never listed these supplements on her forms. I wish I'd specifically asked."

"There's a point when a patient has to take responsibility for her own actions," Weston said.

"He's right," Zack said. "A lot of patients don't think it's necessary to list their supplements, but there are warnings about that everywhere."

"But they think it's safe because it's 'natural'," came Joy's voice over the speaker.

"Still," Myra said, "depression isn't one of the symptoms for serotonin syndrome, so suicide from depression seems like a stretch. Her landlord said she'd been having some trouble lately, seemed to be sick. One of the symptoms for the syndrome is sleeplessness, which might have convinced her to increase her melatonin."

"Which would, in turn, make her symptoms worse." Zack looked at Weston. "If she attended a party on Christmas Eve after dinner and drank even a couple of glasses of champagne or other alcohol, that might have been the trifecta that triggered a full-blown crisis. She wouldn't have needed a whole bottle of anything to kill her, but it sounds less and less like intentional suicide."

"I'll know for sure when Mr. Hawkins calls back if he can find the journal," Myra said. "I'll call you when I've heard from him."

She disconnected. Weston met Zack's gaze. "What would God say about one of His believers taking her own life?"

"I can't claim to know God's mind. I know of Christians who suffered with depression and taken their lives. I blame the depression. It's a physical condition that can overpower anyone."

"What about the passage in the Bible where God says He will never allow His children a temptation so difficult that He won't show them a way out of it?"

"I agree with Myra," Zack said. "I don't believe this was a temptation. I believe it was a tragic accident."

"There were still a lot of pills missing from a recently refilled bottle."

"I think I'll wait and see what else we find out from the landlord," Zack said. "You sure seem to know the Bible more than I expected."

Weston got up and put his mug in the dishwasher. "Would you believe my brother and I attended Sunday school when...before he died?"

"I didn't know that."

Weston took his seat again. "I'm afraid nobody knows much at all about me. After my brother's death, my parents continued to send me to church alone for a while. They never went with me, but the teachers tried to convince me there was a God who loved me and wanted the best for me. I couldn't help wondering why He allowed my brother to die and my mother to switch off."

"She was dealing with your brother's death," Zack said.

Weston stared out the window. "The trips to Sunday school got me out of the house, and that worked for me."

"But you eventually stopped attending?"

Weston nodded. "I tried to pray but it was as if I was praying to a brick wall. Then I got involved in school activities so I didn't have to be home much. Of course, staying away from home led to dating a lot, and then along came Keegan. For many years I thought I was happy. After Keegan died, out of a sense of desperation I tried for a few weeks to find the God from my childhood who was supposed to love me, but I was like one of those pill bugs, turned within myself. Nothing could get through."

"Myra got through to you."

Weston nodded, watching as a coat-clad figure walked across the grounds outside. "Interesting that the first time I decided to oversee operations here the majority of staff was Christian. I realize we're in the Bible belt, but being from the city I don't see that so much."

"How did Joy and I influence you? You had to consider us to be a couple of country rubes."

"I wasn't thinking about other people last year, I was only looking for distraction."

"Except when you tried to save Dustin's life?"

"I can't take credit for that because it, too, was definitely a distraction. Good or bad, I needed to keep my mind off my own miserable life. I saw the engagement ring on Joy's finger and made it a personal challenge to see it removed. Since Keegan's death I became a master manipulator. Everything in life was a challenge to me. Especially living from day to day. Then I came up against two people who had the strength to recover from my attacks. I was curious. When I saw the fallout of my actions over those next few months, I'd come to the end of myself."

"So when you started seeing Myra, you wanted to find out how to change that inner person," Zack said.

Weston stared down at the surface of the table. He nodded. "I'd seen a strength about you that I wanted for myself. I saw it in

Joy and Myra, and yet none of you pounded the Bible over my head. You weren't 'salesmen for God,' you just lived it out."

"You told me you wanted to be a better person," Zack said.

Weston nodded. He still wasn't sure what he wanted, but he didn't want to continue being the person he'd been.

"There's a parable in the Bible about a house that was swept clean of a demon," Zack said.

Weston looked up at him. "Wow. We're kind of jumping right into the deep end," Weston said. "Demons? Yet more biblical mysteries?"

"Especially since the house is a synonym for a human soul."

"Something I've felt for a long time that I didn't have."

"You have one. God's a great mystery to our finite minds, but we don't have to understand those mysteries to put our faith in Him."

"Tell me about this clean house."

"No one else came to fill it so it remained empty. Then the original demon went out and found seven other demons to join him in that same house, and the state of that house at the end was worse than it had ever been."

"Then I don't have a choice?"

"You always have a choice, but it's rare that a person can change his whole character without help, and I'm talking help from God, not just help from a good psychiatrist. It's a total overhaul."

"So you're saying I've managed to push away the so-called demon that caused me to behave the way I have this past year. But that won't stop me from making more wrong choices, hurting more people."

"I only know of one choice you can make that can help you change and grow. Right now you're filled with remorse. I know you continually feel the need to make amends, but you can't live in that state forever. Eventually other thoughts will occur to you, those that will convince you that you are who you are, and you can't change, so you might as well make the most of it. I watched my father take that route."

Weston nearly shoved away from the table. "So there's God, and then there's evil, and nothing in between."

"Unless you have guidance from Someone more powerful than any human, even a good change won't bring you what you want. You can accept the sacrifice of Christ that you learned about in Sunday school as a child, and allow Him to start cleaning house for you, or you can lose your way again."

"And join a church no doubt."

"Not one that resembles Joy's former church, but I'd welcome you at mine. Churches are simply where believers go to support one another in their faith and worship the One who is the reason for their hope. Everyone in that church is human. However, when two or more believers are together, He has promised to be in their midst. That's why church."

Weston rested his arms on the table. He needed so much more than he'd had in his life, and no matter how much money he accumulated, it brought him more stress, less peace. But how much peace did he see in his friends?

"If being a believer in Christ brings peace, how can you explain Myra's fugue state?" he asked Zack. "Or Sarah's death? To me, that doesn't look like peace. Despite how I feel about Myra, just having dinner with her was often stressful because she refused to stop taking calls."

"As I said, we remain human. We don't turn into perfect angels. I told you before God doesn't promise blue skies and perfect days. Our priorities change when we accept Christ, but being human is a messy condition. Trauma in our lives can cause trouble no matter what. Myra is learning and growing, and that's something we'll all have to deal with until the day our promise is received."

"The promise being that we live forever."

"The promise is that Christ's spirit dwells in us and we are never alone, and after this life we find perfection, and reside with Christ."

Weston stared back outside, where the sun had come out and claimed the campus. None of it made sense. It sounded too much like a fairy tale. "I have a lot to think about."

***

Myra listened to Mr. Hawkins telling her about Sarah's journal over the phone. "Dr. Maxwell, I've read the first part of it but didn't find much, but the words I just read are dated in the past week. Listen to this. 'I feel worse every day, but some people tell me that's a sort of die-off of the bad stuff in my system. I guess I should get ready to feel this way for a while. It's no fun. I'll ask Dr. Maxwell about it when I see her next week.' What'd'ya think, Dr. Maxwell? Sound like the flu to you?"

"No, I think her symptoms came from the supplements she was taking. They interacted with the prescription medicines. Have you had any bad reactions to the supplements she gave you?"

"Nope. Feeling better, actually."

"That's because you aren't taking the prescription medicines I had her on. Some meds and herbal supplements were never meant to be taken together."

"I don't take anything but an aspirin and some of these herbs she gave me. I found another section you'll want to hear. Listen to this. 'Now Dr. Maxwell and the pharmacy people are going to think I'm abusing drugs, but I have to get a new script soon. The cap was too tight, and when I finally got it open the pills went flying everywhere. Over half of them went down the sink drain, and since I was running water I lost them. I can't even prove what happened.' What do you think about that, Dr. Maxwell?"

For a moment, Myra couldn't speak. She felt all the strength drain from her, and tears rose to the surface.

"Dr. Maxwell?" Something popped on the phone, as if he was hitting it. "Don't tell me we lost connection," he muttered.

"No." She swallowed. "I'm here. Mr. Hawkins, Sarah didn't commit suicide. What happened to her was a tragic accident, but she didn't intentionally kill herself. I know she thought a lot of you. I believe you helped her more than you know. Thank you for being such a good friend."

Myra and Mr. Hawkins said their goodbyes, and then she told her friends what had really happened as tears of relief and grief mingled and dripped down her face.

She called Weston with the news, and was satisfied with his promise to make sure Sarah's death would be recorded as accidental.

She stared out of the dormer window Molly had put up with a little help from Zack and Joy. The Missouri River sparkling in the sunshine.

Myra knew her future was all in God's hands, and though she felt the frustration with every part of her, and Sarah's death still cast a shroud over her, she knew she could begin to heal now that she knew the truth.

Time to help plan a wedding. In less than a week.

Chapter 25

Joy adjusted the veil for the final time at her grandparents' house on New Year's Day. She checked Laine's reflection in the mirror. She looked perfect, with a dark green dress of satin, clean lines that accented her slender figure. She wore her hair loose. Myra's dress matched Laine's. They would be beautiful bridesmaids, and if Joy wasn't mistaken, one of Zack's groomsmen had his eye on Laine already.

"No sneezing after two nights at Mom's?" Joy asked.

"None." Laine squinted to place her mascara just right, and for her that was quite a feat; she seldom wore makeup. "I even spent extra time with the cats. My experiment is a success."

"Now comes the hard part. All the trials and begging for funds and—"

"Not me. I'm not doing the traditional medical trials. It's going to be considered an herbal remedy only, and I'll patent it, start with local vendors and go from there. But today is about you, and you look breathtaking."

Myra slipped through the door into the large downstairs bathroom to join them. The green in her dress brought out the deep green of her eyes. "Molly's outside in a heated discussion with your grandfather about his tuxedo. He doesn't like the lace on the shirt."

"Then he should have updated his wardrobe since the seventies." Joy wished she'd eloped.

"Weston isn't here yet," Myra said.

"He'll walk in at the last moment," Laine said. "Who wants to face a houseful of people who all know his history?"

Joy fiddled with her veil, couldn't get it to work, and pulled it off. "I can't make this fit."

Myra stepped forward and took the veil, fingered Joy's hair back in the casual fashion that she always wore, then used the comb on the veil to secure it into place. "Laine could have given you an updo. A French braid would be—"

"Too late. We have ten minutes," Laine said. "Myra, I'm proud of you."

"Why?"

"Because you weren't the first one to get married."

"She's right," Joy said. "You were the one with the most guys asking you out during college. You dated twice as much as I did."

Laine grabbed a tissue and dampened it to clean a smudge from her eye. "I was certain you'd end up married before you graduated from med school."

"I might have been, but I had this competition with Joy to see who could hold out the longest. We saw too many divorces in our line of study."

"Tell me about it." Laine dried the eye and tried again. "I had a total of five boyfriends throughout college and med school, and all of them seemed serious while I dated them. None of them lasted when I made it clear I was into school for the long haul. What man's willing to wait for a woman who wants her own career, and won't be willing to follow him all over the country when he needs to transfer?"

"Not the guys I dated," Myra said.

"Maybe that would be a good test of a relationship," Joy said. "Not that I'd advise the emotional fallout. Thanks to Weston, Zack and I ended up proving ourselves more completely because we waited longer."

"I don't think Weston sees it that way." Myra spread the veil out around Joy's shoulders, then together she and Laine pulled the first, filmy layer over Joy's face.

The organ music reached them. It was almost time.

***

Weston stepped through the front door of the palatial Gilbert house, surprised by his first glimpse of Molly's first home. Somehow he'd been of the opinion that she'd come from more humble beginnings, but he'd overheard remarks around town this past week about the sizable holdings of the Gilbert clan.

Impressive. Molly had chosen to raise her daughter on her own instead of depending on her wealthy parents to carry the load.

Not a surprise at all.

He signed the guest book, then placed his gift to the bride and groom on the table already piled high with gifts.

"Pssst!"

He heard the sound slipping through the voices of those who hovered in the expansive foyer. Looking around, he frowned at a hand waving wildly from a door that appeared to lead to a study of some kind. He looked up to see Zack's face, eyes wide, gesturing for him.

With a quick dash through the crowd, Weston made his way to the door and allowed Zack to pull him through. His grip wasn't exactly gentle.

"Would you look at this?" Zack stared at his get-up in the full-length mirror of a library. "What on earth is a cumber bund? And a bow tie? Really?

Weston closed and locked the door behind him. "You do realize the wedding's about to start and you're half dressed."

"I have my clothes on, I just never learned how to tie a bow, and what is a cumber bund?"

Weston got to work on the tie. "Frippery, but it looks good. You don't look happy. Tell me you aren't getting cold feet."

Zack smiled. "No, but they sure do itch. I can't wait to hit the road and be out of this noose."

"Soon enough. I thought all physicians had to take a class in formal wear. Isn't that a required course?"

"All we learned was medicine. I didn't enter this profession to dress up and socialize with the elite. I wish Joy had agreed to elope last summer."

"How can you be such a wise physician when you're so clueless about the woman you love?"

"I'm marrying her today, aren't I?"

"Joy needed this time to get to know you better. Time's an issue too many people ignore. I wouldn't have made nearly as many mistakes in my life if I'd waited and counted the costs."

"This coming from one of the wealthiest people in America."

Weston straightened the tie and looked at Zack, taking a step backward to examine his work and get out of Zack's personal space. "You're the wealthy one. You and Joy have been the best of friends since anatomy lab, right?"

"Yes, and she was my competitor from there on out."

"She isn't your competitor now, so forget that. She's your partner in every way. I wish someone had been able to convince me of that at my wedding."

"She knows I love and trust her."

"Don't ever take her for granted. I've learned that doesn't go over well, either. What about her job situation?"

"You mean you didn't overhear us discussing that last week when everyone at Molly's was watching us through the window?"

"The panes were too thick, and no one's bothered to clue me in since."

"If she goes I go. She'll work on speeding up her work, but if the board still wants her gone they'll have to hire two new physicians, and she and I will pick up shifts in Hermann and Jefferson City, even Columbia until we can build our practice."

Weston grinned. "You might deserve Joy, after all."

"I told the bean counters they'll just have to work with us."

"Watch it with the bean counter remarks. I hire plenty of those. It's a necessity to keep a business open. But your decision to stick with Joy no matter what is a necessity to keep a marriage alive."

"And you know that because?"

"I didn't do it right. What else? You know when I first realized I'd made a mistake firing Joy? It was when I discovered she had my daughter's best interests at heart."

"She still does."

"I know. And it's another reason I've been thinking about what we discussed last week."

Zack's movements stilled. He straightened and faced Weston. "Which part?"

The organ began the wedding march.

Weston shoved Zack toward the door. "It's time."

Zack stopped at the doorway, unlocked the door and then turned back. "What did you decide?"

A large man with silver hair opened the door. "Are you marrying my granddaughter or are you going to stand out here jawing all day?"

"Marriage first," Zack said.

"Then get up there and let's get this done. Kick-off's

coming."

As Joy's grandfather led Zack away, Zack looked back at Weston. "What did you decide?"

"I'm all in."

Zack gave an undignified "Whoop!" that caused people to turn and ladies to giggle, but he didn't seem to care, and neither did Weston. He knew there would still be a lot of decisions to be made and lessons to learn, but he felt a peace and joy he'd never before experienced, and he didn't understand why.

***

Myra had been to Grandpa and Grandma Gilbert's place quite often with Joy, so it was with a great deal of satisfaction that she counted nearly 75 guests crammed into the expansive great room. She also glimpsed the big screen on the far wall, and knew that if Zack's pastor didn't rush through the ceremony someone in this family was likely to switch on the game before the groom could kiss the bride.

When she saw the way Zack looked down at Joy with love shining from his eyes as if they hadn't known each other all these years, she was glad she'd applied water-resistant mascara. She was such a sap for weddings.

Without realizing it, she found herself searching the crowd for a certain handsome man who'd been in her dreams of late. She found him standing at the back of the room, since all the rented chairs were taken. He was watching her.

Joy turned and gave her the bouquet, and Myra nearly dropped her own in the process, causing a few titters from Joy's young cousins perched on the carpeted floor. They'd done a quick run-through with the pastor earlier—much more efficient, in Myra's opinion.

After the ring ceremony, which Zack and Joy had written, themselves, and which had Joy, Myra and Laine sniffing—and half the women in the crowd, along with Grandpa and Grandma Gilbert—the new married couple finally, at long last, sealed the bargain with a kiss.

The crowd of family and friends burst out in applause and shouts, and once more, Myra looked for Weston. He hadn't moved, and his broad smile showed how happy he was for the couple. But he still had eyes only for her.

And God had said to wait. How long? Would this thing be a marathon? Would it even be what she dreamed it could be? She'd caught more and more glimpses of a different Weston Cline in recent weeks. Was she only imagining what she wanted to see?

She'd taught him a great deal in the months she'd met with him, ideas he'd been resistant to at the time, how to speak his thoughts with more honesty and less glib chatter. He'd also taught her a lot—and the most important thing that he'd taught her was how to love the damaged man she saw behind those beautiful blue eyes. She loved him without reservation.

How things had changed.

But where would those changes end? Could he make peace with God? She only knew she would do anything to help him try.

Chapter 26

Weston waited outside and enjoyed a beautiful day with Christmas decorations still gracing the trees, and sunshine and happy people spilling out of the front door of the Gilbert mansion.

Myra stepped through the doorway, and his breath stuttered as everything in his life seemed to reposition. He wanted her in his life forever, couldn't imagine a future without her in it. She searched the yard until she saw him walking toward her. For some reason, he couldn't stop smiling. Unless Zack had already blabbed to everyone in the room after Weston walked from the house, Myra would be the very next person to know the real change in his heart.

He held his hands out to her, and she took them. Hers were soft but strong.

"Wasn't it perfect?" she asked.

He didn't take his gaze from her. "It's most definitely perfect."

Her olive skin tone deepened becomingly, and he had to force himself not to draw her into an immediate first kiss.

He pulled off his jacket and rested it over her shoulders. "I'd love to talk all about it. Want to take a walk with me?"

"Sure. Grandpa Gilbert keeps his ponies around back. Want to say hi?"

Weston glanced toward the fenced pasture behind the house. "So that's where Molly developed her love for animals."

As they stepped along the sidewalk that circled the house he allowed her to lead the way.

She looked over her shoulder at him with a quizzical light in her eyes. "Is something up? You're a little quiet."

"I'm simply enjoying the day, the sunshine and the beautiful company."

She smiled. He was enchanted.

"I don't suppose you missed Zack's shout just before the wedding," he said.

"Who could miss that?" She chuckled. "He and Joy have been waiting for this day for a long time."

"I knew he was. It's all he's talked about these past few days." Weston followed her to the horse paddock and gazed at the pinto ponies that mingled together around a tiny horse barely higher than Weston's knees. "Well, if it isn't Captain Kirk."

Myra looked up at him. "You know this Lilliputian?"

"He was at Molly's this summer. I saw him when I drove to Juliet to see Tressa."

"And Joy."

"That was the day I think I realized she wouldn't be returning to the clinic."

"You were persistent."

"I was a different person then." In so many ways. He smoothed a hand down the soft nose of one of the ponies.

"Since you've spent so much time with Zack this week, have you given him all your business experience?"

"He's not going to learn what he needs to know in a few days. He'll need more than I've told him if he's going to successfully run his own clinic."

"But you'll help him, right?"

"I already told him to call me any time. I'll even send someone from my clinic to help him set up a better office system that will help him deal with all the government changes, but I won't suggest it until he's desperate. Otherwise he'll turn me down."

Myra shook her head. "Men and their pride."

"There are some things I can't teach him. He'll have to learn them on his own." He rested a foot on the bottom rail of the fence as he avoided a curious, slobbery horse muzzle, which was likely checking his pocket for a treat. "There were some things he couldn't teach me, either, though he did a good job of leading."

She looked up at him, the breeze blowing strands of her ebony hair across her face. She pushed them away. "Leading you in what direction?"

"The direction I've been seeking for years, though I didn't realize it."

Myra stepped away from another curious horsey nose that came through the fence toward her. "And what would that be?" she asked softly.

He swallowed, not sure how to say the words. It wasn't as if he'd been raised in the culture and knew the terminology. "I had to learn for myself how to allow Someone more powerful take control of my life. I have a feeling it's going to be a lifelong lesson, and I'll stumble every step of the way."

The thrill of seeing her expression of delight was worth everything. It matched the happiness he'd felt since he'd spoken the words of surrender, and he realized it was real, and he wasn't simply being emotional or desperate or doing this for the wrong reason—such as attracting Myra.

"You believe," she whispered.

"I've done a lot of reading these past few days. I've even studied some good commentaries online. God doesn't hate me as I thought He did. He loves me with more power than I ever dreamed possible." He said it with a sense of wonder.

"How could God hate you when I didn't? He's more capable of love than any of us."

"He stayed with you throughout the fugue state, didn't He?"

She nodded. "Whispering in my ear that I would come through it."

"And look at you now. Easily the most beautiful, thoughtful, wise woman on this property today."

"Now you're just exaggerating because you're riding the high."

"The high?"

"Of fresh new faith. It's an amazing thing to experience." She met his gaze and held it. "Don't forget it. There will be challenges, but today is the beginning of a new life."

He never wanted this moment to end. He could see the joy, perhaps even relief, in her eyes, and he knew why she felt that way. Now they were talking from the same side. Now they belonged to the same God. He had no idea how this beautiful friendship would turn out, only how he wanted it to, but he had a feeling this was only the beginning.

"I can say it now," she said, never looking away from him.

"Say what?"

"I've been grieving Dustin's death for over a year, and I know I'll always grieve. I've watched you continue to struggle with Keegan's death."

"It never goes away."

"Eventually, though, when there's been enough healing, there's room in our hearts for more love if we allow it. I've allowed it, Weston."

"So have I." He turned from the fence and faced her. "For the first time in my life I know what it's like to be truly in love." He touched her cheek, then stepped forward and lowered his lips to hers for the very first time.

She tasted like his finest dreams coming true at last. *Thank you, God.*

Preview of *A Class Act*

Hannah Alexander

Laine Fulton jogged alone in the deepening twilight along the KATY Trail toward her car, disturbed by the lateness of the hour. She studied the open field to her right and saw a herd of deer grazing in the lush June grass—a typical sight for this section of the trail, but she didn't like the long shadows they cast. She'd arrived at the trailhead much later than usual. Most times she encountered cyclers, walkers and runners on this section of the state-wide trail. She didn't want to get back to the car after dark.

Though she'd always found Columbia, Missouri, to be a safe and friendly place to live, a woman alone couldn't be too careful.

She slowed her steps to look behind her. At first she didn't see anything but deer, but then someone stepped around the curve from the cover of one of the myriad trees that lined the trail. A walker headed back to the trailhead, no doubt, not even close enough for Laine to see if it was male or female. Still, she needed to kick up the pace. Should've skipped the exercise tonight.

She turned back and nearly collided with a tall ghost of a man with premature white hair, black eyebrows and a certain intensity in his eyes that had always made her wonder what additional madness might lie behind them.

"Dr. Payson," she said calmly, covering the shock of his sudden appearance. Where on earth had he come from? Had he been following her?

He stood glowering. "Hello Laine." His greeting seemed intentionally menacing.

Gut instinct told her to dodge him and keep on running. Manners, however, as well as her need to control the situation, kept her in place. "I've never seen you out on this trail before." A good reason to use this trail, in her opinion. What was he doing, lurking in the trees, waiting for her to pass by? She suppressed a shudder.

"I think it's time for a talk."

Too bad. "Enjoy your walk," she said, stepping around him. "It's getting dark. Hope you have a flashlight."

He grabbed her arm in a painful grip that jerked her around to face him again. "We need to talk *now*."

Barely resisting the urge to practice a more painful self-defense move, Laine reached up and bent his thumb backward until he grunted with outrage and released her. "Don't touch me again." She stepped away, but didn't turn her back on him.

He took an intimidating step toward her.

She braced herself for a counterattack. "If you need to speak with me I have a phone," she said. "Use it next time." She kept her distance.

"I wanted to see your face."

She wanted to gag. "I should warn you there's someone coming up behind us. I'm sure they'll be a useful witness for me when I file an assault report with the Columbia's finest." She kept her voice calm and practical as always. Practical Laine Fulton.

He looked down the trail then back at her with a glower. With a scowl and a pitying shake of her head she looked down at his scrawny white legs in the ugly, baggy white shorts and tee shirt. He obviously wasn't a runner or even a walker, which affirmed her initial suspicion. He'd specifically followed her here, which meant he'd been watching her for a while. She needed a guard dog.

She met his gaze with narrowed eyes. This wasn't her first difficult encounter with the lecher, but she was prepared this time.

"You've been snooping on me," he said.

She didn't flinch. "That's a common paranoia for a researcher. I could not care less about what you're doing now."

"That isn't what I've heard."

"Then someone's feeding your fear, maybe to get under your skin. You know how it is in the research world." As long as he wasn't unearthing the debacle they'd worked on together two years ago, she'd been requested to simply observe.

His shoulders gave an exaggerated slump of fake disappointment. "And here I thought you might be interested in a job with me again."

"I love the job I have."

"Maybe I'll speak to your employer."

The man was all bluff. Her employer despised Payson as much as Laine did. "As I said, it's getting dark. It's time to get back to my car." She sidled away from him so he wouldn't try to grab her again, and stepped out at a faster pace than her normal jog.

The more distance she could place between them, the happier she'd be.

"I keep tabs on my former employees," he called after her.

She picked up speed. Time to be more careful about the staff members she approached at the hospital. Obviously, some couldn't be trusted to keep their mouths shut.

Her heart rate overmatched her pace, because she knew the darkness in Dr. Christopher Payson. This wasn't the last encounter she would have with him.

About the Author

Hannah Alexander is the pen name of a husband-wife collaborative writing team, and is the author of 30 inspirational novels, novellas and short stories of romance, women's fiction, suspense and medical drama with a dose of subtle humor. All are set in homey small towns. Thank you so much for taking time to read Dandelion Moon. If you enjoyed this novel, Hannah Alexander would very much appreciate it if you would leave a review on the site where you purchased it. Reviews are key to further sales, and sales are key to future novels.

Read more about their work and sample chapters at:
www.HannahAlexander.com

E-book available novels by Hannah Alexander:

Sacred Trust Series:

Sacred Trust
Solemn Oath
Silent Pledge

The Healing Touch Series:

Second Opinion
Necessary Measures
Urgent Care

Hannah Alexander

Hideaway Series Trade Paperbacks:

Hideaway
Safe Haven
Last Resort
Fair Warning
Grave Risk
Double Blind

Love Inspired Suspense—Hideaway Series:

Note of Peril
Under Suspicion
Death Benefits

Love Inspired Historical—Hideaway Series:

Hideaway Home

Jolly Mill Series:

Silent Night, Deadly Night (novella)
Eye of the Storm
Collateral Damage
Keeping Faith (historical suspense)
Alive After New Year

Single Titles:

A Killing Frost (contemporary suspense)
Hidden Motive (contemporary suspense)
The Wedding Kiss (historical suspense)

Hallowed Halls Series

Hallowed Halls
Dandelion Moon

76787462R00133

Made in the USA
Lexington, KY
22 December 2017